5-23-17

Mark,

Always believe in yourself
& your dreams.
The Robinson taught us
a great way to live!
I wish you the very best!

Map of Robinson Island
Year 1815

RETURN TO
ROBINSON
ISLAND

TJ HOISINGTON

AYLESBURY
PUBLISHING

Aylesbury Publishing, LLC

www.SwissFamilyReturns.com

ISBN-13: 978-0-9758884-4-5
ISBN-10: 0-9758884-4-7

eBook and audiobook editions also available:
eBook ISBN: 978-0-9846887-2-2
Audiobook ISBN: 978-0-9776288-6-5

Illustrations by Stanislaf Plonish copyright © 2015 by TJ Hoisington

Library of Congress Control Number: 2015906928

1. Historical Fiction 2. Action & Adventure

Return to Robinson Island is based on the 1812 A.D. version of "The Adventures of Swiss Family Robinson," written by Johann David Wyss and subsequent versions through 1856 A.D., which reside in the public domain.

Printed in the United States of America

First Harcover Edition
10 9 8 7 6 5 4 3 2 1

To the fans of *Swiss Family Robinson*
who have long wondered – *what happened next...*

Also By TJ Hoisington

If You Think You Can!
If You Think You Can! for Teens
The Secret of the Slight Edge
The Power to Shape Your Life
Maximizing Human Performance
Maximizing Sales Performance
The Core Drivers of Leadership
Lessons on Success

Let the journey begin.

Chapter 1

Off the southern coast of Spain, February 1815

A thundering blast rolled across the choppy waves, followed by the scream of a cannon that slams into the ocean forty yards shy of the HMS *Royal George*, sending a plume of water into the air.

"We're being attacked! All hands on deck! To your battle stations!" commanded 1st Lieutenant Ernest Robinson.

Whistles blaring, the midshipmen pick up the chorus, "We're being attacked! We're being attacked! Hands to quarters!"

The ship's crew dart in every direction scrambling to their battle stations.

"Enemy ship starboard two degrees!" a yell comes from the crow's nest.

Captain Charles "Charlie" Williamson was calmly giving orders while making his way to the quarterdeck where Lieutenant

Robinson stood. "Prepare the cannons. Empty numbers five and six into her hull once we pull alongside her. On my orders …"

"Aye, aye, sir." His men quickly obey, pulling the cannons back and loading the heavy iron balls into the barrels.

"Steady. Steady. Fire!" came the order.

Several shots were fired, successfully hitting their mark, before Captain Charlie reached the quarterdeck. Lieutenant Robinson dropped to the deck as a twenty-five-pound cannon ball slammed into the starboard side of the ship with shattering force, sending splinters of wood flying in every direction. Momentarily stunned by the impact, Robinson didn't immediately feel the sharp pain in his forehead until blood began coursing into his eyes. Quickly wiping the blood with his sleeve, he jumped to his feet.

Through the haze of smoke the French ship *Le Tigre* loomed into view. The ship was so close that Ernest could see the frightened expressions of the French sailors on deck, who were clearly beginning to panic.

Although they were returning fire, it was obvious that the French ship was taking on water as it began listing sharply to one side. It was only a matter of time before the ship would be completely crippled.

Ernest stood surveying the scene when a sudden explosion ripped across the sea as fire, smoke, and splintered wood blasted into the air. The men turned to see the *Le Tigre* wheelhouse and foredeck consumed in flames.

"Blimey!"

Ernest turned to his best friend, 2nd Lieutenant John Bennett, standing beside him.

"Mr. Bennett! Get me a report from the nest."

John looked upward and yelled to the midshipman. "A report of other ships."

"Aye, aye, sir," the sailor yelled back as he quickly scanned the seas with the glass. "Two points larboard," he reported.

"What do you see?"

"*Le Tigre's* escort has made a run for it, sir." The French escort had turned tail and was already a distant shape on the horizon.

"Thank you," said John, relaying the information to Ernest as Captain Charlie stepped onto the quarterdeck.

John turned and looked at Ernest. "You look like you tackled some planking." Ernest reached up and pulled a half-inch sliver from his forehead causing a small rivulet of blood to stream down the side of his face. Ernest grinned.

"Obviously just a scratch."

Aboard the *Le Tigre*, screams of panic and agony suddenly filled the air. French sailors ran back and forth in desperation, trying to contain the flames, but the fire was spreading too rapidly. The fire snaked along the decking, setting aflame torn and tattered sails, the wind feeding the fire and spreading the hungry flames throughout the ship. During the fire's feeding frenzy even the longboats were consumed before they could be lowered into the water.

Ernest, John, and other officers joined their captain to watch as the French sailors abandoned ship.

"She's going down, men," Captain Charlie said with pride.

The French sailors plunged overboard into the choppy sea, trying to avoid the burning debris that rained down from the sinking ship.

Executive Officer Bernard Thompson shouted an order to

launch the longboats for a rescue operation.

Captain Charlie immediately countermanded the order. "We'll not be taking Frenchies on board this vessel."

Ernest exchanged puzzled glances with John and the other officers standing nearby.

"But, sir," John said, "You can see that a storm is coming. The men will surely drown if we don't pull them out now."

"Thank you, Mr. Bennett. When I need your opinion, I'll be sure to ask for it."

Speaking to all the officers, Captain Charlie continued, "The impending storm is all the more reason for haste. We can't run the risk of encountering other French ships during a rescue mission. Helping these men would leave us vulnerable to attack. I simply won't allow that to happen. We've used up our run of luck."

The men looked uneasily at one another. Clearly this didn't sit well with any of them. Drowning was every sailor's nightmare. Ernest defiantly spoke up.

"Captain, we can save some. We're fast in our boats. We can do it before another ship arrives and ..."

Captain Charlie interrupted in a menacing voice.

"Robinson, I wasn't aware that lieutenants were in the business of telling their commanding officers what to do!"

After an uncomfortable silence, with many of the men looking on, Ernest tensely replied, "Yes, sir."

It was quiet on board as the men quickly prepared the ship for departure. From the sea they could plainly hear the screams and frantic calls for help from the French sailors. Ernest tried not to look at the drowning Frenchmen pleading for their lives as they floundered in the heaving waves. His face pale with shock and anger, Ernest glanced at John, who returned a look of dismay.

"How many men are we mercilessly leaving to their fate, John?"

"One would be too many."

Yes, it is war, thought Ernest, *but even in war there are certain rules to abide by.* He hadn't joined the British Royal Navy so he could let defeated men drown. He knew this incident would not go unnoticed.

There would be a price to pay.

Chapter 2

Portsmouth, England. Early November 1815

White fog, a trademark of a London fall, was quickly dissipating as it lost its battle with the sun. The steady clip clop of shod hooves and the clatter of carriage wheels on the cobblestone street announced the arrival of a horse-drawn cab at the Navy Court. A young midshipman dashed into the courthouse, getting a frown from the Royal Marine guard at the door, and an admonishment to slow down. The young man slowed to a walk, entered the courtroom, and searched for an empty seat in the rear. He caught the eye of Ernest Robinson who was on the stand.

A respectful silence filled the stately wood-paneled courtroom. The grave issue at hand was the court-martial of a naval officer, Captain Charles Williamson. Lieutenant Ernest Robinson stood confidently at attention in his full dress uniform of navy blue pants and coat, with shiny gold buttons and gold braid adorning the epaulets. He was a handsome, strongly built, twenty-seven year-old man with blue eyes, dark brown hair, who stood six feet and one inch tall.

A stern, older, red-faced Captain of the Royal Navy sat at the defendant's table looking angry and frustrated. His counsel sat beside him. Three judges sat above him, behind a highly polished oak bench in the center of the courtroom. Behind them all, high up on the wall, hung the flag of the Royal Navy.

All of the judges were in full naval dress uniform and wearing the white curled wig of the English barrister. They were all admirals of the Royal Navy and presided like avenging angels, their glare intimidating all before them. Under the military code of conduct, only they could sit in judgment of a fellow officer.

Lieutenant Robinson was the last of several officers to testify, including Lieutenant John Bennett, regarding the unpardonable act of leaving two hundred French sailors to drown. Against all odds, five sailors had survived, and word spread of the heinous act, which became an international conflict between the two countries. Ernest had been the highest ranked officer under Captain Charlie's command aboard the HMS *Royal George* that day.

One of the judges turned his cold eyes to Ernest. "Now sir, if you please, and in your own words, tell the court what you witnessed aboard HMS *Royal George* off the southern coast of Spain, the fifteenth of February, before and after the encounter of two French ships ..." he glanced at his notes ... "*Le Tigre* and *L'Honneur*."

Ernest glanced over at the defendant, his ex-commanding

officer, Captain Charles Williamson, who was often referred to as "Charles the Lucky" because of his reputation for beating the odds. Many engagements that could have gone either way ended in Captain Charlie's favor. The navy was a dangerous job, and sailors tended to be a superstitious lot. Although Captain Charlie would often push the line between law and decency, sailors often sought a slot under his command hoping that some of his luck would rub off on them. Now, however, things had clearly gone wrong. He had pushed the line too far, and his luck had run out.

Taking a deep breath, Robinson started. "Well, sir, the officers and crew knew that Captain Charlie ..."

The judge glared. "Lieutenant Robinson. Please respect the gravity of this proceeding by referring to the defendant as Captain Williamson."

"Yes, sir," gulped Ernest. "We were sailing off the southern coast of Spain when we spotted two French ships."

"That would be *Le Tigre* and *L'Honneur*?"

"Yes. When we got within range, the *Le Tigre* opened hostilities by firing on us first. Captain Williamson called all men to battle stations. We were able to get several broadsides into her while they only got off one good cannon volley that skimmed our deck, killing two of our men." Ernest paused, inadvertently touching a small scar on his forehead.

The judge cleared his throat. "Continue."

"We dismasted her; she started to list to port, and then she began to burn."

"What happened next?"

"Well, sir, there was a terrible explosion on the *Le Tigre* and the fire quickly overtook the ship, including all the lifeboats.

Their crew had no alternative but to abandon ship. Lieutenant Thompson ordered our longboats lowered to pick up survivors when Captain Char ... Williamson countermanded his order."

"Do you know why he did that?"

"No, sir." Ernest glanced at Captain Charlie, who was staring ahead stone-faced. "I think he was worried about French reinforcements coming upon us."

"What you think is of no concern to this court. Do you have any direct knowledge if that indeed was the captain's concern?"

"Well, only because he said as much."

"Where was the nearest French ship?"

"The escort ship …"

"That would be … *L'Honneur*."

"I suppose. I was unable to see the name of the ship, which, by the time the smoke cleared, was out of range."

Snickers drifted through the court, silenced immediately by the judge's stern look.

"She had clearly made a run for it."

"And you saw no sign of other ships in the vicinity?"

"No."

"Go on, Lieutenant Robinson."

"A storm was coming up, and we knew the French seamen in the water would be done for, so naturally Lieutenant Thompson ordered the longboats lowered when the captain stopped him."

"Not one rescue boat was lowered?"

"That's correct."

"As far as you know, were any men picked up?"

"Not that I know of, sir."

"None? Out of a crew of over two hundred?"

The courtroom buzzed with chatter, and the judge pounded his gavel for quiet.

"So, in disobedience of Admiralty rules, the Rules of War, and common decency, Captain Williamson left over two hundred seamen, men like yourself, to drown?"

There was an eerie silence in the courtroom. Ernest thought the question was rhetorical so he didn't immediately answer, but the judge's piercing eyes demanded a response.

Lieutenant Robinson looked directly at his former

captain, who leveled a withering gaze back at him, and said, "Yes, I suppose … yes, sir."

Captain Charlie held Ernest's eye for a few seconds and then slowly grinned. "You'll pay for this disloyalty, Robinson. Mark my words."

The judge's gavel came down heavily as the room erupted in gasps and chaotic conversation.

"Unfortunately, gentlemen, the *L'Honneur* returned to the site to find five French seaman clinging to the wreckage," the judge informed the court.

The room gasped again, as this was the first they had heard of survivors.

After two more days of trial, unable to mount a convincing defense, Captain Charlie was found guilty. In spite of a good deal of bluster and colorful language, arguing that a captain's intuition trumps "hard" evidence, he could offer no substantial proof that enemy ships were in the area.

Captain Charlie was convicted of dishonoring his uniform, and after sentencing by the Admiralty, was dishonorably discharged from the Royal Navy and stripped of his commission and pension. He was also ordered to spend two years in a military prison.

Captain Charlie glared at the prosecutor's table where Ernest, John, and three other lieutenants sat — all formerly his command. Captain Charlie was fuming as he scanned the courtroom packed with Royal Navy officers. *How could they betray a Captain who had served His Majesty's Navy honorably for so many years?* he thought as his anger turned toward the entire navy.

The trial was called to a close as marines marched into the

courtroom with shackles and bound Captain Charlie's hands behind his back. Captain Charlie's supporters looked on, some shaking their heads in disappointment, while others who were not sympathetic looked on in smug satisfaction feeling that justice had been served.

Ernest and John stood talking with their lawyers when the marine guards led Captain Charlie past them toward the courtroom's main doors. Ernest heard his distinct walk, which had an awkward delay between steps, as he came close. Captain Charlie stopped, pulling against his iron restraints in order to level his hateful gaze at his once-trusted lieutenants.

"You will pay," he hissed. Ernest flinched as his former skipper's eyes met his with a malevolence that made Ernest's skin crawl.

Captain Charlie was jerked away and led to the prison transport outside the courthouse. Marines surrounded the carriage as he entered and sat down with his back pressed against the iron bars. The door slammed shut. Captain Charlie dropped his head as the horses lurched forward, carrying him to his ignominious fate. As the carriage rolled past the side of the courthouse, he tilted his head to the side acknowledging the presence of Cyril Wallace, the son of Lord Wallace — their eyes met briefly.

Twilight fell heavily as Ernest and John stepped into a carriage heading back to Southampton.

John said, "He's guilty, you know."

"And it's a darn shame," Ernest sighed.

"Except he's guilty."

"I know, but consider that we're at war, and if Captain Charlie did have intelligence that enemy ships were nearby, then he did the right thing.

"Except that the only other ship in sight had retreated."

"I know, but let's be frank. This wasn't the first time sailors have been left to drown in time of war, and captains have gone unpunished."

"You may have a point there."

"I'm not saying it was the right thing to do, but it looks to me like Captain Charlie is a victim of politics. I think the Admiralty used this case to smooth over political tensions with France now that the war is over. If the Admiralty had wanted to preserve Captain Charlie's name they could have found a way," said Ernest.

"You may be right, but I think you're being too lenient on him. Charlie was the kind of skipper who relied on his own judgment. He rarely consulted with his officers; he saw us as extensions of his authority, people who were there to carry out his orders. And though he was admired by his men, he was close-minded and dictatorial."

"All of that is true," agreed Ernest, "which is partly why he was such a crafty devil. The navy knew of his shortcomings but chose to overlook them because of his brilliance as a fighting commander."

"And with this ... crime ... his luck finally ran out. There were no enemy ships," said John.

"He claimed that his intuition warned him of impending

14

danger. If there had been enemy ships in the area, or if one had suddenly come upon us and we were at a dead stop in the water, it would have been disastrous for us. We would've had no way to escape."

"Except," said John, "Captain Charlie has always had a reputation as a hard fighter. We've been in plenty of tough scrapes with him and he had never been frightened by the 'possibility' of enemy ships before. He left those men to drown, Ernest. Plain and simple."

Ernest said nothing, but agreed. He felt sick at having to testify against his commanding officer, and although he had told the truth, there was a part of him that felt like it was a betrayal. However, he had told the truth, and the truth was that a brave man who had fought his country's battles over the years had done a sinful, disgraceful thing — deserting two hundred men to drown in the sea.

Ernest felt even more distressed to think that perhaps Captain Charlie had lost his nerve. Of course it could happen to anyone. A man was never sure what strength and fortitude he had until it was tested in battle, but Captain Charlie was battle-hardened, maybe too hardened. It took a man without a conscience to do what he did, and for that the punishment had to be severe.

Two and a half hours later, the carriage reached Southampton.

The two officers grabbed their sea bags and exited the carriage. John stretched and said, "It's a good thing the war's over and we've been granted extended leave. I'm looking forward to spending some time on the infamous Robinson Island."

Ernest smiled. "Home. It's definitely more peaceful than

England, and infinitely more beautiful. You are going to love it! I just wish Miss Cole could join us. Then it would be truly perfect."

Chapter 3

———⊱✦⊰———

Robinson Island, Indian Ocean, November 1815

A soft offshore breeze whispered through the fronds of the coconut palms. William Robinson and his son Francis moved noiselessly along a mountain trail, the pristine blue ocean sparkling below. Suddenly, he raised his hand to stop Francis, and both men gazed down at a set of animal prints. William gently brushed some leaves aside and examined them carefully. The Robinsons had a knack for tracking game. They could quickly tell by the touch of the hand how old tracks were, and these were fresh. William paused quietly, listening to the sounds of the jungle.

A light breeze made its way through the jungle canopy. He looked up and signaled to Francis; forty yards in front of them, a red stag deer was carefully making its way through the thick vegetation, unaware of the Robinson men behind it.

Fortunately, the breeze was blowing downwind in their favor.

The deer paused briefly to graze, unsuspectingly eating the leaves off a tree. Francis silently lifted his crossbow to his target, steadied his aim, and fired. The arrow struck the animal just below the neck. The deer attempted several large leaps trying to escape, but by the time William and Francis caught up, it was lying dead on its side. The men set their weapons on the ground and felt the deer with careful hands to ensure that it was indeed dead.

This was the way of life for the Robinsons. There were no markets on the island to buy food and supplies, so survival on the island required the Robinsons to know all aspects of hunting and food preparation. With knives in hand, William and Francis began to gut and clean the deer. In addtion to the meat, they used virtually every part of the animal, wasting nothing, including the liver and heart. The hide would be made into leather and used in a hundred different ways. The entrails would be saved for bait; even the sinews would be used for making bowstrings.

They stuffed the remains into leather bags, which they carried on their backs. The legs of the deer were tied to a long branch, each man lifting an end onto his shoulder to transport the carcass back home.

William, well into his sixties, was an educated man. The family was originally from Switzerland where he had been a pastor. He was a curious man who had learned many practical skills throughout his life including carpentry, animal husbandry, use of firearms, and knowledge of wilderness survival. These skills had proved vital when they were shipwrecked on the island fifteen years earlier. Strong and wise, he was loved by his wife and children and revered as the family patriarch.

Francis, on the other hand, was headstrong and rambunctious, and at twenty-one, he was adventurous and impulsive. He possessed an infectious sense of humor that kept his family laughing. Living almost his entire life on the island, he had become a skilled hunter like his older brothers, Fritz and Ernest.

William and Francis slowly made their way down the mountain along animal trails when, for the first time ever, they were startled to see a man's leather boot and an aged bottle half-buried in the ground. Father suddenly stopped and motioned to Francis to set the deer down.

"What is it, Father?"

William signaled Francis to come closer and study the items. He flicked rocks off the boot and brushed away the dirt. "Someone has been here before."

"Certainly not the Baraourou," said Francis.

"No. Boots of this type have never been worn by the Baraourou," In a somber voice William continued, "Pirates, most likely."

"But why would they come all the way up here, Father?"

"I don't know, son. One thing is certain though; no one has been here recently. This boot is very old and has been here quite some time."

The island had a history of pirate activity, but the only visitors to the island in recent years were merchant ships bringing supplies and the occasional naval ship seeking fresh water and a safe harbor to make repairs.

"Do you think pirates left treasure on the island, Father?" Francis asked, barely suppressing the excitement in his voice.

"I sincerely doubt it."

"Why?"

"There haven't been unwelcome guests here for many years. Any pirates who left treasure here would surely have come to retrieve it long ago."

"Unless they were dead."

"In that case, knowledge of it would be lost anyway," said Father, smiling. "Let's get the real treasure home," he said, directing Francis to lift the deer.

"Do you ever worry that pirates might come back to our island?"

"It's unlikely, but if they do, the hunting traps we've put all over the island should help discourage them."

During the long walk home, they reached a familiar trail running alongside a freshwater stream. Suddenly, they heard rustling in one of the large traps set just off the path. Once again lowering their burden, they approached the trap and could see broken branches and scattered leaves. Something large had obviously been in the area.

Francis cautiously approached the edge of the trap. To his great surprise, two yellow eyes and a long, angry howl emanated from the trap as a large and angry panther leapt at Francis, sending him running back to the trail.

William grabbed his gun.

The cat favored its left paw, probably injured while struggling in the snare.

William raised his rifle and began to level the animal in its sights.

"Do we have to kill it, Father?"

"I'm sorry, Francis," William answered. "He's dangerous

enough even without the injury, and there is no way to safely get him out of the trap without bringing harm to ourselves."

"You're right. Besides, it would be cruel to let him suffer with its injury or leave him to slowly starve," Francis agreed.

William carefully aimed and pulled the trigger. The gun jumped in his hand. When they were sure the panther was dead, they gutted and skinned it.

"Mother will be able to make good use of this animal."

They walked down to the nearby stream and washed their hands. Returning to the carcass, they draped the panther over the pole and continued making their way toward home, slower than before.

Stopping to rest from time to time, they inspected the snares and traps that were regularly set alongside the trail. One small snare consisted of a hole in the ground with fifteen needle-sharp bamboo spikes pointing down at an angle. Beneath the pointed spikes at the bottom of the hole was bait, which attracted smaller game. When an animal crawled into the hole to get the bait, the spikes would prevent it from crawling back out of the hole, thus trapping it. It was a simple but effective way to catch food.

The first snare William and Francis checked was empty.

As they descended down the jungle trail to the family home they called *Falconhurst*, they saw nine-year-old Nicholas inspecting the traps that had been set and baited earlier that day. As William and Francis came within range, they suddenly heard him shouting to himself, "Yes! That's the one I set."

Nicholas was triumphantly holding a dead squirrel in his hands.

William commented to Nicholas as he and Francis walked past, "Food that comes from one of God's creatures is a gift. We should always remember that."

Humbled, Nicholas said, "Yes, of course, Grandfather."

Nicholas noticed the larger kills that William and Francis were carrying and was amazed.

"What is that?" he asked, pointing to the black hide.

"It's a panther," said Francis.

"Wow. I've never seen a panther before."

Together they continued walking until they finally emerged from the jungle into a large clearing. Several large Australian Banyan Fig trees towered above them, two of which had grown to a height of 150 feet. Large roofed platforms were nestled high in the branches.

"Falconhurst," Francis sighed.

On closer inspection it was evident that there were two distinctly separate tree houses suspended in the trees about thirty feet off the ground. Both tree houses consisted of several roofed platforms on multiple levels. The bottom levels including a living room, dining room, and kitchen. Above the main gathering rooms were several private bedrooms suspended higher up in the trees. All of the rooms were made of solid wood and the walls were plastered with clay. Wood bridges and ladders connected the rooms, and the overall effect was fanciful and breathtaking.

Near the base of the trees, the island's main river divided. The smaller branch of the river ran deep and had a strong current, which fed a large waterwheel and pulley system that provided the two homes with an abundant supply of fresh water. Vegetable and flower gardens, fruit trees, small animal pens, and various outbuildings surrounded the elaborate tree houses.

"Pa, Pa," Nicholas yelled to his father, Fritz. "Grandfather and Francis got a panther!"

Fritz, the oldest of the Robinson's four children, came out to the balcony of the tree house. Looking down, Fritz saw Nicholas proudly holding the squirrel he had snared high above his head.

"This is from the trap I set."

"That's marvelous, son." Fritz slid down a thick rope to the ground and patted Nicholas on the back. "You ready to clean this critter?"

"Yes, Pa."

Together the four Robinsons walked toward the smokehouse at the edge of the clearing.

Outside the smokehouse, William and Francis hoisted the panther and deer carcasses onto a rough-hewn worktable. Francis massaged his shoulder, took a deep breath, and sighed with relief.

"Long day?" Fritz asked.

"I don't think I've ever gone in that far before," said Francis.

"Where'd you go?"

"A fair distance up the mountain," William replied.

Fritz grabbed the head of the deer by the horns and said, "Nice kill."

"Francis brought him down with one clean shot," William boasted.

"This guy couldn't hit a tree at ten yards," laughed Fritz.

"Brother, I could outshoot you with my eyes closed."

Fritz suddenly faked an uppercut blow to his younger brother's gut, while Francis retaliated with a quick fake jab at Fritz's head. The two brothers tussled like that for a minute or so until William finally put a stop to it.

"Come. Come. There is still a lot of work to do before it gets dark."

"Father!"

Standing by the henhouse was William's wife, Elizabeth, and Fritz's wife, Jenny, who was holding their one-year-old daughter on her hip and grasping their son Jacob's hand. The door to the henhouse was carefully secured before the small group made their way across the family establishment to the smokehouse.

"It's about time you returned," said Elizabeth, embracing her husband and son. "I was starting to worry."

"You know nothing could keep me away from you," William replied with a twinkle in his eyes.

William and his two sons turned their attention to the meat lying on the table in front of them. Jenny put the baby down to play with an assortment of stick toys on a pile of soft straw and asked Jacob to keep an eye on her. Preserving a large animal required everyone's help to prepare the meat for smoking.

After skinning the hide of the deer and hanging it to dry, William and Fritz carved away the layer of fat covering the meat, putting it aside, and cut the meat into small strips. Elizabeth and Jenny cleaned dirt and stray hairs from the meat, then gathered the strips into baskets and took them inside the smokehouse. Each strip was dredged heavily in a mixture of salt, sugar, and spices to give the meat a rich flavor. The seasoned meat was then hung on racks that reached from the floor to ceiling.

The process was then repeated with the panther meat. Panther meat was not as flavorful or as tender as deer meat, but the Robinsons had learned to not be finicky. It was their belief that all food was a gift, and they were always grateful for the food that the island provided them.

Once the meat was hanging securely, they built a small fire inside the smokehouse and hung a canvas sail as a barrier between the meat and the fire.

"Why do you do that?" asked six-year-old Jacob, who had just entered the smokehouse. Jenny strained to secure the far corner of the sailcloth. Her arms ached with the effort and she marveled, not for the first time, at how strong her mother-in-law was.

"This is important because if the fire is too hot or if the flames come in contact with the meat it could burn and dry it out," Elizabeth said, wiping her hands on her apron. "Separating the fire from the meat will allow the meat to be preserved by the smoke and not by the heat of the flame."

"How long will it take?"

"Anywhere from eight to ten days. We'll check it every day until the meat is just right."

William entered the smokehouse holding the baby and said, "What a great blessing this is. One never knows when we will have another successful hunt."

"Here, let me take her," said Jenny.

"Let's all get out of this smoke," said William. "You two have done an admirable job, as always."

Night was falling fast as it always does in the tropics. As they all walked together back to the tree houses William took Elizabeth's hand and said, "The past fifteen years have been good to us."

"Indeed they have."

"Good thing we get regular supplies from Jenny's grandfather!" Fritz said.

"That's right," said William. "It was just our luck you married the granddaughter of a successful merchantman."

"I've almost forgotten what the civilized world was like," sighed Jenny. "Almost."

Fritz hugged her close. "Do you wish to return to civilization, my love?"

Jenny looked into his face and laughed. "Only when my husband's face is covered in animal blood!"

Fritz hastily rubbed his face with his sleeve, but to no avail, as the shirt was bloody too. Everyone laughed.

"But, no," continued Jenny. "I know too well how chaotic the outside world can be. It's peaceful here, and with my family around me, what more could I want?"

Chapter 4

Southampton Harbor, England, Late November 1815

Among the many vessels that lined the harbor in Southampton was the merchant ship *North Star*, docked at Tisbury Pier. The *North Star* was fully stocked and ready to set sail. Her mast was one in a forest of masts and spider web rigging.

Ernest and John, duffel bags on their shoulders, steadied themselves on the gangway. Sir Ian Montrose stood waiting at the top of the gangway with a smile. A wealthy old Scot seaman, he had a long, craggy face, which tended to accentuate his twinkling blue eyes. Sir Montrose was the owner of several merchant ships and was a respected and successful businessman. He had earned his title and reputation through exemplary service to his country during time of war. In his many years of business, he had made many inroads with the English aristocracy and was very well connected. Sir Montrose was Jenny Robinson's grandfather, so to the Robinson family he was simply Grandpa.

"I'm glad I caught you before you left," he said. "Please give my heartfelt regards to the family and tell the children that their Great-Grandpa Montrose misses them."

Ernest flashed his warmest smile. "You can be sure I will," he said as he reached out and shook Sir Montrose's hand. "Thank you for letting John and I travel with your crew. It's been a long time since I've been home."

"It's my pleasure."

Just then, out of the corner of his eye, Ernest noticed a striking young lady walking briskly down the pier toward the ship. His heart skipped a beat. It was Miss Elizabeth Cole. She was so beautiful that Ernest found it difficult to breathe. Being away from Elizabeth for so long was going to be more difficult than he had thought. He and John would be gone for at least ten months. Ten long months away from the charming Miss Cole. Ernest drew in a deep breath and steadied himself.

Elizabeth had almost reached the ship before Ernest dropped his sea bag at the top of the gangway, and hurried back down to the pier, closing the distance between them.

The couple had been courting for several months and had developed a strong attachment to each other. Ernest and John's trip to Robinson Island had been planned for quite some time, and although Elizabeth would miss Ernest terribly, she understood how important it was for him to see his family. He would be gone for the better part of a year, but she was confident that the depth of their attachment would see them through the long months ahead.

Elizabeth had come to Southampton six months earlier to do the social season with her cousin Rebecca. Their mothers were sisters, and her Uncle, Lawrence Crawford, was a well-respected lawyer. Elizabeth, the daughter of a successful banker, was an educated and vivacious eighteen-year-old. Elizabeth and Rebecca were the same age, and dear friends. They looked forward to all the parties and balls they would attend together. Indeed, Elizabeth was very happy to be staying with her dearest cousin.

Shortly after arriving in Southampton, the Crawfords were invited to attend a ball at Sir Montrose's home on the hill high above the harbor. The occasion was to celebrate Sir Montrose's seventieth birthday, and many influential and affluent guests would be attending.

On the night of the event, the carriages lined up at the front steps to the Montrose estate. Ladies were dressed in their most elegant gowns, and the gentlemen wore their most stylish suits. The guests gathered in the ballroom as music danced through the air. The atmosphere was festive with music, dancing, dining, and conversation.

Elizabeth accepted many invitations to dance throughout the evening and was surprised and flattered when Cyril Wallace, a distant member of the royal family, had asked her to dance. Cyril was well known in Southampton as a gambler and womanizer, but, being new to the area, Elizabeth was unaware of his spotty reputation. One dance was all it took for Elizabeth to guess at Cyril's questionable nature. It wasn't that he did anything obviously wrong, but Elizabeth felt that he tried to hold her too close during the dance, and the way he looked at her gave her the chills. Indeed, by the time the dance ended, Elizabeth's arms were shaking from the great effort it took to keep her body at an appropriate distance from his. Elizabeth promised herself that she would never be alone with the man again, regardless of his high station in life.

Later in the evening, Sir Montrose's butler stepped to the door and announced that Lieutenant Ernest Robinson had arrived. Sir Montrose and his wife stepped forward to greet him. Elizabeth and Rebecca were present at his arrival.

"Lieutenant Robinson, we're so glad you could make it."

"I wouldn't have missed it for the world." Presenting a box from under his arm he continued, "I made a little something for you. I hope you like it."

"Ernest! You shouldn't have."

"I only wish I could have done more."

Sir Montrose opened the box to find a beautiful miniature replica of a three-masted ship. It was beautifully carved with intricate details.

"Good Heavens! You did this?"

Earnest smiled broadly. "Indeed. I carved it myself while aboard the HMS *Royal George*. Being a seaman yourself I thought you might like it."

"It's beautiful. How long did it take you?"

"About three months, when time permitted. I'm just glad it made it back in one piece. Happy birthday, sir."

"Thank you," said Sir Montrose as he reached forward and grasped Ernest's arm.

"That was very thoughtful of you, Ernest. He will treasure it," Mrs. Montrose remarked.

Those who were privy to the conversation clapped in respect, Elizabeth and Rebecca among them. Elizabeth found herself immediately drawn to Ernest. There was a special quality about him, she felt, something noble and admirable.

Ernest was approached by several naval officers and soon found himself conversing about politics and military life. He quickly lost track of the conversation, however, the moment he looked across the room and noticed Elizabeth smiling at him. *She's beautiful,* he thought. *Who is she?* Their eyes met for only a moment before she blushed prettily and looked away.

A few minutes later Elizabeth's conversation was interrupted by Sir Montrose and his wife.

Mrs. Montrose, speaking to Sir Montrose, said "My dear, allow me to introduce you to Miss Cole. She is in town visiting her aunt and uncle, the Crawfords."

"It is a pleasure to meet you, Miss Cole."

Elizabeth curtsied, "The pleasure is all mine, Sir Montrose. May I wish you a very Happy Birthday?"

"Thank you, and welcome to Southampton. I do hope you enjoy it here."

"Thank you. I've taken a strong liking to this beautiful city."

Leaning in, he continued, "The gentlemen present here tonight seem to have taken a strong liking to you."

Elizabeth blushed, quickly changing the subject. "Are you enjoying the evening, sir?"

"Oh yes, but I can't believe I'm seventy. I don't really feel it you know."

"My father always told us that one's age is nothing more than a state of mind," said Elizabeth.

"If that's the case, then I'm not a day over thirty-five," Sir Montrose laughed. "Now I must introduce you to my grandson-in-law. He was just asking about you. He is the finest gentleman in Southampton. In all of England, if I do say so myself."

Elizabeth hoped her smile didn't betray her racing heart.

"Miss Elizabeth Cole," Sir Montrose said with pride, "Allow me to introduce you to Lieutenant Ernest Robinson."

"Miss Cole. It's a pleasure to meet you," Ernest said with a bow, kissing Elizabeth's hand.

As the evening progressed, Elizabeth marveled at how easy and natural it was to talk with Ernest. There were no awkward lapses and they found that they had similar interests. A waltz was just starting when Ernest took Elizabeth's hand and asked her for a dance.

As they danced Elizabeth noticed Cyril watching them with a malicious look, but she ignored him. She didn't want anyone or anything to spoil the evening for her.

From that evening on Ernest became a regular caller at the Crawford home. The spark that had begun at Sir Montrose's party grew steadily until the bond between the two was strong and dependable. And now, six months later, Ernest was boarding the *North Star* for an extended visit to Robinson Island. Being separated from each other would be difficult, of course, but it had been several years since Ernest had last visited Robinson Island and he was anxious to see his family again.

Ernest and Elizabeth were standing on the pier together when the signal came from the ship that it was time to board. Ernest reached down and gently touched Elizabeth's cheek. He looked into her eyes. "I'll miss you."

"I'll miss you too," she whispered.

"I love you."

Moisture gathered in Elizabeth's eyes as she replied, "I love you too."

Ernest would return in ten months. For any other relationship this could be a trying time, but Ernest and Elizabeth had developed a strong and abiding love, the kind of love that couldn't be weakened by time and distance.

"Here are some things for your nephews, my love." Elizabeth handed Ernest a bag, which was tied securely at the top. "Once you're underway you'll find a gift in there for you as well."

The ropes to the ship were being released and the wind was straining against the ship's sails.

Captain Briggs yelled, "Lieutenant Robinson, this ship is about to leave without you!"

Knowing that his time was nearly out, Ernest reached into his coat and presented Elizabeth with a large, beautifully carved silver locket. As the final bell sounded, Ernest took Elizabeth's hand and looked into her eyes. Then he turned and raced up the gangplank just as the ship began pulling away from the pier. Once on board, Ernest ran to the stern and waved to Elizabeth and Sir Montrose, who were already fading into the distance. Elizabeth waved with a smile on her face, but sadness in her heart.

Ernest returned the gesture and yelled at the top of his lungs, "Miss Cole, you take my breath away!"

A few of the seamen nearby roared with mocking good humor, "Oh, Elizabeth, you take my breath away..."

Sir Montrose, seeing the tears in Elizabeth's eyes as she watched the ship slip out of the harbor, took her hand. "He is a great man and he's blessed to have you."

"Ten months seems so long."

"He'll be back soon enough."

It was then that she opened the locket to find a beautiful miniature portrait of Ernest within.

"He never ceases to amaze me. Wait until he opens my gift," she grinned.

"May I ask what it is?" Elizabeth whispered it into Sir Montrose's ear. He grinned.

"I knew you two would make a fine pair."

Still at the stern, hands on the rail, Ernest bowed his head and said a prayer thanking the Lord for placing Elizabeth in his life, and asking that she would be safe and comforted during his absence.

Chapter 5

Aboard the North Star, *at sea*

One night a few days into their journey, Ernest and John were standing on the main deck watching the heavy sun sink into the swelling sea. Since Ernest and John were granted extended leave, it was nice to be passengers rather than part of the ship's crew. They were relishing that wonderful "on leave" feeling known only to military men. However, Ernest and John were not accustomed to, nor comfortable with, being idle, so they would often assist the crew on deck with the rigging and cleaning. In the evenings, they would dine with Captain Briggs in his quarters and reminisce about seafaring days.

Ernest and John particularly enjoyed playing card games with the crew, but rather than gamble for money, Ernest insisted they use corks and other small objects in the place of currency. Ernest's excellent poker face in contrast to John's numerous "tells" added humor and camaraderie, helping the long evenings pass more swiftly.

One evening, while playing a game of cards, Elizabeth entered Ernest's thoughts and he suddenly remembered her telling.him that there was a gift for him in the bag. He was so overcome at their parting that it had completely slipped his mind. His anxiety at having forgot about the gift overcame him and he stood abruptly, telling the men to hold the game.

"Where are you going?"

"I'll be back shortly," he called over his shoulder. "And don't look at my cards!"

The men groaned with frustration that their game had been interrupted. Ernest hurried to his quarters, opened the bag Elizabeth had given to him, and began pulling out items that were intended for various members of his family. *How thoughtful and kind she is to send gifts to my family,* he thought.

At last he pulled out a hard, flat, rectangular object. It was wrapped with paper and tied neatly with a string. Ernest held the package to his face hoping to capture some remnant of Elizabeth's scent. He then carefully untied the string and peeled back the paper. A note fell to the floor, which he quickly retrieved.

My beloved Ernest, although we are thousands of miles apart my heart will always be close to yours. I shall miss you deeply and pray that you return quickly and safely. May this gift help to keep me close to your heart. I will always be yours.
—Elizabeth

Deeply touched, he continued peeling off the wrapping

paper and to his surprise, he discovered a detailed sketch of Elizabeth in a simple wood frame. Her eyes seemed to dance in the candlelight, and he found it impossible to look away. *She's beautiful,* he thought. *I am the luckiest of men.*

Before leaving to go back to the card game, Ernest took another long look at the beautiful sketch and marveled at how they had each given each other such similar gifts.

Several weeks into the voyage, Ernest and John were enjoying a quiet conversation with Captain Briggs in his quarters.

"Where exactly are we on our route, sir?" John asked.

"Let me show you," Captain Briggs answered, pulling out a set of charts and spreading them across his desk.

"We started here and crossed the English Channel. We then joined the Celtic Sea and will then sail down the west coasts of France, Spain, Portugal, Morocco, and the Cape Verde islands to Africa."

John leaned over the captain's shoulder as he traced their way past western Africa, and on to Cape Town, South Africa.

"Once around the southern tip of Africa, we skirt the southern coast of Madagascar and sail on into the Indian Ocean."

"Are we currently on schedule?" asked John.

"Yes. Barring any unforeseen events, we should be dropping you two gents off in paradise in about three months."

The journey, however, was anything but "smooth sailing." Rough weather plagued them for several weeks, slowing them down, and then, just off the coast of West Africa, the *North Star* had the misfortune of trying to outrun a fierce gale and in the process sustained damage to the ship. They were in a sorry state when they limped into Table Bay, Cape Town, South Africa, for repairs.

Cape Town was a fast-growing city, especially in the area surrounding the harbor, as it was here that many ships stopped to resupply and sell goods. Cape Town's economic life thrived on commerce, and there were several warehouses, merchant stores, and taverns in the area. The town had officially passed into British control a year earlier, although it was mainly occupied by the original Dutch settlers. Eighty ships or more docked in Table Bay each year to do trade, and as a result the town was growing fast.

On their first day of shore leave, while Captain Briggs was conducting business on behalf of Sir Montrose and overseeing repairs to the *North Star*, Ernest and John hired horses and rode to Table Mountain. They gazed in awe at the majesty of the huge flat rock formation that was the trademark of Cape Town. It measured two miles from end to end and 3,563 feet at its highest point.

Making their way down from Table Mountain into the city of Cape Town, they stopped in at The Dark Temple, a rowdy tavern frequented by sailors, to meet up with the crew. John was happy to share a drink with the men, but Ernest, who did not drink, preferred the quiet company of Captain Briggs, who was sitting at a table in the corner. Captain Briggs, who fancied himself a world-class draughts player, challenged Ernest to a friendly game. Chess was the preferred game among Royal Navy officers, but Ernest was happy to accommodate the captain. It was a close game but prudence, and diplomacy, prevailed, and Ernest eventually let himself fall behind on the score.

"A rematch once we're back on the ship?" Ernest suggested.

"Indeed," replied Captain Briggs.

"Sir, let me ask. Have you ever beaten Sir Montrose at this game?"

"Never! The old scalawag is the stealthiest cheater on the high seas. And you?"

Ernest laughed. "No. Never."

Fortunately the repairs to the ship were not as extensive as first thought and a week later the ship set sail for the Indian Ocean. From the deck they watched as Table Mountain receded beyond the waves. Within a month, they would reach Robinson Island.

Four weeks later, after chasing fair skies and gentle seas, the *North Star* dropped anchor in Safety Bay on Robinson Island. They fired three cannon blasts as a signal to the Robinsons that a friendly ship had arrived. John and some of the crew who had never before sailed to Robinson Island crowded the rails, curiously gazing out at the remote island. Robinson Island was gaining notoriety in England as an island paradise, and first impressions did not disappoint. For Ernest though, it was simply home and the place where he had shared many adventures with his castaway family.

Ernest always had a thirst for knowledge, and as a boy he

had learned a great deal in theory from the books he read, but he had little formal schooling. Life on the island had taught him more than any classroom ever could have, and it was under the backdrop of the lush tropical jungle, turquoise water, and soft white sand that the young and naive boy had grown into an intelligent and practical man. The years spent enlisted in the Royal Navy had allowed him the perfect environment to apply his vast intelligence in many useful and practical ways.

The crew lowered a rope ladder and a longboat. Captain Briggs met Ernest and John as they were about to disembark. Ernest and John shook his hand warmly and thanked him for all he had done for them.

"We'll fire the usual three guns when we return for you in about two months time."

"Aye, Captain."

Captain Briggs grinned at Ernest. "If you had beaten me at checkers, I would have deserted you here to protect my reputation."

"Then we'd have the Royal Navy looking for us," laughed Ernest, extending his hand once again. "We'll see you in two months."

Ernest and John dropped into the longboat and were rowed ashore along with supplies for the family. As they approached the island, John's eyes widened. They stepped from the foaming surf onto a white sand beach edged with swaying coconut palms.

"What a beautiful place," John breathed, gazing about.

Ernest was overjoyed to be home. It had been five years since his last visit and he had missed his family terribly. "We'll have a great time, John. You're not going to believe the fishing and hunting here."

Stepping out of the longboat, Ernest shouldered his duffel bag and carried the bag Elizabeth had given him. He turned and waved to the crew as they began rowing back to the *North Star*. Then, hearing movement coming from the trees, Ernest and John turned to see several of Ernest's family members hurrying through a jungle trail to greet them.

"What a wonderful surprise," William said as Ernest dropped his belongings and embraced his father.

Fritz stepped forward to embrace his brother, Nicholas and Jacob hanging back shyly.

"It's good to have you back, brother."

"It's good to be back. It's been too long."

Looking down at his nephews Ernest marveled, "Nicholas, you have grown so much. And Jacob, you don't remember me. Last time I was here you were just a baby. Let me guess, Nicholas you're nine now, and Jacob, six?"

"That's right. Nicholas was four and Jacob was the same age as baby Anne is now," Fritz replied.

"You've had another baby? A little girl?"

"Indeed we have, and she is a delight."

"That's wonderful."

The boys smiled, and Nicholas stepped forward to give Ernest a hug.

"And who do we have here?" Father asked, directing the conversation toward John.

"This is my best mate, Lieutenant John Bennett. We served together on the *George* and have been through a lot together. I told him so many stories of home that he said he had to see it for himself. So here we are."

"Welcome to our home, Lieutenant Bennett."

"Thank you, sir. Please, call me John. I've been looking forward to this visit for some time now."

"Well, let's head in and get you settled. If we don't get back soon Mother and Jenny are going to be beside themselves," Father said as he and Fritz shouldered supply boxes.

The group set off down a path leading through the jungle, the young boys running ahead and John bringing up the rear. Ernest yelled back to John who was taking in the scenery, "It can be surprisingly dangerous here in paradise, so stay close."

John was overawed with everything along the trail and he barely noticed when Ernest stopped for a moment, took out his knife, and cut a stalk of sugarcane. He broke the sugarcane into two pieces, handing John one of them. Unfamiliar with the plant, John watched as Ernest began gnawing on the woody cane before he tried it himself. Biting into the sugarcane and sucking the juice out was exquisite; the sugar and juice were sweet and refreshing after their long journey aboard the *North Star*.

The men continued marching on but John, enjoying his sugarcane, was distracted by a monkey sitting on a branch next to a carved wooden mask hanging from the tree.

Overcome with curiosity, he approached the little primate, calling softly, "Hey there, little monkey."

The monkey stared at him, a look of bored indifference on its face. John moved closer, his outstretched hand holding a piece of sugarcane. "Here you go, want some sugarcane?"

Fritz whirled around and yelled with alarm, "Stop! Stop right where you are! Don't take another step!"

Everyone stopped and looked back. Ernest dropped his bag, ran back to his friend, and picked up a stick, using it to lift up a clump of leaves that covered a lethal animal trap within inches of where John stood. It was a pit, seven feet deep, with sharpened bamboo spikes pointing upward. Heart beating in his throat, John wiped the sweat from his brow with his forearm. "What is this?"

"There are traps all over the island."

"Traps?"

"We use traps like this for hunting the large animals, and if you don't know about them you will quickly find yourself skewered. They can protect us from unwanted visitors."

"Unwanted visitors?"

"Years ago, pirates sailed these waters, and although they haven't been here in recent years, we continue to keep the traps. You never know when we might need them," Fritz interjected.

"What about friendly visitors?"

"Friends to the island know to stay strictly to the center of the paths."

"Kind of takes the blush off of paradise, doesn't it?"

The Robinsons laughed. Ernest moved forward, "Come along, I'm anxious for you to meet the rest of the family and see our beautiful home."

Three hundred yards ahead the jungle suddenly opened up to one of the most extraordinary sights John had ever seen.

"This is majestic! You weren't exaggerating."

They had finally reached home.

Chapter 6

Robinson Island, April 1816

"Welcome to Falconhurst."

The establishment before him surpassed anything John could have ever imagined. As a child in rural England, he had often dreamed of living in a tree, but it was the simple imaginings of a child. Now, here in this large clearing, was a warren of charming dwellings nestled far above him in the branches of two towering trees of immense height and girth.

The houses, suspended in the air, were obviously built by a master craftsman. Wide overhanging roofs of bamboo and woven tree limbs protected the structures of two distinct homes, connected by a rope and a plank bridge, the sides of which were about four feet high and made of woven reeds and rope. Around the front and one side of the tree houses was a large balcony, and solid wooden bridges and ladders connected all of the structures.

A nearby river fed an ingenious waterwheel and conveyer system that delivered water to a wooden barrel nestled high in the branches, which provided the kitchens a constant source of water through hollowed-out bamboo pipes.

The ground structures included a smokehouse, slaughterhouse, various storage sheds, and a two-bedroom guesthouse nestled along the tree line surrounding the tree houses.

There were vegetable and herb gardens in neat raised beds protected by netting and connected by paths of flat stones surrounded by soft green moss. The Robinsons cultivated all manner of vegetation including beans, lentils, barley, pineapples, cucumbers, carrots, onions, oats, barley, and millet — to name a few.

Farther away from the living areas, sturdy wooden pens held pigs and goats, as well as a large chicken house. In the distance beyond Falconhurst, there was a field where the family maintained a herd of animals including sheep, zebras, ostriches, and cows. John later learned that the domesticated animals had been delivered to Robinson Island by Sir Montrose's merchant vessels over the years.

The magical scene was shattered when a border collie leaped out of nowhere, racing past Father, and came at Ernest and John growling, her teeth bared.

"Down girl. Down," Fritz immediately commanded the family dog. Ernest crouched down, reached his hand out, and quietly said, "Sunshine, you old fake. Come here, it's me, Ernest." Sunshine approached slowly, still skulking low, ready to attack, before she sniffed Ernest and recognized his scent. Her demeanor instantly changed and she leaped on him, yapping and licking his face. Ernest scratched Sunshine behind the ear and patted her on the back, laughing.

John stood quietly, grateful the threat was over. Ernest explained, "Sunshine can be a bit overprotective."

John smiled tightly. "Ah. I see that."

"Sunshine is very special to us," Ernest clarified as he rubbed Sunshine's back, calming him down. "Her parents were Turk and Flora, our original dogs who were shipwrecked with us when we first came to the island. We were blessed with six puppies, but Sunshine was the only one who survived. So you see, we are very lucky to have Sunshine since her parents passed on years ago."

"Well, you are a special one, aren't you?" John cooed at Sunshine, as he reached out his hand so she could get a sniff of his scent.

Ernest directed, "John, look up."

John craned his head back to look up at the enormous trees. The roots, which ran above ground for several feet before disappearing into the earth, were half as high as a grown man. There was a solid wooden ladder leading up the exterior of the huge trunk, which had been built to be raised like a drawbridge to protect the homes if necessary.

"Magnificent. Unbelievable," John breathed.

"The ladder can be pulled up so that nobody can get at you. And you'll see later that there are other escape routes if the need should ever arise," Ernest added. "But wait, there's more."

Ernest and John took the measure of the huge trunk. It measured thirty-four footsteps around its base. After walking around the trunk, Ernest opened a hinged door that was cleverly concealed in the trunk and bark, and when opened led into a hollow trunk.

"Here, take a look. This is the main entrance."

John leaned into the trunk and looked up. A stream of light shone through a small window cut in halfway up the tree. He could see a circular staircase spiraling up the middle of the trunk. The staircase had a pillar in the center taken from the mast of the wrecked ship that had brought them to the island fifteen years before, and starting from the base of the tree there were thirty wooden planks that circled the mast leading up to another door that led into the living room of the main tree house.

"How is this possible?"

"What do you mean?"

"How it is possible that a tree could live with a hollow trunk?"

"You will notice that the wood on the outer part of the trunk is thick and strong. Father believes that the tree was struck by lightning long ago and the tree simply grew around it. Like our willow tree back in Switzerland, it receives its nourishment through the bark."

"Fascinating! I've never seen such a tree before."

"There's probably no other like it in all the world," Ernest boasted.

John closed the trunk door and followed Ernest to the center courtyard where Father and Fritz stood.

"Fritz, Jenny, and the children live in that tree house and my parents and little brother live in this one," Ernest explained, pointing out the various structures in the tree.

Just then, rushing out to a suspended porch on Fritz and Jenny's tree house, Mother appeared calling, "Ernest, is that you?"

"It is!" Ernest replied with a grin.

Then Jenny appeared with Nicholas and Jacob. "Ernest?"

We heard the cannons, but we didn't know you would be on the vessel. What a great surprise."

Mother wiped her hands on her apron, rushing across the rope bridge connecting the two houses, and made her way down the hollow trunk staircase. Jenny picked up the baby and followed.

Within a matter of moments, Mother encompassed Ernest with a fierce hug. Wiping her eyes, Mother cried, "I've missed you so much, son."

"I've missed you too, Mother. I've missed all of you. It's so good to be home," Ernest said, wiping the tears from her eyes.

"Where are our manners?" Mother asked, flapping her apron to cool her face. She reached her hand to John. "I'm Elizabeth Robinson."

"This is my friend and shipmate, Lieutenant John Bennett. We serve together in the Royal Navy."

"Welcome to our home, Lieutenant Bennett."

"Thank you, Mrs. Robinson. I'm honored to be a visitor to your beautiful island. And please, call me John."

"John, this is Jenny. You remember Sir Montrose? Jenny is his granddaughter."

"A pleasure to meet you. I'm a great admirer of your grandfather." John replied.

"And this is our little Anne," Jenny said. Ernest took the baby into his arms, giving her a kiss on the cheek.

"What a beautiful addition to the family."

"And she has been a treasure to us all," Mother said affectionately.

Anne, suddenly shy, reached back for her mother.

Just then, a young man of twenty-one years burst into the clearing. He paused, took in the scene at a glance, unslung a brace of rabbits and his hunting bow from his shoulder, and came running.

"Ernest!"

"Francis!" Ernest called.

"I heard the cannons, and came back as quickly as I could," Francis panted, catching his breath.

The two men embraced warmly.

Ernest ruffled Francis's unruly hair. "How have you been, little brother? Here, meet Lieutenant John Bennett, my good friend."

They shook hands. "You've been hunting, I see," said John.

"I hope you hunt better than the last time I was home," joked Ernest.

"That crossbow you brought him on your last visit has worked wonders for his marksmanship," Father said. "He can bring a deer down at forty yards."

"That I will have to see," Ernest laughed. "When I left he could hardly lift it!"

"He uses the traditional bow as well as you ever did, and he's a better shot than his old man!"

"Impressive," Ernest replied, "I look forward to seeing you in action."

With the introductions complete, John asked, "Does anyone else live in this beautiful place?"

"No. This is it. We do get visitors from time to time, but they don't stay long," Father answered.

Walking back to the main tree house, Jenny said, "Maybe Ernest would come back to live too if he ever decided to settle down and get married."

"That won't be long," John quipped. "Soon you might have two Elizabeths in the family."

"I see you have a lot to tell us," Mother said, a smile dancing on her lips.

Later that evening, when Ernest and John had settled into their room, the family gathered to share a large dinner. Mother had set the table with her best china, and together she and Jenny were finishing the final preparations on what promised to be a delicious meal. The men and boys were sitting in the living room relaxing and waiting to be called to the dinner table. Nicholas and Jacob had been on their best behavior all afternoon, but they could stand it no longer and began to pepper Ernest and John with questions.

"What's it like to be a captain on a Royal Navy ship?" asked Nicholas.

Ernest threw his head back and laughed. "Captain? Nicholas, you have promoted us. We are lieutenants. Our job is to do what we are told, and do it well or feel the captain's wrath."

Everyone laughed.

"Ernest and I are assigned to serve on the HMS *Royal George* and she's a beauty for sure," John replied. Telling the boys about the ship and the duties performed by a lieutenant put John at ease, and it didn't take long before John felt at home and comfortable with the Robinsons. It was in every way the family that he had always dreamed of, but never had.

Finally gathered at the table, the family joined hands to pray.

"Our dear Lord," Father prayed, "we bow our heads and thank Thee for this food. Please bless it that it will nourish and strengthen our bodies. Lord, we thank Thee for bringing Ernest and John safely home. Amen."

Chapter 7

D inner was a time not only for eating but for enjoying each other's company as well. Nestled up in the trees, sitting at the large dinner table, the family shared the day's activities and accomplishments. It was a time to strengthen bonds or, in John's case, to create new ones.

The food was passed around the table, and tonight the family feasted on a variety of meats, potatoes, and several varieties of fresh vegetables in delicious sauces.

"I've never seen children with such manners," John remarked, turning his attention toward Nicholas and Jacob. "I think the admiral of the Royal Navy would be duly impressed." The young boys beamed at him with complete adoration.

"Would you like more hickory tea, Mr. Bennett?" Mother asked.

"Yes, please. I must say this is a delicious meal you have prepared," John said, acknowledging both Mother and Jenny.

"Thank you, John," Mother said as she busied herself around the table.

"Ernest tells me this beautiful island was stumbled upon by a twist of fate?" John asked, turning toward Father. He lifted the silverware, which was intricately crafted with gold inlay. "It is a rare treat to dine in such splendor."

"Indeed. The silverware was one of the few valuables we were able to salvage off the wreck before we destroyed the ship," Father explained. "But, I'm getting ahead of myself. I'm not sure what Ernest has told you, but sixteen years ago, we left England en route to Port Jackson, Australia. We are originally from Switzerland where I was a clergyman. Times were difficult so we decided to leave Switzerland and immigrate to England. It was freedom and space that we craved, which we didn't find in England, so we booked passage on a ship bound for Port Jackson, Australia. It was our hope to begin a new life—an adventure— starting over with the prospect of owning land."

John nodded. This was something he understood.

"During the voyage to Port Jackson we made a brief stop on the island of Otaheite. Afterward, we were sailing off the coast of New Guinea when a violent storm arose and for days drove us off course. We finally ran aground on the rocks of this island. It was a terrible night. When the storm finally calmed, we left our quarters and realized we were the only survivors on board."

Father paused, remembering those who had died. Fritz and Ernest sat silently, recalling the fear and horror of that experience. Nicholas and Jacob sat absolutely still, wide-eyed and anxious to hear every detail of this well-loved family story.

"We decided to sink the ship because at that time pirates frequented these waters. We didn't want them to pass by the island and see the wrecked ship. The last thing we wanted was to draw the attention of pirates to our situation."

Fritz chimed in. "Before we destroyed the ship we salvaged as much as we could off of it, especially food, medicine, tools, rope, guns, and ammunition."

"And fabric, kitchen supplies, fuel, and whatever books we could find," Mother added.

"We even managed to retrieve a cannon from the ship and bring it to the island," Francis said.

"And where is it now?"

"We keep it in the cover of the trees along the beach."

"What a lot of work that must have been," John marveled.

"Indeed it was. Mother and our four boys worked day and night to take every useful provision off the ship. We didn't know when another storm might arise and destroy what little remained. We had to salvage all that we could."

John asked, "Four boys? Will I have the privilege of meeting your fourth son?"

"Unfortunately no," said Father, the mood immediately becoming somber. "Jack died shortly after leaving the island about the same time Ernest did."

"He was stricken with scurvy during a long sea voyage," Ernest explained.

"I'm so sorry to hear that," John said.

"It was a difficult time for us all, but through the Lord's grace, we made it through. We will see him again," Father said, looking at Mother, who smiled warmly.

The family continued eating in silence for a time. Mother and Jenny had learned to use exotic spices to season the meals, and this evening they had sautéed a variety of meats. They had cooked the recently caught rabbits and, at the request of Francis, a small portion of "surprise" meat from the smokehouse.

John took another bite of the meat, savoring the unusual flavor. Francis turned to him and asked, "Can you guess what it is you're eating?"

"No, but it's tasty!"

Everyone was smiling. John noticed and looked up with his mouth full. He mumbled, "What is it?"

Giggles erupted and Francis, laughing, told him, "It's panther meat!"

"What?" John sputtered, nearly choking on the meat. He had had no idea what kind of meat he had been eating. John swallowed quickly and looked around the table at the highly amused faces surrounding him.

"You eat this?"

"Indeed," Fritz laughed.

Laughing and nodding at John, Ernest popped the meat into his mouth. John shrugged and took another bite too, both men purring like cats. The family roared with laughter.

As the meal was coming to a close, Mother explained to John how they made use of every animal and plant on the island. She told how they used certain plants to make ointments for burns and irritations, potions for fever, and medicines for infections as well as for pain.

"We even make poison," Nicholas said proudly.

"Poison? For what purpose?"

"There is a thin green cactus on this island that produces a foamy white sap that, if touched, is highly irritating and in large amounts can even be deadly," Fritz explained.

"We use the toxin for hunting. We dip the end of our

arrows in it which can be very handy for killing the larger, more dangerous animals," Ernest added.

"Does the toxin spoil the meat?" John asked.

"We use the toxin in small doses that have no effect once the meat is cooked," said Fritz. "We're always very careful, though. Even when the cactus is dead and withering, we don't burn it for any reason. The smoke will carry the poison into the air which could be dangerous, maybe even fatal, if breathed in."

"I'll be sure to remember that," John said uncomfortably.

When supper was over, the family moved to the comfort of the living room to enjoy a light dessert of fruit and cheese. "Mrs. Robinson," John began, "I have eaten in some of the finest eating establishments in London and Paris, and none equal this experience."

Mother dipped her head in acknowledgement.

Ernest slapped John on the back. "Well said, John."

"How has the Royal Navy been treating you fellows?" Father asked.

"Just fine, Father. In fact, I'm coming up for a promotion soon."

"To … ?"

"To captain."

"Captain?" Father raised his glass. "Well, that calls for a toast. To Ernest," he announced and they all joined in.

John raised his glass, unenthusiastically, feeling a sharp and ugly pang of jealousy, which he quickly hid behind a smile.

"Tell us about Elizabeth," Mother said. "You only mentioned her briefly in the last letter you sent months ago."

"She's simply wonderful, Mother."

"Any future plans you have neglected to disclose?" asked Fritz.

"All of Southampton is wondering the same thing. When will they marry?" John quipped.

"It sounds to me that you formed a strong attachment to this young lady," Father added.

"Yes. It is true. She has quite stolen my heart. I'm just waiting for my promotion before I ask for her hand," Ernest admitted. "She gave me a drawing of herself before we left. I'll show it to you later."

"And you, John?" asked Jenny. "Is there a wife or fiancée back in England waiting for you?"

John coughed. "No. For the moment I'm married to the navy. Although I wonder, how did you and Fritz meet?

Fritz smiled at his wife. "Soon after we were shipwrecked, Ernest, Jack, and I decided to explore and make a map of the island. We had been out a couple of weeks when we came to the far side of the island. Out in the breakers we saw a capsized longboat with a couple of bodies washed ashore. We were young and foolish then, actually hoping to see pirates."

"Speak for yourself, brother," said Ernest.

Fritz continued, "We crept up to the edge of the tree line to take a look. When we moved in closer around the boulders along the beach, we were surprised to see a cabin boy hiding among the rocks. Like us, his ship was lost at sea, and he was the only survivor so we took the lad home with us. Of course during our hike home we learned that the cabin boy was not a boy at all, but a girl. A rather beautiful girl, I must say." Fritz's eyes danced remembering that memorable time. "Jenny had disguised herself as a boy by keeping her hair tucked in a cap and wearing baggy clothes so that no one would discover her secret and harm her. Quite a clever idea, I must say. When we found out her true identity she got scared and started crying, and being the strong, brave gentleman that I am, I reassured her and told her she would always be safe with me."

Jenny, who was rocking Anne, snorted.

"Anyway," Fritz laughed, "We made it back home and I've been in love with her ever since."

The story was greeted with applause all around. "What an extraordinary story," John said. Then, turning to Father, "Have you thought about someday returning to civilization — to Switzerland or England? Or perhaps going on to Australia as you originally intended?"

"Early on, that's all we thought about, but this island has become a part of us. It is home. We have come to realize that the constrictions of society are not for all of us."

The evening was growing late, and Ernest noticed Nicholas and Jacob struggling to stay awake. "Boys," he said. "I have some gifts for you."

The children instantly perked up as Ernest made his way upstairs to his bedroom, grabbed his duffle bag, and the bag Elizabeth had given him, and brought them down to the living room where everyone was anxiously waiting. He set the bags down in the middle of the floor and pulled first from his duffle bag the portrait of Elizabeth.

Ernest took a good look at it before handing it to Mother.

"She is indeed beautiful," Mother said as the family crowded around to see for themselves.

"She's even more beautiful in person," Ernest said proudly.

Ernest continued sifting through the duffle bag.

"What do I have here?" Ernest smiled, enjoying himself.

"Ah. Here you go, Nicholas," he said, handing him a slingshot made of polished teak with a band of strong rubber with a flexible leather pouch attached.

The boy's eyes lit up. "This is much better than the one I made out of an old tree branch," he cried. "Now I'll be as good a hunter as Uncle Francis. Thank you, Uncle Ernest," he said, leaping into his arms for a big hug.

"You're already a better hunter than most of those who live in the civilized world," Ernest said praising the boy.

Nicholas grinned with pleasure.

"But remember," Ernest cautioned. "This isn't a toy. Never sling anything at a person, especially your brother or Anne."

"I know. Pa already told me," said Nicholas solemnly.

Ernest reached into his bag and pulled out another gift for Nicholas.

"Here you go." He handed him a small folding knife with a beautifully carved wooden grip.

Nicholas's eyes glowed. "Thank you, Uncle Ernest. Thank you! Thank you!"

"That was kind of you, Ernest" Jenny said.

After more searching in the duffel bag, Ernest produced a finely crafted wooden toy gun for Jacob and a long knife with a tooled leather sleeve for Francis.

Handing the knife to Francis, he said, "This knife was taken as bounty from a Spanish ship during the war. I believe it belonged to an admiral."

Finally, Ernest pulled out two new compasses, one each for Fritz and Father, a silk scarf for Jenny, and the latest printing of the King James Bible which he reverently presented to Mother.

Stroking the high-quality leather binding of the book, Mother gave Ernest a kiss on the cheek.

"Thank you, son. I love it, but having you home is the most wonderful gift I could have asked for."

Father, daring not to speak, nodded.

Ernest leaned down and gently massaged baby Anne on her head. "I'm sorry sweetie, next time I come, I will have something really special for you."

The one-year-old took no offense to the gift giving as she was entertaining herself on the floor.

"And, finally," said Ernest, opening Elizabeth's bag, "Elizabeth sent these." He pulled out two beautifully crafted wooden boxes. "These are for Nicholas and Jacob."

The boys took the boxes, not quite sure what to think of them.

"I believe they are your own treasure boxes," said Jenny, "to put things inside that are special only to you."

"Oh, I see," said Nicholas, opening the box and putting his slingshot and folding knife inside. Jacob followed his brother's example, putting his toy gun in his box.

It was hard to get the children to settle, as excited as they were with their new gifts. "It's off to bed for my family," yawned Fritz. "Good night Father, Mother, Ernest, Francis, John."

"Good night," the boys called, already racing each other across the suspension bridge to their house, their treasure boxes in hand.

"Fritz and Jenny have decided to stay and raise their children here," said Father, folding his arms behind his head. "When the boys get older they can choose to stay or leave just as Jack and Ernest did, but for Mother and me, I doubt we'll ever again long for the rules and confinements of society. Of course the lure and excitement of society is greater for the young. They may need new people, new experiences, new challenges, and ... " sneaking a peek at Ernest ... "perhaps even a spouse."

After visiting a little while longer, John and Ernest felt exhaustion overcoming them. Mother escorted them up the stairs to their rooms. She kindly pulled the sheets back for each of them, wishing them a good night.

Chapter 8

The sun had already risen when John woke to the sound of voices somewhere below him. He could also hear the sound of hammering in the distance as he made his way downstairs and into the dining room, where Ernest was eating a breakfast of eggs, ham, fresh fruit, and bread.

"Good morning," Mother called to John as she took freshly cooked eggs off the stove in the kitchen.

"Good morning, ma'am."

"It's about time you got up, lieutenant," Ernest said, sipping his warm cup of hickory tea sweetened with sugarcane. "Sleep well?"

"Superbly. It was the most restful sleep I've had since leaving England."

"Would you like some breakfast?" Mother asked.

"Yes, please," John said, sitting at the table across from Ernest.

Mother placed a heaping plate in front of John before heading back into the kitchen.

John marveled at the cast iron stove that had been hauled up into the tree house, a gift from Sir Montrose. It was placed on several slabs of stone to prevent it from burning the wooden floor beneath, and it was a much more reliable and safer method of cooking and heating than having an open fireplace.

John once again became aware of the sound of iron hitting iron. "Father and Fritz are forging something in the blacksmith shop," Mother called from the kitchen.

John grinned. "Blacksmith shop? Of course. No home would be complete without one."

He also couldn't help noticing the elaborate water system that flowed from the island's main river and up into the tree houses.

Water was not only necessary for drinking but was also conveniently used for bathing, washing dishes, and cleaning. The waterwheel at the river powered the pulley system of buckets, made from cut sections of bamboo, that carried water high up in the trees to a large wooden barrel. When the barrel was filled they could release the gears of the pulley system preventing it from overflowing. However, because the water often carried unseen particles that could make one sick, it first had to be purified before drinking it. To do this, they boiled a pot of water every night before going to bed. Through the night, it would cool down and be ready for use the following day.

Just then Francis came running up the stairs and into the kitchen.

"Ernest, how about we give John a quick tour?"

"Sounds good to me," Ernest replied.

John took one last sip of water, stood up, and took his plate to the sink.

"Don't worry about cleaning up," Mother said. "I'll take care of it. You go on. Have fun and be safe."

Thanking Mother again for the delicious breakfast, they followed Francis down the spiral staircase.

The first stop on the tour was the smokehouse, which at its base was surrounded by large boulders three feet high to protect against digging, marauding animals.

A short distance from the smokehouse was the pig enclosure where Nicholas and Jacob were working. When the three men arrived they noticed the boys struggling to dump a large wooden basket of spoiling sweet potatoes and broccoli into the trough.

"Good morning boys. Your pa has you up early doing chores."

"No. Ma said we had to get the chores done before we could come see you."

"Well, perfect timing then. We'll help you with that basket, and then you can come walking with us." Nicholas and Jacob could hardly contain their excitement and ran around the three men as they resumed their walk.

Over a hill and some distance away was an area covered with thick vegetation and large boulders. They called the area Tent Holm, because it was the first place the family had lived for several months in makeshift canvas tents after being shipwrecked, and before construction on Falconhurst was completed.

After moving into the tree house Father and his sons discovered a large cave not far from Tent Holm. They called the cave the "Grotto," and it later became their winter home. Living in a tree during a typhoon was very dangerous, and finding a more secure place to live during the winter months had become a priority when Mother seriously injured her leg while climbing the stairs at Falconhurst during their first major typhoon.

The Grotto was camouflaged behind several low, thickly leafed trees. They had planted the trees years earlier for the purpose of concealment. To keep the Grotto secure they built a door from wood remnants of the shipwreck, which sealed the cave, keeping it dry and free of small animals and rodents.

The cave was partitioned into three bedrooms, a storage room, a kitchen, and a living room. The ceiling was high and the walls were covered with natural rock salt that sparkled like a starry sky, providing the family with an unlimited supply of much-needed salt.

The floor was lined with wooden planks that were secured with clay grout. The raised floor kept the Grotto dry throughout the year and the floor level. On top of the wood planks was a felt carpet to provide warmth and comfort. They made the carpet using natural resources from the island. First they covered the wooden planks with sailcloth and then blanketed it with a mixture of wool and goat's hair. They then poured isinglass, a natural glue-like substance, over the cloth and hair mix. Finally they rolled up the carpet and beat it until it became soft and pliable.

Because the cave was large and dry, and maintained a constant temperature, the Robinsons found it a useful place to store gunpowder, ammunition, blankets, lanterns, guns, oil for lanterns, spices, and all manner of provisions.

Just as with everything else, the Grotto was a place of wonder and fascination for John. He couldn't believe how creative and resourceful the Robinson family was. He wondered, not for the first time, if he would have been able to survive and thrive as well as the Robinsons if he had found himself stranded in the same way.

As the days flew by, John adapted easily to the tempo of Robinson life. There was a seemingly unending amount of work to do to keep the family supplied with food and other essentials. Washing clothes by hand was a chore performed daily by Mother and Jenny. There were implements to be fashioned, shoes and clothes to be made, and repairs to the houses and other buildings to complete—all of this in addition to caring for the garden, crops, and animals.

One day, John helped Mother make candles. This was done by cutting portions of bamboo about seven inches in length; one end cut below a solid joint and the other end above the solid joint. This left a seven-inch tube with one end open and the other end closed. In the solid end of bamboo she carved a small hole with a knife, then cut the bamboo tube vertically in half making two pieces.

A tightly woven cord of sailcloth was tied into a knot at one end making a candlewick. Mother placed the knotted end below the hole she had created in the solid joint end of the tube and rejoined the two halves in their original position with the cord stretched in the center running the full length of the tube. She wrapped the tube with twine made from vine fibers. At the opened end, she also tied a small twig to the cord, keeping it taut as it hung.

Finally, extracting the liquid from candleberry bushes, Mother made liquid wax and poured it in the tube and set it aside to cool and harden. Once the wax hardened, she removed the twine and split the mold apart to uncover the candle within.

On this day he and Mother created a dozen candles. John was again amazed by the ingenuity of the Robinsons, and immensely proud of his efforts.

Life on the island was not all work, John reflected. He recognized it was a peaceful life full of adventure. There was time for hiking, swimming, fishing, and hunting or simply lazing away a few hours swinging in a hammock reading. It was a beautiful place and the epitome of what many sought as the ideal life free from the stress, worries, and concerns that plagued most who lived in civilization. *This is real freedom,* thought John.

The Sabbath was strictly observed on the island. Other than milking the cows and feeding the livestock, the day was spent in rest and spiritual reflection. The Robinsons devoted time to reading Scripture, visiting with one another, having dinner together as a family, and maintaining a reverent tone in all they did. This was a new experience for John who was not raised in a religious home.

One day after working hours in the hot sun, the family decided to take a break and have a picnic at a freshwater lagoon. The lagoon was a thirty-minute hike inland, but it was well worth their efforts. The lagoon was a placid turquoise pool of water surrounded by boulders and thirty-foot cliffs. The lagoon was fed by the main river on the island in the form of a graceful waterfall that fell from the cliffs into the water, casting a fine mist and sending gentle ripples through the crystal clear water.

When they arrived, Nicholas and Jacob climbed up the face of a giant boulder. Nicholas grabbed a rope, which hung from a tree ten feet above the water, and swung out, dropping into the pool with an exhilarating whoop.

Ernest threw off his shirt and shoes, dove in, and came up yelling, "John! Come on in!"

Francis, Jacob, and Nicholas took turns on the rope swing as Mother, Father, and Jenny sat at the water's edge, cooling their feet. Fritz was wading in the shallow with baby Anne.

John took off his shoes and shirt and jumped off one of the boulders, diving into the clear blue water. He came up yelling, "This is amazing!"

Not to be outdone, Nicholas and Francis scaled the rock wall and jumped off one of the twenty-foot cliff ledges, whooping all the way down.

"Wouldn't it be nice to have that kind of energy again?" John asked Ernest.

"What do you mean? Let's show, 'em how it's done!" Ernest cried, jumping to his feet. The two men swam to the other side of the lagoon and climbed up the boulder face. Ernest grabbed the rope and ran forward, yelling, "Wahoo!" With the same skill he had enjoyed as a boy, he reached the end of the swing's arc high above the water and, letting go, executed a perfect flip and dove straight into the water.

The family sitting on the shore was generous with their applause.

Now it was John's turn. He performed the beginning of a flip, but as this was his first attempt on the rope swing, he let go too early and landed on his back in the water. He was a good sport, however, and quickly swam to the edge of the pool for another attempt.

Jacob grabbed a low-hanging vine and called, "Uncle Ernest, John! Watch me." The boy swung on the vine and did a dead drop into the water.

Again the family clapped from the shore.

From atop the cliff next to the waterfall, Nicholas yelled, "Give cliff diving a try, John."

Grimacing, but game, John responded by taking a deep breath. "All right." After all, he was a brave and battle-tested naval officer. Surely he could do anything a boy could do.

"I've got to see this," Ernest taunted.

Nicholas dove gracefully off the cliff into the water. Finally Fritz, who was a skilled diver, could stand it no longer. He handed the baby to Jenny, stripped to the waist, and headed for the cliffs.

By now, John had made it to the top of the cliff. He stood looking down for a moment, took a deep breath, and jumped off. His wet foot slipped on the smooth rock causing him to lose his balance. He tumbled uncontrollably, his legs and arms flapping, into the water.

John hit the surface hard and sank far below the surface. When many long seconds went by with no sign of him, Nicholas and Jacob started to scream, "John has drowned!"

Fritz, Ernest, and Francis dove into the pool, frantically searching, when suddenly, John popped up, roaring like a sea monster and grabbing at Nicholas and Jacob.

The boys screamed, then laughed.

"You dog," laughed Ernest.

"Yes," Fritz agreed. "You fit right into this family."

Mother called the divers in for lunch, and then they spent some time warming themselves on the boulders.

Finally, Francis said to Ernest, "Should we show him?"

"Absolutely," said Ernest. Then, to John, he said, "Come on John. This is the best part of the lagoon."

They took off in the direction Francis and Nicholas were swimming. "Get ready to hold your breath," Ernest instructed.

Francis and Nicholas dove deep in the water and Ernest and John followed. Just at the point they could not hold their breath any longer, they popped up behind the waterfall and found themselves in a spacious cave. Light filtered in through the waterfall, which created a perfect curtain hiding the cave's entrance. Francis climbed out of the water on all fours, and began climbing a steep rock wall at the rear of the cave, which slanted back sharply about thirty-five feet. Nicholas quickly followed.

"Where are they going?" asked John.

"Wait, 'til you see this."

John pulled himself out of the water and sat on the rock ledge, looking up at Francis.

When he reached the top, Francis flipped around and started to slide on the smooth and slippery rock surface that had been formed by thousands of years of water dripping from an underground spring. He picked up speed as he descended, then when the bottom of the rock wall suddenly leveled off, he shot out of the cave through the waterfall and landed in the middle of the lagoon.

The family members outside the cave clapped and shouted. Nicholas then cannonballed through the waterfall and everyone waited in anticipation to see who was next.

They heard screaming and echoing from inside the cave as John emerged through the roaring curtain of water, landing feet first in the pool. Finally, Ernest shot out, spinning his body in midair and making as big a splash as possible, showering Mother, Father, Jenny, and Anne. The baby sent up a mighty howl of protest.

"You'll pay for that, brother," laughed Fritz, who dove in after Ernest. The others joined the fray and a great water battle ensued. It was a day John would never forget.

Chapter 9

One evening, after dinner, Francis invited John to go hunting. It was an invitation he eagerly accepted.

"We hunt a little differently out here ... no firearms," Ernest explained.

"No firearms?" John asked. "What do you use then, may I ask?"

"Crossbows, spears, darts, bow and arrow. A skilled hunter can get by with the basics," Francis answered. "We have plenty of firearms, but Father doesn't like to waste ammunition hunting unless absolutely necessary. Every year we test our supplies of gunpowder to made sure they're in working order, and our supply has always been maintained thanks to Sir Montrose, but it is still a precious resource for us and we guard it carefully."

As John prepared for the hunt he was certain that he could do at least as well as Francis. He was, after all, a highly trained officer in His Majesty's Navy.

They set out after breakfast the next day. Mother had packed plenty of food in case they were out late, and they had several flasks of water and a quiver full of arrows, so they were well provisioned.

"Francis, you know the island well. Be sure to look after our guest and be careful," Father cautioned.

"Of course, Father." Francis said.

After a few minutes hiking in the jungle, John asked, "Why is your father so overly concerned about danger? This seems like a peaceful place."

Francis grinned but said nothing. He decided they would skip the clearing and hike farther inland on the south side. After brushing aside a giant spider web, they entered a canopy of trees. Ducking under branches and climbing over them was harder than John expected.

"There are all kinds of dangers out here that you might not expect," Francis finally answered. "There's quicksand right there, for one."

The ground just beyond John's feet looked like any other barren sandy spot, but when Francis threw a log into the middle, it slowly sank from sight.

"Good Heavens," whispered John.

As they pushed through some hanging vines, Francis listed other possible dangers. "Dense undergrowth, snags, and animal holes—you could easily twist an ankle; or steep cliffs where you could fall to your death. Then there are the big cats, snakes, and boars, all of which are in the area where I'm taking you, and they can be deadly."

"Boars? They're just big pigs, aren't they?"

"Yes, but these are wild boars."

"So?"

"They are cunning, devilish animals with sharp, curved tusks. They can charge and outrun a man. When we hunt boars we always do it in pairs because a person could easily stumble and be gored."

"I see," said John, a bit more respectful of the young man and his knowledge of the island.

After an hour of slogging through tangled jungle, they stopped by a small pool of water to rest.

"I was thinking you could take a few practice shots with the crossbow if you'd like. Get the feel for it," Francis suggested.

"I don't know how good I'll be with a crossbow. I've never shot one before."

"All the more reason to get some target practice in before we move on."

"Okay. I am at your disposal."

John found that accuracy with a crossbow was an elusive thing. After some practice shooting, missing, and retrieving the errant arrows, he finally hit the target, a small tree fifty yards away.

"Good shooting," said Francis. "Now let's eat."

The men were hungry after their long hike through difficult jungle, and they made quick work of the cheese sandwiches Mother had packed for them.

"What is the water supply for pools like this?" John wondered.

"The pools are all over the island and mostly fed by underground springs, and rain, of course."

After lunch, John was tempted to doze off but Francis kept him on the move.

"Let's go. From here on in, be as quiet as possible. Male boars are usually out at this time of day to hunt while the females are in their dens taking care of their young. The only boars we're going to encounter today are hunting males and they are aggressive."

A short while later, John heard the telltale grunting and snorting before he actually saw his first boar. Francis held his hand up and signaled quiet, but John unwittingly stepped on a twig that snapped loudly under his boot. The boar heard it, his head snapping up as he sniffed the air.

"Luckily we're downwind of him. He may not smell us," Francis whispered.

John had been skeptical of the danger until he saw the boar for himself. Large, curved, and thrusting upwards, the tusks were menacing to say the least. John could see why one would want to avoid contact with this creature.

They moved slowly toward the animal. The boar was loudly rooting up wild vegetables and failed to notice the two hunters as they moved in to shoot.

John had the crossbow in his hand when Francis whispered, "Shoot. Shoot now."

John was a bit nervous as he released the trigger mechanism. The arrow thunked into a tree two feet from the boar, startling it. Hands shaking, John reloaded and fired again but the boar was up and running away now.

"We've lost him," Francis said.

"Sorry. I … " began John, embarrassed.

"No worries. I think you've the idea now."

John was eager to redeem himself with Francis, who he was respecting more with every passing minute.

It was late afternoon before they found another boar. Again

it was a male that was busily chasing a rabbit.

"Let's follow him," Francis suggested. "When he makes his kill, he'll be too busy to notice us."

John nodded. They were winded by the time the boar brought the rabbit to the ground. The large jackrabbit lay skewered and quivering on the boar's bloody tusks. "Let's fire together," Francis whispered, "it will ensure we get him that way. On the count of three. One. Two. Three."

They shot. John missed but Francis hit the boar on the shoulder which only enraged the beast and he turned, looking for his assailant. John and Francis were reloading their arrows when the boar spotted them and charged.

"Split up!" Francis yelled.

The boar was running at them when they bolted in different directions.

The boar chose to go after Francis. John was horrified to see that the infuriated animal had almost reached Francis who, in a desperate move, had slung his bow over his shoulder and was clambering up a tree. The boar, snorting and spitting, began leaping up and down at the tree trunk, trying to catch Francis with his deadly tusks.

John raised his crossbow and took aim.

"Aim low! I don't want to get hit today," Francis yelled.

John breathed in and out, and then fired. The boar squealed in pain and dropped like a stone to the ground, the arrow firmly lodged in its throat. Francis dropped from the tree, moaning as he grabbed his leg.

"Are you hurt?"

"He only nicked me. I'll be okay."

John watched with admiration as Francis grabbed a nearby

guava leaf, split it in half, and held it on the gash. If he was feeling any pain, he didn't show it. It was obvious that growing up on the island had made him tough.

The boar was at least 140-pounds. Francis gutted it as John stood watching, crossbow at the ready, for any encroaching predators that might try to move in on their kill. They then cut a strong branch, just as Father and Francis had done many times before, trussing the boar's front and back legs to carry it home.

Sometime after dark, the hunters arrived home. They were tired and Francis was limping, but they were triumphant. They were greeted by Ernest and Fritz, who had been watching for them. They helped John and Francis take the boar into the slaughterhouse.

Father examined the boar. "Nice kill, boys."

"John put an arrow through his throat," Francis bragged.

Father called out to Mother who was in the main tree house. "Fresh pork for dinner tomorrow, dear."

Chapter 10

One of the major projects undertaken while Ernest and John were visiting on the island was the construction of a fish farm. Father had wanted to start this project for a while and now with the help of two extra men, it was the ideal time. The area designated for the fish farm was upriver from the bridge that lead to the trailhead at the south end of the beach. The men began by digging a pool six feet deep and thirty feet wide. When that was completed they constructed a dam by rolling boulders down from the ridge above. The small spaces between the boulders ensured that water would continue to flow downriver while at the same time maintaining a constant level of water in the pool. As a precautionary measure, a sixteen-foot section of the dam was made by stacking heavy logs on top of each other and lashing them together with thick leather straps. If for any reason the pool needed to be drained, that could easily be accomplished by removing the logs one at a time or cutting the leather straps altogether.

While the men were working on the fish farm, Mother and Jenny were busy working on a net to cover the pool. The net was very important as it would keep birds and other wildlife from removing any fish from the pool. The net was created by unwinding many strands of rope into hundreds of smaller strands of twine, which they then wove into netting. The net took just as long to make as the fish farm, the women often working long into the night. It was painstaking and tedious, the strands of rope cutting into their fingers, but work on the hatchery was a priority because the year's spawning cycle was nearing an end.

Several weeks after construction began, the net was secured over the pool. "I think we're done," Father announced. The entire family stood admiring their work. A vibrant red sunset sent crimson fire across the sky. Turning to Ernest and John, Father said, "Thank you for your help. We couldn't have done this without you."

"It was a privilege, Father. I wish I was able to do more," said Ernest.

"Hear, hear," John added.

Fritz turned to Mother, "Didn't you remind me the other night that we haven't had turtle soup in a long time?"

John looked puzzled.

"We'll go turtle hunting first thing tomorrow," Ernest said. "It'll be a nice change from digging holes and moving rocks."

The next morning, Fritz, Ernest, John, and Francis set out for the beach, Sunshine yapping at their heels. They untied their outrigger boat and prepared nets and lines. "How is this done exactly?" John asked.

"We net them," Ernest said as they pushed off and rowed

gracefully through the surf.

Sunshine leaped into the water after them but soon turned back to shore where she paced back and forth, a faithful sentry waiting for them to return.

They rowed out just beyond the low breakers then waited quietly, watching for the large green creatures to swim along not far beneath the surface of the water. Fritz stood patiently, a net in his hands.

"There," whispered Ernest as a dark shadow passed under the boat.

Fritz waited until the moment was right, then he threw the net over the turtle as he dove into the water. Fritz moved quickly to tie the net with a rope to prevent the turtle from diving into deep water and breaking free. With the net secure, the turtle struggled to free itself, but the rope held tight. Fritz threw the end of the rope to Ernest, and Francis and John began to pull the animal to the boat. Ernest leaned out and grabbed the turtle by the back flippers, and summoning the last of his strength, pulled it into the boat. It landed wildly, flipping and snapping its powerful jaws.

"Stay back, John, if you want to keep your toes!" Fritz warned as he climbed into the boat.

With one heavy blow using a short wooden club, Fritz hit the turtle squarely on the head, killing it instantly.

Arriving on shore, they transferred the turtle to a cart and pulled it up the main trail to Falconhurst. Spirits were high, and they all agreed it had been an exhilarating day.

The large turtle provided enough meat for tender turtle steaks and turtle stew. The steaks were stored in the meat house where they would soon be smoked. Whether it was the shell, fat, or meat, little went to waste, and under Mother's capable hands turtle soup and biscuits were served that night for dinner.

The following day was Sunday, a much-needed day of rest. As the Robinsons observed the Sabbath, they readily acknowledged God's hand in their lives and were humble and thankful for the many blessings He had afforded them. As John noted their devotion, he began to see this was what much of the civilized world was missing, the peace and balance that came from gratitude and religious observation.

Later that evening after the children had been put to bed, the adults gathered out on the balcony of the main tree house. A light shower began falling from the sky. John gazed up at the overhanging eaves of the tree house. "I've been meaning to ask how in the world you made the roof?" he asked.

"When we first moved here we built a roof of palms and long-stemmed leaves," Father explained. "But when storms continually damaged the roof, we decided to replace it with something more permanent. We used a combination of solid wood and giant bamboo shoots with a diameter of six inches or more. The roof was latticed first with the wood beams, which we caulked with clay, sealing all gaps in between. Then we split the bamboo vertically. We learned quickly how dangerous a process that can be. You have to be very careful when working with bamboo."

"Why is that?" John asked.

"Bamboo can literally explode into razor sharp slivers. Fritz can attest to it."

"Yes," Fritz grinned, brandishing his arm. "See these scars on my hands?"

John nodded.

"Bamboo shards."

"Thank goodness it wasn't your face," said Jenny, touching his cheek.

"Or your eyes," agreed Mother.

"Amen to that!" Fritz nodded.

Father continued. "We laid the bamboo halves by alternately interlocking them, nailing them to the wood beams beneath. After a few days in the sun the clay dried rock hard and we had a permanent roof that hasn't leaked once."

"Very impressive," said John. "I must say, you are the most ingenious and industrious people I have ever encountered."

"I believe it was Plato who first said, 'Necessity is the mother of invention,'" Father reflected philosophically, while sipping his warm drink.

"What do you say about giving John one last look around the island," Mother suggested to her sons. "I hate to bring it up, Ernest, but you've been here nearly two months now, and it won't be long before the ship returns. This may be the last chance you'll have to take John exploring."

John perked up at the idea.

"That's a great idea," Francis said, always up for an adventure.

"Sounds good to me," Ernest agreed.

Fritz sat thinking. "I say we give John the grand tour. If we're going to do it right, we should give ourselves a few days. We don't want to rush."

"Sounds good," everyone agreed.

Chapter 11

The next morning Fritz, Ernest, Francis, and John set out on their final adventure on the island, Sunshine nipping at their heels. They carried rope, bedrolls, flint for starting fires, shoulder bags filled with food, one rifle, and machetes. Francis took his bow and quiver of arrows along with the new knife Ernest had given him.

About an hour into the hike, a small parrot swooped down from the trees and seemed to follow the men, returning again and again in spite of Sunshine's continual barking. At one point it flew to Fritz's shoulder and nipped his ear in a playful way. Fritz batted at it, but it merely flew to a nearby branch.

"Looks like you've found a new friend," Ernest teased.

"It does, doesn't it?"

"Do you think it will follow us back home?" Francis asked.

"Well, if it does then the little ones will have a new pet," laughed Fritz. The dog, seeming to understand, set up an aria of disgruntled whining.

Later in the day, after several hours of hiking through the thick jungle in the broiling sun, they came within view of the summit of the island's tallest mountain. The parrot, which had obviously been listening to the men talk, suddenly squawked the word "Hot. Hot. Hot."

"Did you hear that?" Francis asked.

"I did. But I don't know if I believe it."

"This could be a lot of fun," Francis said, a twinkle in his eyes.

"Or a headache," Fritz lamented.

Francis kept trying to cajole and handle the parrot, but the only person who seemed to have any control over it was Fritz. Fritz finally reached out his arm and whistled. The parrot immediately swooped down and rested there.

The bird had beautiful cobalt blue feathers with bright yellow accent feathers adorning the sides of its head and wing tips. A patch of delicate ruby red feathers framed its piercing black eyes.

"Ahoy," cooed Fritz. The bird inched its way sideways along Fritz's arm, bobbing its head up and down, watching Fritz's mouth with intense interest. "Ahoy," Fritz repeated.

In a raspy voice the bird repeated, "Ahoy. Ahoy."

Everyone laughed. The dog sidled up to Fritz, clearly suspicious, but Fritz gave her a warning look and said, "Down, Sunshine. This is a friend. See?"

He lowered his arm slowly toward the dog. The animals eyed one another cautiously, then the bird suddenly jumped on top of Sunshine's head. When she started to react, Fritz warned, "Down, girl! Good dog. It's okay. This is a friend."

The bird squawked "Down," and jumped back to Fritz's shoulder.

This made everyone chuckle, which set Sunshine barking and running in circles.

"I think that's a good name for him," said Ernest, wiping tears of laughter from his eyes. "Friend."

"You're right. 'Friend' it is."

Later, when they had reached the base of the mountain, Francis remembered that he and Father had been hunting in this location before.

"Follow me. I want to show you something Father and I found," he said, leading them up an old worn game trail.

"We were hunting here several months ago, when we stumbled onto this." Francis pointed to the remnants of a worn leather boot and glass bottle partially embedded in the ground.

"This is strange," said Ernest, kneeling down to unearth the aged objects. "These didn't get here by accident. What reason would someone have to come this far inland?"

"Maybe someone was stranded on the island but never survived," Francis suggested.

"It's possible," Fritz said, "but we may never know for sure. By the look of it, this boot has been here much longer than we have."

Farther up the trail they passed the location where Father and Francis had gutted and dressed the deer several months earlier. Continuing on, the jungle became very dense and the men were forced to clear a path with their machetes.

An hour later, they came to a narrow ledge with a rock wall about forty feet high on one side and a sheer drop four or five hundred feet on the other.

"Watch out for loose rock," Fritz warned from the lead.

"Watch out. Watch out," repeated the parrot.

They took their time navigating the narrow path, keeping as close to the rock wall as possible, and were considerably relieved when the path widened and they were able to comfortably continue their upward trek.

Finally, reaching a spot near the mountain summit, the trees and foliage fell away, and they could see the entire southwestern expanse of the island and the beach far below. It was a magnificent view with the white sand beach and the startlingly beautiful azure ocean beyond.

The men decided to take a short rest before continuing on to the summit.

As Ernest looked out at the huge expanse below him, his mind drifted to thoughts of Elizabeth back in England. He pictured her mahogany brown hair; the white softness of her skin; her sparkling, mischievous eyes, so full of intelligence; the lovely grace of her figure; and her proud bearing; and he longed to hold her in his arms.

Where is she right now? he wondered. *Does she think of me, or has she transferred her affections to another man?* His heart raced at this thought. After all, she was so lovely, and surely other men would notice her beauty and intelligence. *No!* he thought, bringing himself up short. *She loves me, and will be there when I get home.*

Suddenly, the stunning scenery before him and the endless expanse of ocean became an ugly barrier, and he felt nearly panicked to return to England. He surveyed the horizon, straining for sight of the ship that would make that possible—the sooner the better.

Then, just as suddenly, he longed for Elizabeth to come to the island. *What would my family think if they met her? Would she be as intelligent, lively, and beautiful to them as she is to me? Perhaps one day we'll decide to return to the island to raise our family.*

"Awe-inspiring," John mused, clapping Ernest on the shoulder, rousing him from his thoughts.

"Yes. Mere words are an insult to the beauty around us."

Francis and Fritz joined them, surveying the miles of jungle terrain, the green peaks and fertile valleys and the rivers and waterfalls spread out before them.

"Most people only dream of a place like this," Ernest said.

Marveling how the dark blue sea brightened to a brilliant aqua before dissolving into the lacy foam of curling surf rolling up onto the soft white sand, John exhaled, "Do you think the time will ever come when this island will become populated?"

"I'm sure it's inevitable," said Ernest. "Stories of Robinson Island abound in England and Europe. There are visitors from time to time, and some will inevitably stay."

Fritz quickly interjected, "I hope not anytime soon. If it has to happen though, God willing it will be on our terms."

"Some of our shipmates back home in England are envious of the castaway Robinsons. They imagine the ideal," John remarked.

"And what do you think?" asked Francis

"It's more than I could have ever imagined. Much more. Ideal for sure, but I'll be sure to tell everyone that it has only come about through hard work, ingenuity, and faith."

"Faith?"

"Yes. Faith. Only men and women of great faith in God and themselves could have accomplished what your family has."

Just then, the parrot began squawking and flew about fifty

feet to a tree growing out of a grassy knoll. Curious, Francis followed it to see why it was so excited.

Looking skyward Ernest warned, "We only have about an hour of daylight, and it looks like a storm is on the way."

Francis ran to the crest of the knoll when, abruptly, they heard a loud grunt as Francis dropped from sight.

"I could use some help," Francis yelled in a distressed voice.

The others ran up the hill and found that Francis had broken through the turf, falling into a hole on top of the hill. He was hanging from his armpits, having saved himself from falling all the way through by snagging dense grass and vines running along the ground.

Grabbing an arm each, Ernest and Fritz pulled him out.

"Are you all right?"

"Yes," Francis panted, brushing himself off, trying to catch his breath. "It looks like I've found another cave."

"Indeed you have," said Ernest.

Everyone chuckled.

The laughter ceased when Fritz, studying the ground, murmured, "Someone has been here before."

Surprised, the others turned as Fritz picked up a weathered sword that was half-buried beneath the undergrowth. Remembering the shoe and bottle they had seen earlier he wondered, "Why would someone come all the way up here?"

"No idea," said Ernest. "But whoever it was, they were here for a reason, and this hole must lead somewhere."

"Or lead to something. Maybe there's something in there," John mused, thinking out loud.

"I say we take a look," Francis responded.

Fritz asked for the rope that John had been carrying and

secured it around the trunk of the nearby tree.

"Ernest, Francis, you two go down. John and I will wait up here."

The parrot, squawking loudly, flew around the heads of the men, finally landing on Fritz's shoulder. Sunshine, sensing the bird's anxiety, whined as Ernest and Francis lowered themselves below the ground.

Ernest and Francis descended about twenty feet to the bottom. The cave was really only a shallow bubble about thirty feet wide and thirty feet long. Without candles or a lantern, the only source of light into the cave came from the hole above, and they could only see the areas immediately surrounding it. Luckily, the light illuminated a five-foot-wide gash close to where Ernest and Francis were standing. Francis tossed a rock into the gap. They heard nothing for several seconds, then a small splash. It was obvious that falling down this particular chasm would be fatal.

"I can't believe we didn't bring a torch down with us. One of us could easily have fallen into that," Ernest reflected.

"Yes," agreed Francis, shivering. "But, look at this," he said, pointing out three thick wooden planks laid across the chasm.

"Fritz," Ernest called up. "Someone has definitely been here before. There are wooden planks bridging a crevasse in the cave floor."

Francis lowered himself onto his belly and slowly wriggled

himself up to the crevasse. "It's blacker than night down there."

As their eyes slowly adjusted to the heavy gloom inside the cave, Ernest and Francis noticed that there seemed to be small beams of light flickering on the far wall beyond them. Thinking there might possibly be another opening to the cave, they carefully picked their way along the wall to investigate.

From the opening above Fritz yelled, "You're moving out of the light and I can't see you. Keep talking so we know that you're okay."

"Alright."

"What do you see?" Fritz called.

"Nothing yet, but we think there might be another opening," Ernest yelled, his voice echoing upward.

To Francis, Ernest said, "Stay close to the wall. We don't know how secure the ground is here, or if there are any more crevasses."

After several tense moments of inching along the wall, they reached the small shafts of light and found a large hole leading outside. Years of undergrowth had almost completely covered it. They took out their knives and began cutting away the vines and debris to allow more light into the cave. Once reasonably cleared, Francis stepped outside onto a narrow ledge overhanging a precipitous drop of several hundreds of feet. Unaccustomed to the light, he lost his footing on some loose rocks and — in an instant — had fallen, and was hanging off the ledge. Panicking, he reached to grab whatever he could.

"Ernest!" he screamed. "Help!"

Ernest grabbed a vine hanging on the outside of the cave, quickly testing its strength before going out on the ledge, reaching for Francis's hand. Their fingers barely touched but did not connect.

"Francis!"

Unbalanced by his reaching, Francis slid over the edge. His body raked across a wiry bush growing out of the side of the rocky cliff, and he managed to grab hold.

"Ernest!"

Still holding onto the vine and leaning out on the ledge, Ernest stretched as far as he could and was just able to grasp his brother's right arm.

Francis let go of the bush with his right hand and grabbed hold of Ernest's arm. Using every ounce of strength he had, Ernest managed to pull Francis up over the ledge. Francis scrambled back to the cave opening, sitting with his back against the rock wall, panting. Ernest pulled his brother into his arms, holding on to him fiercely, too overcome with emotion to speak.

Finally, Ernest said, "I swear to you. If you're not more careful, you are going to end up dead!"

Both men smiled.

"Never! Not when I have my brother around to save me," Francis laughed. "Thanks, Ernest. I owe you my life."

"No you don't. We're brothers. This is what family does," he said, still breathing a sigh of relief.

"What's going on down there? What happened?" Fritz, who could hear the commotion, shouted from above.

Ernest and Francis, still facing outward and sitting on the ledge, looked at one another, and started laughing with relief and emotion.

"What in the world? Are you all right?" Fritz shouted.

"Yes," Ernest finally managed to holler back.

"We found another opening to the cave," added Francis,

wiping his eyes.

"And that's funny?" yelled Fritz. "Get serious, you two. Daylight's almost gone."

Ernest carefully stood up on the ledge, clearing away loose rock and debris. With the debris gone, he could see that the ledge ran along the outer rock wall of the cave for about ten feet before meeting a clearing with a path that ran up the back side of the rock-strewn hill.

While Ernest was outside clearing the pathway, Francis turned to step back into the cave that was now flooded with light from the newly discovered opening. He could see the entire cave from wall to wall and he gasped.

"Oh my ... Ernest. Ernest! You're not going to believe this. Get back in here."

Ernest stepped back through the cave opening. Looking up, he paused, rubbing his eyes as if waking from a dream. This was no dream though. Overwhelmed, all he could say was, "Unbelievable!"

On the opposite side of the cave, across the crevasse, accessible only by the wooden planks, was a treasure hoard of immense wealth. Five large wooden chests held jewelry, gold, silver artifacts, and gold coins that gleamed and sparkled in the light.

Ernest and Francis fell into a stunned silence. Fritz, also now able to see more clearly into the dark hole below him, yelled, "What's that over there?"

Ernest looked up, laughing. "You're not going to believe this."

"Coins. Gold and silver coins," Francis interjected. "We found treasure! Real treasure!"

Fritz and John reached for the rope, eager to descend into the cave, but Ernest told them, "It would be quicker if you come around the knoll. There's a narrow path leading to the cave's main entrance. Walk around, but watch your step. It's extremely dangerous!"

Telling Sunshine to stay, Fritz and John left the rope attached to the tree hanging down into the cave and made their way around the rocky hill where they easily discovered the narrow path leading down to the cave opening. Fritz and John finished clearing the path, cutting vines away and knocking down loose rocks until they reached the main entrance.

Stepping into the cave, they stood alongside Ernest and Francis as Sunshine yapped down from the hole above. They were stunned when they saw the five overflowing chests full of treasure lined up against the cave wall.

To get to the treasure, the men would have to cross over the wooden planks.

"We'll need to strengthen them," said Fritz. "Let's lay two planks side by side, and center the third plank on top."

When the bridge was ready, Francis offered to go first.

He danced across the narrow plank bridge with the ease of an acrobat. He went straight for the chests, and started inspecting the treasure.

Ernest and Fritz crossed over easily, but John, more cautious, inched over the planks, cringing at every creak and groan made by the old wood.

The content of the treasure was more substantial than they could have ever imagined. They had never seen such wealth.

Francis reached into one of the chests and picked up a handful of coins, letting them fall between his fingers.

"We're rich! We're richer than the king of England!"

Ernest carefully examined a coin. "I suspect the treasure's been here for quite some time. This is not modern currency."

"You all know that finding this treasure changes everything in our lives," said Fritz. "If word gets out about this, there could be some very dangerous consequences."

"I agree. Father will know best what to do," said Ernest.

"Let's camp for the night and take some of the treasure back with us to Falconhurst tomorrow," Fritz suggested.

Moments later, a loud crack of thunder echoed through the cave.

"I guess we're sleeping in here tonight," said Ernest. "We haven't much time. Let's get Sunshine and gather some firewood."

Leaving the cave, they crept carefully along the ledge and began searching for firewood.

"We had better get some old man's beard before it starts to rain or we'll have a devil of a time getting a fire started," Francis commented.

"Old man's beard? What's that?" John asked.

"Dry tree moss."

It was not easy to find dry wood on a tropical island. The climate kept everything in a perpetual state of dampness, but the Robinsons had learned how to overcome this problem by skinning pieces of wood with a knife to expose the dry center.

"Come on, Sunshine," Ernest called.

Fritz whistled for the parrot, but it was nowhere to be seen. "I guess he knows how to take care of himself in a rainstorm," he said.

They returned to the cave just in time. Typical of the tropics, rain began to fall in torrents. A column of water flowed through the hole in the roof and ran across the cave floor into the crevasse.

Striking their flint and steel into the old man's beard, they added kindling and pieces of wood, and soon a nice fire was burning. The smoke rose to the ceiling and vented out of the hole in the ceiling.

Sitting around the campfire, they bowed their heads and gave thanks for the food that Mother had prepared for them, and asked for wisdom concerning the discovery of the treasure. They ate strips of smoked meat, biscuits, and fruit.

With their backs against the cave wall, watching the fire, each man could not help but dream of all the possibilities this newfound treasure presented. The flickering flames amplified the glow of the treasure. In addition to the heaps of jewels and gold, there were finely crafted swords, gold and silver goblets, and exquisite jewelry. There were candelabras adored with rare gems, gold wine goblets, daggers and swords with intricately carved hilts, and even normal household implements.

Fritz suggested that the next morning they fill their bags with what they could carry and hike back home. Everyone agreed, especially John, who now considered himself a rich man.

"Do you think there might be others?" John asked.

"What do you mean others?"

"Others that might still know about the treasure."

"I doubt it. The treasure is old, and best we can tell no one has come looking for it since pirates stopped sailing these waters years ago," Ernest answered.

As the conversation slowly came to an end and the evening grew late, Fritz fell asleep and began snoring. Ernest lay staring at the treasure, and couldn't help but think of his lovely Elizabeth and how this might affect their lives together.

The fire had burned low when Sunshine started to growl. Out of the corner of his eye, Ernest detected movement. A large snake slowly slithered around the boulder that John was leaning against. Without hesitation, Ernest leapt to his feet, drew his machete, and lunged at John, the machete swinging in a large arc. The dog began to bark wildly. John yelled, terrified, thinking Ernest was attacking him. Instead, the machete sliced the air above his head and thwacked the rock with a thunderous, sparking clang.

Looking down, John was startled to see two bloody halves of a snake twitching at his feet.

"You could have warned me," John cried, scrambling away from the serpent.

"No, I couldn't."

Fritz, now awake, grabbed the snake, cut its head off, and threw it into the fire.

"Was it poisonous?" John asked.

"Extremely."

"It's a black tiger snake," said Francis. "The most poisonous on the island."

Fritz deftly skinned and cleaned the snake, tossing the entrails into the crevasse. He positioned a forked branch between three rocks at an angle over the fire, draping the long pieces of meat over the embers to cook slowly through the night.

Looking unsure, John said, "We're going to eat that thing?"

"Oh yes. It's actually quite good," Ernest replied.

"We'll have it for breakfast in the morning," Fritz clarified.

By the time the snake was cooked, everyone had dozed off for the night, except Sunshine who laid keeping watch, alert for any other intruders.

With first light, Sunshine left the cave, sure-footed along the ledge, eager to explore. The men, still sleeping, were woken by the parrot outside, squawking near the entrance of the cave. The fire had burned out and the rain had stopped, leaving the sky clear and bright. Rubbing their eyes and stretching their bodies, they stood gazing at the treasure to make sure it wasn't all a dream.

It was real.

Fritz handed pieces of the snake meat to John and the others. The Robinson brothers watched John, curious how he would react. "Hmmm. Not bad," he pronounced. "Not as good as turtle, but not bad."

The men carefully filled their bags with as much treasure as they could carry, being sure to take as much variety as possible to show the rest of the family. They left the cave, sidestepping carefully along the narrow ledge, to find Sunshine waiting at the top of the hill, with the parrot perched happily on her back.

"That bird was waiting for us all night. Can you believe it?" Francis laughed.

"Come here, Friend," said Fritz. He whistled and held out his arm. The parrot flew to him and sidled up to his shoulder for the long journey to his new home.

Chapter 12

Robinson Island, June 1816

When they returned to Falconhurst the following evening the sun was dropping below the horizon, and the creatures of the night were beginning to stir. The forest was subdued, as though it was holding its breath.

The brightly lit houses suspended in the air against the blackness of night were a beautiful and welcomed sight. As they approached the tree houses, Fritz whistled three distinct times to alert family members they were approaching.

Father was sitting in his favorite chair reading. Hearing the whistle, he whistled back three times.

The three brothers and John opened the tree trunk door and quickly ran up the stairs.

"Father, Father. You are not going to believe this. Look what we found," Francis blurted, unable to contain his excitement.

Father tried to quiet him down, not even noticing the pieces of treasure in Francis' hand.

"Shhh! Mother is helping Aunt Jenny put the children to bed."

"Sorry Father, but look," Francis whispered as the others made their way into the living room. Triumphantly he handed Father a small gold urn.

Father calmly closed his book, making sure he put the bookmark in the correct spot, and put it down on the end table.

"Are any of you hungry?"

No one moved or said anything. Feeling the gravity of the moment, Father took the urn from Frances and examined it.

"Looks like solid gold. Where did you find this?"

"You won't believe it," Francis laughed.

"We found a large treasure trove," Ernest calmly explained.

"Treasure? Where?"

"We were following a game trail about halfway up the base of the mountain. You know the trail where we discovered the boot and bottle?" Francis chimed in.

Father nodded.

"We continued hiking up the mountain from there when we stumbled upon a cave," Ernest continued.

Once again, Francis couldn't hold himself back. "There are five chests full."

Ernest reached into his pocket and pulled out a handful of coins, handing them to Father. Fritz and John walked over to the kitchen table carefully removing items from their bags. Fritz lit another candle and placed it on the table. Father placed his candle on the table as well. The treasure glimmered in the candlelight, enticing and promising.

Just then, Mother came in. Too shocked to speak, she covered her mouth.

"Mother, are the children asleep?" Fritz asked.

"Yes. We just laid them down."

Fritz was about to call for Jenny but turned to see her standing in the entryway. She moved toward Fritz and took his hand. "It's good to have you home."

It was strangely quiet. Jenny glanced around the room. Fritz stood with a grin on his face, and Francis couldn't contain his huge smile. It was then that she looked down and saw the treasure spread across the table.

"Merciful heavens," she breathed.

"We found it hidden in a cave up on the mountain."

"And there's more where that came from," Francis interrupted. "Much more."

Carefully examining the coins under the candlelight, Father muttered, "They appear to be at least a hundred years old according to the markings. If I were to guess, I'd say these coins are from Spain."

"This treasure is probably why pirates were so interested in the island years ago," Ernest guessed.

"I imagine you're right."

"What are we going to do with it?" Francis wondered.

"What do you mean?" Father asked, his brow furrowed. "This kind of wealth has no real use to us on the island, and knowledge of its presence will only attract every pirate from here to the Caribbean."

The room grew silent and serious.

"Let me think for a moment." Father sat in his favorite armchair turning the Spanish coin over and over with his fingers, deep in thought. The family stood waiting for him to speak. It was several long moments before he broke the silence.

"If rumors get out that treasure is on this island, it will only be a matter of time before thieves and treasure hunters arrive." He paused, letting the thought hang before continuing. "The only way to keep our family safe is if no treasure leaves the island. No one must speak of it either. If word of this got out, our very lives could be at risk. Do you agree?"

The jovial mood of a few minutes earlier was gone as the gravity of Father's words started to sink in. Slowly the family members agreed, although Francis gave his assent reluctantly.

John, however, hesitated.

"Of course, I have no right to ask this without consulting your feelings on the matter, John. You have just as much claim on the treasure as we do."

John looked around the room at his friends, candlelight dancing across their grave faces. The mood was somber and expectant.

"I won't deny that I feel torn about this. It's no secret to any of you that I don't come from a wealthy family. I've had to work very hard to earn my lieutenancy in the Royal Navy."

"True," said Ernest. "So many men purchase their military commissions, but John has earned his position through skill and force of will."

"Thank you, Ernest. The same applies to you, of course. So, perhaps you can understand how even a small part of the treasure could change my life."

The others nodded their understanding.

Mother quietly began moving about the kitchen, reheating food from dinner earlier that evening. Jenny picked up a large basket from the corner and carefully moved the priceless objects off the table into it.

"I imagine you men are hungry," Mother said.

Father motioned for everyone to sit while Ernest, Francis, Fritz, and John ate.

After the meal, "Would any of you be interested in berry pie?" asked Mother.

"Dare I decline the best pie from Australia to England?" said Ernest.

"How about you, John?" Father inquired.

"Yes, please," said John, who had been uncomfortably detached during the meal.

When the meal was finished John continued. "Thank you. That was delicious, as usual, and typical of the great kindness and generosity you all have shown me from the moment I set foot on the island. I would never want to do anything to bring harm to your family, or to Ernest, who is the finest friend any man could ask for."

John paused, swallowing.

"I don't know what your lives were like in Switzerland, Mr. and Mrs. Robinson, but it was the desire for a better life that propelled you to seek out a place where that could happen. And that led you here to this island."

Father and Mother looked at one another.

"You worked hard, and you've given your children an idyllic home and childhood."

"But, I … my childhood … " John's voice broke. "Well," he said, recovering himself, "Let's just say it wasn't idyllic. I ran away at fourteen to join the navy, and I swore I would never experience such poverty again."

Understanding glances passed around the table.

"And," interjected Father, "the treasure guarantees that pledge for you, but it will have to come in time. Our family cannot run the risk of others learning of the treasure just yet. Can you agree not to mention anything of it for the time being?"

"Yes, sir," John said, looking into Father's eyes.

The others sat quietly, feeling heavy with sympathy.

"I meant what I said. I would not want to do anything to put you or your family in jeopardy."

Father nodded. John looked into the kind faces looking back at him. He shrugged and smiled. "It would be less than honorable for me to do anything else."

"Good man!" Fritz said, thumping John on the back, the tension in the room released.

Ernest stood, reaching out his hand. John took it and Ernest pulled him to his feet. "Bully for you, old man. I'm proud to be your friend."

Father stood. "I can only say this, we are indeed grateful. Thank you."

Seeing that these expressions of gratitude were making John uncomfortable, Ernest said, "It's getting late, and that ship will be here any day now to take John and me away. We need a good night's sleep, because heaven knows we won't know another one in the next few months!"

Everyone laughed and said their good nights.

Later that evening while everyone slept, Father woke Ernest.

Ernest sat up and quietly followed Father downstairs. He paused for a moment and looked back as he heard John stir in his sleep.

They spoke in the living room, talking in low tones.

"I've been thinking about what John said," Father began. "Perhaps another solution can be considered. Let's gather a few pieces of the treasure and take it to Sir Montrose. Perhaps he'll know of a way to divest it honestly and quietly. It may belong to Spain, and we may not have any claim to it at all. However, if we do, John deserves his share. It's not right that we hold it from him."

Ernest agreed.

The living room was not far from the bedroom where John was sleeping. Ernest went up the stairs to retrieve his duffel bag. Trained to sleep lightly, John woke. Lying on his side, his eyes open now, he heard Ernest quietly descend the stairs and continue his conversation with Father. John adjusted his body until he was lying on his stomach peering through a small crack in the floor. Through the living room window he watched Ernest set the duffel bag on the table, pull out a few articles of clothes, and hand them to Father. He watched as they took several small pieces of the treasure, including a ring and several coins, wrapped them in the clothing, and put them back into the duffel bag.

As John watched, a feeling of frustration flared within him. He reflected on how stern Father had been when he singled him out, wanting a clear commitment of silence. *He's sending Ernest back to England with treasure,* he thought. *What a fool I've been!*

"Be sure that no one besides Montrose knows you have this treasure," Father admonished, "or even that the treasure exists at all."

"Not even John?" asked Ernest.

Father's voice was stern. "Nobody. Not until we know more."

Although John was unable to hear all that they were saying, he did distinctly hear his own name. He did not, however, hear Father whisper, "It's best for everyone's safety, including John's. Now let's get back to bed. It's late."

Ernest put the duffel bag down on the floor against the wall and made his way back upstairs to his bedroom.

John rolled over and stared at the ceiling, seething with anger. *So the Robinsons were as duplicitous as anyone else,* he thought. Disappointment in them and in himself fueled his anger. He was devastated, thinking that he had been betrayed. In the long, sleepless hours that followed, he decided not to confront Ernest right away. He would watch and bide his time. He was determined. He would not let the Robinsons, or anyone else, take away what he deserved.

The next morning Father and Fritz took the remaining pieces of treasure to the Grotto at Tent Holm to store them safely.

That afternoon, Ernest and John were alone on the beach relaxing. The sky was a brilliant cobalt blue, the sand white and relaxing. Occasionally they stirred from their lethargy to cool down in the ocean before returning back to the beach to bask in the warm sun.

"We won't be seeing the sun like this back in England, you know," Ernest reflected sadly.

"Indeed we won't," John laughed

They lay watching the gulls float on the gentle ocean breeze, the sound of the breaking waves lulling them into a state of deep relaxation.

"Come on, old chap," Ernest said rousing himself. "It's time we earned our keep."

John groaned, but stood and followed Ernest to the shore. Spears in hand the two men waded chest deep out into the water a fair distance apart. In only a few minutes, both had speared a number of fish. Ernest was aiming for a fat grouper when he caught sight of a fin in the distance moving toward John.

"Shark! Shark!" Ernest shouted, pointing in the distance. However, John couldn't hear Ernest over the crashing waves. John stood, confused for a moment, watching Ernest frantically yelling. Then, in a moment of sickening clarity, John saw the fin cutting through the water coming right at him. In a blind panic he turned and started racing toward shore, his progress slowed by the soft sand and the pull of the water.

Ernest watched with growing dread as John struggled toward shore, the shark gaining on him. In a desperate final attempt to save his friend, Ernest flung his string of groupers directly in front of the shark.

The surface of the water turned into a foaming, bloody froth as the shark tore into the fish. As John, then Ernest, made it to shore, they stood hunched, their hands on their knees, panting, trying to catch their breath. Their hearts were beating in their throats from fear and adrenaline.

John finally gasped out, "That was an exceedingly clever tactic, Ernest. Thank you."

The following morning, the sun beamed into the tree house

through celestial shafts of light as the entire family gathered for breakfast. It was another peaceful morning as the family ate, the birds twittering away.

The new family pet, Friend, was rehearsing his latest word, "Jenny," over and over again. Nicholas and Jacob began mimicking the bird playfully. Soon the room was filled with a chorus of "Jenny," "Jenny," "Jenny." Anne giggled with delight.

Exasperated, Jenny said, "Oh, you two bird brains! For that you can add feeding the chickens to your list of chores."

"Awk. Bird brains," squawked the parrot as everyone roared with laughter.

Without warning a cannon blast interrupted the fun, echoing through the jungle toward them. Then another. And another. The jubilant mood was instantly overshadowed by sorrow. Below, Sunshine barked and circled in a frenzy of excitement.

"It's the *North Star*," Ernest said, pushing his chair back. Ernest and John went to their rooms to gather their belongings.

The family walked quietly to Safety Bay. When they arrived at the cove, the *North Star's* longboat had already reached the shore, and had unloaded the few provisions they were leaving for the family. Standing on the soft white sand, Mother let her tears fall freely as she held Ernest in a final embrace and wished him well. Ernest dropped to his knees to say good-bye to the children, who were trying desperately to hold back their tears.

"Come back soon," they cried.

Ernest hugged Jenny, Fritz, Francis, and Father as they each gave their good-byes.

"I intend to return for another visit," John said, thanking the family for their kindness and hospitality, his thoughts drifting toward the treasure.

Ernest hoped to return soon, but knew it might not be possible for a long time, and it showed in his eyes. He loved his family deeply, and it was always difficult to leave not knowing when his next visit would be. It was at times like this that they were all aware that England was a world away.

Father took Ernest aside. "Remember what I told you. Speak to no one about the treasure except Sir Montrose. I'm confident he'll know what to do."

The family stood as the two naval officers, their bags over their shoulders, climbed into the longboat. As the boat began rowing back to the ship, Jenny called, "Give our love to Grandpa Montrose, and tell Elizabeth we are all anxious to meet her."

Ernest smiled and waved. "Good-bye! I'll miss you all."

The *North Star* was swinging idly on her anchor chain as Ernest and John climbed up the rope ladder to the deck. Captain Briggs was waiting for them. "I hate to take you from this paradise, but we are in a hurry to make the outgoing tide."

Soon they were sailing away, Robinson Island slipping slowly into the distance. *I will miss home, but now I must look to the future with Elizabeth.* His heart soared at the thought.

Chapter 13

Southampton, England, July 1816

M ore than 7,000 miles away, while Ernest was at sea, Elizabeth went with Rebecca to a dress fitting at the local dressmaker's shop. It was an unusually cool day with gray skies. Drafts of summer air invaded the shop each time a customer entered or left, causing the oil lamps to gutter.

Elizabeth pulled her shawl closer around her shoulders. Ernest had been gone nearly eight months and if all went well, he would arrive back in England in three more months. Eternity, she thought to herself, as she watched the dressmaker mark and pin Rebecca's dress.

"Missing him?" Rebecca asked as she watched her cousin in the mirror.

"Yes," Elizabeth sighed. "Perhaps this gloomy weather makes the longing worse."

"You know," Rebecca said, "You don't have to be lonely. There are any number of balls and socials this season and you have received invitations to most of them."

"Yes, but … "

"Ernest would not expect you to stay away from the gaiety. He would not want you to … "

"I know, but … "

"As the daughter of a respected banker, you do have an obligation to be seen."

"Now you sound like my mother," Elizabeth laughed.

"Of course I do. Our mothers are sisters, and I agree with her. Besides that, I need you by my side this season, or I'll never be noticed."

"You don't need me cousin. You are a beautiful, charming woman."

"Yes, and eighteen years old, practically a spinster! And you, dear cousin, are nearly nineteen! If it weren't for the fact everyone knows you're promised to Lieutenant Robinson, you would be a spinster too."

Elizabeth laughed at her cousin's absurdity. "So? Why, then, must I attend the season?"

"Why? If you stayed home all of the young men in Southampton would be devastated," Rebecca teased. "Even in your old age, you are the most beautiful woman in England."

"Oh, go on, you conniving minx."

Just then, a bell chimed as the door to the shop opened.

A shop girl went to greet the customer.

"Is Miss Cole present?" a man asked. "I was told I could find her here."

"Yes. She's in the fitting room."

The man handed the girl a card, which she delivered to Elizabeth in the fitting room. Cyril Wallace, the son of Lord Wallace, distant cousin of the royal family, was in the front room.

What on earth is he doing here? Elizabeth wondered. She distinctly remembered her last encounter with him at Sir Montrose's birthday party more than a year ago. She had been very careful not to see him in the months since, but she couldn't see any way around it. She would have to go out and see the man, or risk bringing embarrassment to the dressmaker, who was the best in town.

Cyril stood in the middle of the room, impatiently holding his gloves and tapping them into his hand. He applied a smile to his face and touched the brim of his hat but did not remove it.

"Good day, Miss Cole."

"And you, Mr. Wallace," Elizabeth said, smiling back tightly.

Cyril paused awkwardly, then began to stroll around the shop, inspecting the window dresses.

"May I help you Mr. Wallace?" Elizabeth finally asked.

"No. Yes. I ... you look tired, Miss Cole."

Cyril knew instantly that he had said the wrong thing by the bemused look on Elizabeth's face. He tried to recover.

"May I offer you a ride home in my carriage?"

"Thank you, Mr. Wallace, but I'm here with my cousin, and we will be walking home together. It isn't far."

"I insist."

"You are very kind, but I'm afraid that would not be appropriate, Mr. Wallace. We're not very well acquainted."

"A situation you seem to perpetuate by your determined avoidance of me, Miss Cole. I would like to change that. Perhaps you'd consent to have dinner with me at my home tonight. Then we could finally get to know one another better."

Elizabeth felt uneasy with the direction the conversation was taking and retreated behind the shop counter. She was shocked when Cyril followed her and grabbed her arm.

"Mr. Wallace! Please unhand me. You're making me very uncomfortable."

"I like to think I make you uncomfortable. You've made me feel that way a good deal."

"It was never my intention to do anything of the sort. Now, if you please … "

Cyril suddenly pulled Elizabeth close. "I have desired you from the moment I saw you."

Elizabeth put both her hands on Cyril's chest. "Please, sir. You know I am promised to another man."

"Yes," he laughed. "Lieutenant Robinson. A poor choice for a woman of your caliber. I offer you my attentions, Miss Cole. You know I am of royal blood and well connected. I could give you a life you've only dreamed of."

"What do you know of my dreams?" Elizabeth asked, squirming under his grip. "Lieutenant Robinson is a thousand times the man you are. Now let me go at once or I'll scream!"

"That's what I like about you, Miss Cole. You have fire. Courage. Traits I admire in a woman—to a point. With a little guidance, you would make a fine companion for someone of my status."

Elizabeth spun away from Cyril, knocking over a fabric display.

An inquiry came from the back dressing room. "Miss Cole, is everything alright?" asked the store owner as Elizabeth bent down to pick up the display.

"Yes, sir. Bumped a display, but everything is fine."

Delayed, finally Cyril stepped forward to assist Elizabeth and her skin crawled in disgust being near the man.

Once in place Elizabeth turned toward Cyril squarely and erect. "I suppose I should be flattered by that endearing statement, Mr. Wallace, but I assure you, I am not!"

Rebecca, hearing the commotion, rushed into the shop room.

"Is everything … ?"

Cyril turned calmly, and walked to the door. He turned and looked at Elizabeth, his eyes cold. "Miss Cole. You would be a fool to reject my offer. Think about it. I hope to be seeing you soon."

He pulled the door shut roughly behind him.

Rebecca rushed to Elizabeth. "Are you all right?"

"Yes," said Elizabeth, trembling with fear and anger. "That man is … so … insufferable!"

"Come on," said Rebecca, retrieving her wrap. "Let's go home. I think we should tell my father about this."

"No. Please don't. I think he's harmless. Repulsive, but harmless."

The girls talked aimlessly on the way home, but underneath the banter, Elizabeth couldn't shake a cold sense of foreboding.

Chapter 14

———◆———

At Sea, Indian Ocean, July 1816

The *North Star* was on a starboard tack just off the east coast of southern Africa when the lookout spotted a ship well astern and just above the horizon. Captain Briggs and Ernest went to the stern rail where the captain studied the ship through his telescope. Typical of telescopes used on board ships in the nineteenth century, the tapering barrel was covered in leather and had a panel showing signaling flags used by ships at the time. The captain utilized a single brass drawtube to bring the glass into focus.

"Who is she?" Ernest asked.

"I can't tell much at this distance, but we'll keep an eye on her. We are in the Indian trade routes so there's always a lot of shipping around here."

"Aye."

"One need always keep abreast of European wars," the Captain mused. "You never know who has declared war since we left port. It has been my experience to leave port in peacetime, only to find months later that we are at war with Spain or France. We could blunder into a man of war of some nation we didn't even know was our enemy."

Before the midday bell rang out Captain Briggs was back at the stern rail. Ernest and John joined him. The captain was again peering through his glass. "She's flying a Spanish flag." He handed the telescope to Ernest who studied the ship.

"She's gaining on us. That's for certain," the captain said.

"It's odd she travels in our wake," John noted.

"Especially because she's not flying any signal flags," said the captain, checking the panel on his telescope.

Ernest had been quiet. "Ernest? Something on your mind?" John wondered.

"I was just thinking about the conversation we had with Father a few weeks ago. Remember? He told us he got a good look at a ship that sailed close to the island."

Captain Briggs leaned in, listening with interest.

"Father spoke of how she was rigged oddly, and we were speculating as to why."

"I remember," John said. "She seemed to carry too much sail on her top gallants."

"That's right. She was a brig, like the ship back there, and she was top heavy with sail. As you both know, brigs are popular among pirates because of their speed and maneuverability."

"I remember we guessed she wanted as much speed as she could to overtake potential victims."

"Let's have another look," the captain said. "Yes, she's closer.

I'd say she's about a mile and running fast. No doubt about it. This is beginning to disturb me."

"Well, it's good that Sir Montrose had the forethought to arm his merchant ships," Ernest pointed out.

"Yes. Sir Montrose has decided that it's better to arm us with a few tons of cannon than carry that much more in freight and be taken by pirates."

"Do you think," John asked, "we might move a gun to the quarterdeck? Maybe it will discourage this stranger if we send a shot across her bow?"

"Good thinking. My cabin might be best as the stairs leading to the quarterdeck are narrow and difficult to negotiate. Come, we don't have much time. She's gaining steadily on us."

It took eight crewmen with the aid of pulleys and ropes to wrestle the 3,400-pound cannon up to the main deck and into Captain Briggs's cabin. The sailors trained her muzzle out the large aft window.

They studied the mystery ship again. "Look at her sails. There's no doubt she's pushing to catch us," Ernest pronounced.

Ernest turned to Captain Briggs. "Sir, I have no authority to fire a cannon on your ship, but if you will allow it, I am at your service. You have only to give the command."

The Captain gave it some thought. It certainly wasn't friendly to fire across the bow of any ship. Still, he was aware that pirates still sailed in these waters and he didn't want the mystery ship to pull alongside where she could easily overwhelm them with a broadside. Captain Briggs made up his mind.

"Sir?"

"Put one over her teeth. Let's see what her intentions are."

"Aye, aye, sir."

"Brigs usually carry anywhere between ten to eighteen guns. They're fast and maneuverable, but require a large crew to handle the rigging," said Ernest. He was a proven leader and strategist. With John's help, he supervised the crewmen designated as gunners who loaded the weapon.

"This is a demicannon," said Ernest, assessing the weapon. "She fires a thirty-two-pounder about three hundred feet."

Using a gunner's quadrant, Ernest checked and rechecked the cannon's angle of elevation. He decided to aim the ball to fly high and land harmlessly, but definitively, in front of the oncoming ship.

"Watch the recoil, gentlemen," he cautioned, and then ordered, "Fire!"

The gun roared, recoiling back into a network of heavy ropes controlled with great difficulty by the six gunners. Acrid smoke and heat filled the cabin instantly. The crew at the stern rail watching the action saw the shot splash about twenty yards in front of the pursuing ship's bow.

The mystery ship kept coming.

John ordered the gun reloaded. Ernest adjusted the angle of elevation lower, which would change the trajectory of the ball. The gun roared and the shot splashed closer to the stranger's bow. Captain Briggs trained his glass on her then handed it to Ernest.

Still, the ship came on. Suddenly, she altered course ever so slightly, veering off but still on their tail.

Ernest took notice and remarked, "As you know, a skilled captain can maneuver a brig with ease and elegance. It can turn around almost on the spot. This brig is trying to get an angle on us so she can bring her broadside to bear. There's no other possible reason for the course change. In fact, the brig was a smaller target before she changed courses."

"We don't even know if she's armed at this point," Captain Briggs pointed out.

"She's armed, sir. No doubt about it. Look how low she's sitting in the water. Few freight shipments have that kind of weight. And if they were only carrying freight, they certainly wouldn't be pursuing other ships. I'd say she's armed—and heavily."

Captain Briggs decided that if they erred, it should be on the side of caution. "I'm sure we cannot outrun her. She carries a lot more sail than we do."

Standing nearby, John said, "I agree, sir."

Meanwhile, Ernest was deep in thought.

"She's not turning away from warning shots, so that tells me she's hostile," he said. "I would engage her while we have the advantage, Captain. If she widens that angle, we will be in range of her broadside. I think our only chance is to demast them."

"That will take some precision shooting," replied Captain Briggs, nodding his head.

"These round balls are capable of penetrating several feet of solid oak. At close enough range, we can blow the main mast to splinters. We have to draw her in closer though first, sir. If we take in sail, he's going to guess our intentions," Ernest pointed out.

"What if we just let her catch up as she's been doing?" John suggested.

"That's an idea, too," agreed Ernest.

So they played the waiting game, allowing the ship to close the distance on them. When it came within three hundred yards, close enough for a ball to hit her main mast, Ernest ordered the crew to prepare the cannon.

"Did you know cannons were invented by the Chinese hundreds of years ago?" Ernest asked as he made his calculations.

"Great news," said John. "We must remember to thank them."

The men waited to light the gunpowder. Ernest calmly said, "Fire."

The shot whistled through the air, tearing through the mystery ship's mainsail about ten feet from the mast. With that shot, it was obvious that the *North Star* was not interested in issuing warning shots.

Ernest ordered the men to reload, when a blast from the other ship suddenly sent a cannonball screaming over their heads, landing in the water.

The enemy was now within two hundred yards. While calculating the gun's angle of elevation, Ernest carefully checked the direction of the wind and height of the waves before again ordering, "Fire!" This shot glanced off the main mast.

As Ernest guessed, the brig changed course, but Ernest had already made his calculations, needing only to see if the ship was moving to port or starboard. They made their decision, and Ernest made his. His next command sent a ball screaming squarely into the main mast, splitting it with a crack loud enough to be heard clearly aboard the *North Star*. It splintered and came down in an avalanche of smashed rigging, spars, and billowing sail. The *North Star's* crew cheered lustily.

Without wind power, the mystery ship drifted until she was dead in the water as the *North Star,* under full sail, quickly created distance between them.

Captain Briggs smiled. There was little doubt that the

mystery ship was either a pirate or some other form of wartime profiteering vessel. He knew that the two Royal Navy officers had saved them and called for three cheers from the crew.

Hours later, as the sun was beginning its final descent, and evening was approaching, Ernest was above deck immersed in a book and the crew was midship enjoying a celebratory feast that the captain had ordered for them. It was then that John took the opportunity to go below deck.

The waves were rocking the ship side to side, and below only a few candles were swinging back and forth. John had only one thing on his mind. Entering the small quarters he and Ernest shared, he retrieved Ernest's duffel bag from under his bunk and quickly rummaged through it looking for the treasure, his eyes sparkling with malice and greed.

He knew he had done an excellent job hiding his feelings of betrayal and anger from Ernest, playing the role of good mate and loyal companion. Back on the island he had given his pledge not to divulge the secret of the treasure, while Ernest and his father were scheming to hide the wealth with Sir Montrose, obviously planning to cut him out of his share. Well, he would see about that. All his life he had been exploited by the upper classes. He had bowed and scraped, taken abuse, shown obeisance and loyalty, and worked his way up the ranks through the navy. He had not come this far only to once again be cheated out of his due.

He paused, looking back over his shoulder to make sure he was not being watched. He quickly pocketed a few coins, and a heavy gold ring set with emeralds. He wasn't exactly sure what he would do with these items, but he at least wanted to be able to prove that the treasure existed. He carefully righted Ernest's belongings and returned the duffel bag to its rightful place under the bunk.

Over the next few months, they sailed around the Horn of Africa into the Atlantic, and with the exception of a few bad squalls, the *North Star* had favorable passage and dropped anchor in Southampton just north of Portsmouth four months after leaving Robinson Island.

Southampton, October 1816

As Ernest and John prepared to disembark the *North Star,* Captain Briggs thanked them heartily for their service, and promised to send letters of praise not only to Sir Montrose but to the Royal Navy as well.

A carriage was flagged down to take them to the naval barracks just outside Southampton. As John was climbing into the carriage, Ernest told him that he would meet him back in the barracks later. He needed to see Sir Montrose.

"Of course," John said, struggling to keep sarcasm from his voice. "Family first, right?"

Ernest made his way to Sir Montrose's office in a prosperous section of Southampton's bustling waterfront district. He was ushered into a luxurious office with dark paneled walls and a large, finely crafted mantle. Sir Montrose, sitting at a huge teak and mahogany desk, carved in intricate Chinese symbols, looked up from his work, surprised. He stood and greeted Ernest with a cheerful hug.

"Ernest! How was your trip? How is the family?"

The old man was anxious, of course, for word of his granddaughter and great-grandchildren.

Ernest happily caught him up with news of the family, delivering letters from Jenny and describing Sir Montrose's three great-grandchildren in great detail. When talk of the family had wound down, Ernest asked permission to close the door.

Sir Montrose sensed the change of mood in the room.

With the door securely closed, Ernest dug into his bag and retrieved the silver dagger, a gold urn, and a few gold coins, handing them to Sir Montrose.

Sir Montrose's eyes widened. He studied the bejeweled dagger, a look of pure amazement on his face. "Where did you get this?"

"From a cave on the island. We found five chests full of treasure."

"Five chests?"

"Yes. Five overflowing chests. We all agreed that other than these few items, the treasure mustn't leave the island for now, and we all agreed not to speak of it."

"Wise." Sir Montrose sat silently fingering the gold urn, thinking. Finally, he looked up. "Is Mr. Bennett aware of this?"

"Yes. He was with us when it was discovered. Other than

me, John is the only person off the island that knows about the treasure. Not even Captain Briggs."

"Hmmm," mused Sir Montrose.

"Father instructed me to give these items to you. He said you would know what to do."

Ernest frowned, remembering something. He dug through his bag, fumbling through the pockets of the clothes inside looking for an emerald ring he thought Father had included. Shrugging, he finally abandoned the search because he wasn't entirely sure that Father had actually put it in the duffel bag.

"Father thought you could likely determine dates and country of origin on some of these things."

Sitting back in his chair Sir Montrose gazed steadily at Ernest. "It looks to me like your family has suddenly become very wealthy. Congratulations. I'll look into these items for you discreetly, and let you know what I find."

He took the pieces of treasure and opened his iron safe. The treasure would be safe with him, just as Father had thought. Ernest felt a great burden lifted because he was confident that in time Sir Montrose would have the answers the Robinsons were seeking.

Chapter 15

Southampton, England, October 1816

Ernest entered the living quarters he shared with John and two other Royal Navy officers, Malcolm Everett and Iain Wilde. John was at a table talking to the others and showing them the blowgun and darts he brought back from Robinson Island. Malcolm and Iain were amazed at the velocity and speed as they blew darts across the room into a wooden board they had fixed to the wall. Unfortunately, due to their lack of skill, the darts often missed the board, hitting the plaster and sending chunks flying off the wall. The men were wildly amused.

"What are you gents thinking?" Ernest said, shaking his head as he stored his duffel bag. He turned to find the others with their heads together, sniggering. "What's so funny?" he asked.

"Oh nothing. It's just that Miss Cole and I ... well ... began courting while you were gone," Malcolm said, barely suppressing a laugh.

"In your dreams," Ernest replied with complete confidence.

"Wait! She and I are engaged I'll have you know," Iain said, joining the fun.

"Not true," Malcolm persisted, "the lady is mine."

"You wish," Ernest laughed.

"How is Miss Cole anyway? Have you seen her?" Ernest asked his friends.

Iain couldn't pass up the opportunity to tease Ernest. "She came by yesterday hoping you were back, and she said if you didn't show up soon she would happily be mine."

With a shake of his head, Ernest washed up, changed clothes, combed his hair, and headed for the front door.

"Don't be out late, Lieutenant Robinson," Malcolm said in a mocking tone. "We have to report for duty first thing tomorrow morning."

"Where are you off to?" John asked.

Ernest placed his hat squarely on his head and opened the door. "To see the beautiful Miss Cole, of course!" The door slammed heartily behind him.

"That, my good fellows, is a man in love," Malcolm lamented.

"I'd be in love too if I had a lady like Miss Cole," said Iain.

"Indeed," John agreed.

Ernest stepped down from the hansom cab in front of the Crawford's three-story red brick house. On a whim, he plucked a flower from the immaculately kept front garden and hurried up the steps. He lifted the heavy doorknocker, letting it fall several times.

A servant answered the door, and invited Ernest into the foyer while Mrs. Crawford was informed of his arrival. Mrs. Crawford's face lit up at the news that Ernest had finally returned to England.

"Oh. Do send him in."

Mrs. Crawford stood and gave a small curtsy as Ernest entered the room. "Lieutenant Robinson! How good it is to see you."

Ernest bowed. "The pleasure is all mine, Mrs. Crawford."

"We have been counting the days, anticipating your arrival."

"Is Miss Cole presently home, ma'am?"

"She is not, I'm sorry to say. Elizabeth is down at Thompson's upholstery shop choosing a new fabric for her settee."

Just then, Mr. Crawford entered the room. A generous smile spread across his face. "Good afternoon, Lieutenant Robinson. I'm glad to see you home," he said as the two men stepped forward to shake hands.

"Thank you, sir. "

Ernest realized he was still holding the flower he had picked and presented it to Mrs. Crawford with a bow.

"Thank you," she said, smiling, recognizing the bloom as one from her front garden.

"We've been placing bets on when you would arrive," Mr. Crawford informed Ernest.

"You have? Now that I'm here, tell me, who is the victor?" Ernest said smiling.

"If my memory serves, I recall you chose today. Did you

not?" Mr. Crawford said turning to his wife.

"Well, yes. I did. Poor Elizabeth thought you would arrive yesterday. You should have seen her excitement."

"And her disappointment when you didn't appear," added Mr. Crawford.

"It makes no difference now," Mrs. Crawford smiled. "Elizabeth will be thrilled to see you. She should be arriving soon. Would you like to sit, Lieutenant Robinson?"

"Thank you," said Ernest, "but ... I think ... I'll just ... "

"Yes. Quite right. Go. She has waited long enough," said Mrs. Crawford.

"Hurry along now. She'll be delighted to see you," Mr. Crawford encouraged.

Ernest thanked them, returned to the street, and hailed a carriage to the upholstery shop. Standing at the window, he could see Elizabeth standing at the counter looking at fabric samples. The sunlight played across her chestnut hair, which was arranged in a fashionable twist at the crown of her head.

Standing taller than most women, she looked elegant in her long black-and-white striped dress, nipped tightly at the bodice in the empire waist style. Ernest longed to see her face. Just then a customer walked through the front door, making the bell ring. Elizabeth turned and Ernest quickly moved away from the window, not wanting to be noticed.

Ernest crossed the street and entered a stationary store where he purchased five blank note cards with envelopes. He found a quiet spot where he could write notes on each of the cards. He planned to send Elizabeth on a surprise adventure.

Ernest wrote five clues on each of the cards, and placed them in their envelopes and addressed them to Miss Cole. He did all of this quickly as he was unsure how much longer Elizabeth and Rebecca would be at the shop. He put the first card in his pocket, and gave the second card to the proprietor of the stationary store. "There will be a young lady, Miss Cole, coming in asking for this note. All you have to do is give it to her."

"And what shall I say?" the proprietor asked uncertainly.

"Nothing at all. The message in the envelope will tell her all she needs to know." The proprietor looked at Ernest carefully, and decided that he could be trusted, so he agreed.

Ernest thanked the man and went on to the next location. It was a hat shop three blocks down the street. There he gave the milliner the third envelope, and then left the fourth card with the doorman at a respected hotel.

He then took the fifth and final card to Kings Park Carriage Service four blocks away and handed it to the groom.

Once again Ernest explained, "When a beautiful young lady comes and asks for a sealed envelope, simply give it to her if you wouldn't mind."

"No problem a'tall."

"The two ladies will need a ride," Ernest explained, producing money from his wallet. "Drive the lady and her companion to the entrance of Kings Park."

Ernest noticed a flower cart nearby. He quickly ran over, bought a rose, brought it back to the groom, and asked if he would make sure it was lying on the passenger seat when Elizabeth entered the carriage.

With all the cards delivered, Ernest raced back up the hill to the upholstery shop. He noticed a young lad walking toward him. Ernest pulled the sealed note from his coat pocket, along with a coin, and stopped the boy.

"Would you like to earn a little something?" Ernest asked the boy, holding the coin in front of him.

"Yes, sir!"

"Take this envelope into this upholstery shop, and ask for Miss Cole. She's the lady wearing the black-and-white striped dress. Hand it to her. That's all."

The boy eagerly agreed, eyeing the coin hungrily.

Ernest watched from the corner of the window as the boy opened the door and walked in.

"I have a message here for Miss Cole," he announced. Elizabeth heard her name and turned around.

Ernest caught his breath as the warm glow of the gas lamps enhanced the extraordinary beauty of her face.

"I'm Miss Cole," she said, a bit confused.

The boy handed the envelope to her. "A man asked me to give this to you, Miss."

"And what did this man look like?" Elizabeth asked.

"I cannot say. I was told only to give you the envelope and leave."

"I see, but tell me, did he seem like a nice man?"

"He did, Miss."

"Was he tall and with brown hair?"

"He was wearing a navy ... "the boy stopped short, realizing he had said more than he should have.

Elizabeth dazzled the boy with a smile. "Well done. You may be on your way, and thank you!"

Once out the door, the boy received his payment. "Thank you, sir," he yelled, running down the street.

Elizabeth opened the sealed envelope with shaking hands.

"Well, what does it say?" Rebecca asked, peering over her

shoulder.

Elizabeth read the letter to herself, and then a second time aloud.

When work is done, don your coat and bonnet.
At yon stationer, receive the note with writing on it.

Recognizing the handwriting, Elizabeth's heart began to race. Ernest watched as Elizabeth and Rebecca rushed through the store, gathering their coats and bonnets. Elizabeth nearly dragged Rebecca out the door and across the street to the stationary store with the most radiant smile Ernest had ever seen.

The note in the stationary store read:

In the millinery shop on Front Street,
A message you will find.
Please go there, my love,
If you would be so kind.

Ernest was careful to stay one step ahead of the ladies as they hurried from one location to another retrieving the messages.

In the hat shop they giggled with mirth as Elizabeth read the note waiting for her there.

The concierge at the Pelican Hotel
Has another note for you as well.

Winded, her cheeks rosy with anticipation, Elizabeth arrived at the Pelican Hotel. Ernest was hiding behind a column in the lobby watching her. *She is so very beautiful,* he thought.

The note given to her read:

> *To Kings Park Carriage Service you must go,*
> *The last of these notes they will show.*

Beside herself now with excitement, Elizabeth nearly flew out the door. Rebecca gasped and pulled Elizabeth's hand stopping her.

"Elizabeth, I must catch my breath," she gasped.

"Oh, dearest Rebecca! I simply cannot wait one second more. It is nearly killing me knowing he is here and I have yet to see him."

"Very well."

With quick strides the ladies hurried to Kings Park Carriage Service. Seeing them leave the hotel, Ernest had hailed a coach, knowing he had very little time to arrive at the arranged meeting place.

When they arrived at the carriage service, Elizabeth spoke to the wizened, old groom. "I understand you have an envelope for me?"

"That depends on who you are," said the man with mock severity, the twinkle in his eyes giving him away. "Your name, if you please."

"Miss Elizabeth Cole."

"Let me see," he said rummaging through the paper on the desk. "No. No. Nothing here under that name."

Elizabeth's face fell. She and Rebecca looked at each other puzzled. Elizabeth felt frantic. "Would you be so kind as to check again, sir?"

The man would have liked to continue his ruse, but he couldn't bring himself to tease the lovely ladies standing before him a moment longer. He reached into a cubby in his desk and with twinkling eyes said, "It seems I do have a little something for you."

"Oh, thank you, sir," Elizabeth gasped. She moved one or two steps away, taking a deep breath to calm herself, as she opened the sealed envelope.

> *A carriage is waiting to bring you to me.*
> *Dear Elizabeth, my darling, I wait there for thee.*

The ladies were guided to a beautiful white carriage. On the seat Elizabeth found a red rose and caressed the petals tenderly, beaming with joy. As the horse slowly drew the carriage through the crowds, Elizabeth's heart raced with anticipation.

"I'm so happy for you," Rebecca said, taking her hand.

The driver looked back and asked, "You have someone special to see?"

"I believe I do. Someone very special," Elizabeth answered shyly.

"Not your typical Englishman to dream up such a lovely adventure for his lady. He must be very kind," the old man commented.

"He is the very finest of men," she said with pride.

"Here we are ladies," the groom announced as the carriage pulled up to the entrance of Kings Park

Ernest stood at the gate looking dashing in his Navy uniform. Removing his hat, and tucking it under his arm, he extended his hand to help Elizabeth down from the carriage. Elizabeth met

Ernest's eyes and her breathing slowed.

"I am very happy to see you, Miss Cole. I have missed you deeply."

Elizabeth blushed prettily. "It is a pleasure to see you Lieutenant Robinson. I have long awaited your return."

Ernest turned to help Rebecca down for the carriage. "It's a pleasure to see you as well, Miss Crawford."

"I'm so glad to see you Lieutenant Robinson. Another day of waiting would have devastated my cousin, and driven me to distraction."

As the carriage began to pull away, the driver called out, "I wish you two the very best."

Elizabeth smiled, and waved good-bye to the driver.

"I see you have won another heart," Ernest teased.

The three entered the park and began to stroll. Rebecca walked several paces behind the couple, giving them some privacy.

"How is your family?" Elizabeth asked.

"They are all well. Of course they are anxious to meet the lady who has won my heart." They both smiled as they walked.

Time passed quickly as the young couple talked of their families and the adventures on Robinson Island. As the light began to fade, Ernest led them back to the park entrance where a carriage was waiting for them.

Ernest helped Elizabeth and Rebecca into the carriage, and climbed in behind them. Before sitting down he retrieved a blanket and draped it over the ladies' legs. Elizabeth and Rebecca sat together with Ernest taking the seat across from them.

When they arrived at the Crawford residence, Ernest generously tipped the driver, adding his thanks, and sent him on his way.

Mr. Crawford met them at the door. "Lieutenant Robinson, come join us in the drawing room." Mr. Crawford inquired of Ernest's family and the island. Ernest entertained them all with stories of his niece and nephews.

When the topic turned to the navy, Ernest turned toward Elizabeth. "Miss Cole, the Royal Navy's annual ball is next Friday evening, and I would be honored if you would accompany me."

"Of course. I would be delighted!" Elizabeth responded.

"May I call on you tomorrow, Miss Cole?"

"Of course you may," Elizabeth answered quickly as they made their way to the front door.

"Goodnight, Elizabeth," whispered Ernest, holding her long slender hands.

"I'm very angry with you, you know."

Amused, Ernest pulled away. "Oh? What did I do?"

"Your infuriatingly long hunt! I nearly died of anticipation," Elizabeth pouted.

Not fooled for a minute, Ernest touched her chin. "You're even more beautiful when you're angry. I shall have to make you angry more often."

"And I shall have to say goodnight, you scoundrel," smiled Elizabeth as she turned toward the door. Turning back she said, "I had a lovely time tonight." The door slowly closed, leaving Ernest craving more of her attention.

Ernest turned and walked the quiet, misty streets of Southampton in a daze of happiness, arriving back at his quarters long after his mates were asleep.

Sleep, however, eluded him as he replayed every moment of his reunion with his lovely Elizabeth.

Chapter 16

Friday arrived. The Royal Navy Ball was an annual tradition sponsored by the Admiralty, and was intended to bolster the morale of officers. It was a lavish event featuring the finest in music, food, and spirits. The ladies wore their best gowns and jewelry, and the men looked dashing in their dress uniforms. It was a glittering affair, and Ernest and Elizabeth were enjoying themselves. Several officers stopped them as they moved through the crowd. "Welcome back, old chap. Good to see you."

"Thank you," Ernest said. "It's good to be back."

Leaning over to Elizabeth he murmured, "The only difficult part of being away was missing you."

Elizabeth smiled back at him, brilliant and sincere.

Ernest was surprised some time later when Admiral Weatherford joined them. "There's a rumor going around about you, Lieutenant Robinson."

"What rumor would that be sir?"

"It's about your promotion to captain."

"I believe that particular rumor is premature, sir."

"We at the command staff are happy for you. You have proved yourself to be a worthy leader."

Before Ernest could respond, the admiral turned and walked away.

Ernest was perplexed by what the admiral had said, but before he could even think of it Commander Samuel and his wife, Sarah, joined them. "I see you made it back in one piece," Commander Samuel said.

Shaking hands, Ernest said, "Yes, and happy to be back, sir."

"I meant to tell you before you left. I am glad to see that you did the right thing at the court martial of Captain Charles Williamson."

"All I did was tell the truth, but I took no pleasure in testifying against a man whom I once admired and respected."

The commander's brows lifted. "Respect?"

"Yes, sir."

The commander seemed bewildered. "How can you respect a man who did such a terrible thing?"

Separating themselves from the conversation, Elizabeth and Sarah drifted off together to visit with a group of ladies.

"I said, sir, that I had once admired him. I served under him for two years and always found him to be a competent leader. He certainly had his share of successes in battle." Ernest explained to the commander that one of the things he liked about navy life were the high ideals expected of men. True, the captain of a ship needed to be a strict authoritarian, but he couldn't be successful unless his crew liked and respected him.

"In the case of Captain Williamson," a fellow officer

interjected, "especially in recent years, he made one too many questionable decisions. However, with all due respect, a scapegoat was required in Captain Williamson's case because of the political situation with France. Someone had to take the fall in order for the government to save face."

"Or perhaps he committed a crime against humanity. Simple as that," Ernest mused.

"Yes. By the way, did you hear Williamson was released from prison?" the commander asked.

Ernest was dumb-founded. "Sir? And what about his two year sentence?"

"It seems he had the help of influential friends who also happen to be members of the royal family. They managed to get him released from prison much earlier than his sentence dictated. He is now captaining a merchant ship out of the Southampton harbor."

"May I ask who the influential friends are?"

"Lord Basil Wallace and his son, Cyril," the commander said with contempt. "Lord Wallace is second cousin to the king, and unfortunately, a very influential man. Captain Williamson is obviously more useful to the Wallaces as a free man."

Throughout the course of the conversation several other officers had drifted into the circle. When Commander Samuel spoke of Captain Charlie's release from prison, the conversation went quiet.

Eventually an officer spoke up. "Williamson has a dangerous grudging nature. He is no longer the gallant officer you remember, Lieutenant Robinson. He is a drunkard, and when in port spends much of his time in pubs. From what I hear, he's up to no good."

"Pity," Ernest mumbled.

Bringing an end to the unpleasant conversation, Commander Samuel abruptly asked, "Officer John Bennett? Is he around?"

Ernest scanned the ballroom, spotted John across the way talking to a group of officers, and pointed him out to the commander.

Meanwhile Elizabeth and Sarah returned to the group. The officers all bowed, greeting them politely.

Speaking to Elizabeth, Commander Samuel asked, "I assume you're pleased to have this wandering seaman back?"

Taking Ernest's arm Elizabeth said, "I certainly am."

The tinkling sound of metal on glassware subdued the conversation. All eyes were on the head table as Admiral Weatherford stood. When all was quiet he began, "I'd like to welcome all of you to this year's Royal Navy Ball. There is plenty of food and wine, so please enjoy." After making several other announcements the admiral continued. "It is my honor to make a special announcement this evening regarding our latest promotion. We weren't sure if he was going to make it back in time, but fortunately this man has proven time and again that he is worthy and qualified for this promotion."

Raising his glass, he added, "So without further delay, it is my privilege to officially recognize Lieutenant Ernest Robinson, and promote him to the rank of Captain in the Royal Navy."

The ballroom immediately erupted in boisterous cheers. Ernest bowed his head, overwhelmed with the honor being bestowed on him.

Across the room, John turned and lurched through the door, nearly tripping on his way out, spilling his drink on the floor.

"Lieutenant Robinson, will you honor us with a few words?" Admiral Weatherford asked.

Holding tight to Elizabeth's hand, Ernest led her to the front of the room and stood. "Thank you Admiral Weatherford, commanders, officers, ladies, and gentlemen. It's marvelous to be back. I only wish my family were here on this special occasion. It is because of them I am the man I am today. I pray I'm able to live up to this great honor. I am deeply humbled."

The room erupted again in cheers.

As the audience quieted down, Ernest became serious. He raised his glass. "Ladies and gentlemen, a toast. To England and the Royal Navy and all the best she stands for."

"Here, here," roared the crowd.

"God save the King!"

The crowd suddenly stood at attention and sang as the orchestra took up the national theme.

God save our gracious King!
Long live our noble King!
God save the King!
Send him victorious,
Happy and glorious,
Long to reign over us,
God save the King.

As the final refrain drifted away, the orchestra began playing a waltz and the ballroom filled with whirling dancers. Several officers surrounded Ernest, pounding him on the back and shaking his hand.

"I'd be proud to serve with you, sir."

"We needed a good man to replace Captain Charlie."

Ernest, gracious as ever, thanked them all. Finally, he turned to Elizabeth.

"Let's step outside for a minute. I could use some fresh air."

He led her out of the ballroom. Soon they were strolling through the beautifully manicured gardens and along walkways lit by candles. They came to a small pond that sparkled with the reflection of a million stars. Ernest guided Elizabeth to an ornate stone bench in a quiet secluded spot where light from the ballroom windows cast an ethereal glow on her face.

Ernest took her hand and dropped to one knee.

From his tunic pocket he withdrew a small black velvet box. Elizabeth's heart started beating rapidly in anticipation.

He opened the box. A thin gold ring set with tiny garnets and rubies sparkled against the soft velvet.

"Miss Elizabeth Cole, I have loved you from the moment I first saw you. I promise to always honor and cherish you, to protect you and love you with all my heart. Will you marry me?"

Tears gathering in her eyes, Elizabeth responded, "Yes. I would be honored to be your wife."

Ernest took the ring from the box and gently slid it onto her finger. It was a perfect fit. Ernest sat next to her on the bench. Elizabeth's eyes went from gazing at the ring to Ernest's blue eyes. Ernest and Elizabeth melted into each other's arms.

"The ring is beautiful. I will always hold it dear to me," said Elizabeth.

"I know you will," Ernest replied.

"And all those wonderful promises you made to me; I too promise to love and cherish you with all my heart."

Music from the ballroom danced through the air. The stars seemed to shine a little brighter as Ernest cupped Elizabeth's face in his hands. He stroked his thumbs on her cheeks as he took in all her beauty. She was the most exquisite woman he had ever known. Ernest leaned toward her, and gently, sweetly, pressed his lips to hers.

Chapter 17

After leaving the Royal Ball in a jealous stupor, John wandered the streets until running into a couple of fellow officers at a local pub. He joined them for a drink. Then another. And another until he was drunk, disheveled, and red eyed.

Raising his glass he called, "Another pint if you will," his words slurring.

The corpulent bartender sauntered over, placing another tankard on the table.

The conversation lulled and John, needing to be the focus of attention, and reckless in his drunkenness, made a startling admission. "I'll give you something to drink about, lads," he slurred. "We found treasure on Robinson Island," he finished triumphantly.

Dubious glances were exchanged between the officers. "I didn't know you were a storyteller, Lieutenant Bennett," one mocked.

The bartender's ears, always attuned to conversations that might benefit him, eased closer to the table. Finally the center of attention, John found he couldn't, and didn't want to, stop.

"I tell you there is treasure on the island."

"Treasure?" laughed the men. "Like what? Shell necklaces?"

"I said, treasure!" John slammed his hands on the table. "We found chests full of gold and silver and jewels."

The officer, still disbelieving, said, "John, you drunken fool. You've had your fill of drink for this evening."

John straightened, needing to be believed. He reached into his pocket and pulled out his proof. He placed several gold coins and the large emerald ring on the table.

The men leaned in closer for a better look. One fellow picked up the ring. "I know a little something about emeralds," he said. "I once worked for a jeweler in Grosvenor Square in London." They all waited while he examined it.

"Unbelievable. Unless I am mistaken, this emerald is genuine, and I'd say worth a king's bounty, based on the size of it."

An excited murmur went through the men. The bartender was careful to see and hear everything.

Another officer picked up the gold coin and bit it, examining it as carefully as his blurry eyes would allow. "It's at least a hundred years old, based on the markings."

"That makes it more valuable," said John triumphantly. "Don't tell me I'm a drunken fool. I say there's treasure on that island and lots of it. Five chests full."

Staring defiantly into the faces of his companions, John felt satisfied with his suddenly elevated position. He snatched up the items and returned them to his pocket.

In a darkened corner of the pub and unbeknownst to John, Captain Charles Williamson was immersed in a game of cards with Cyril Wallace. Cyril's father, Lord Wallace, was considered the black sheep of the royal family. Although Lord Wallace and Captain Charlie had developed a mutually exclusive business arrangement, he would not risk the scandal of being seen in public with a convicted felon, as it would not reflect well on him or the royal family. Instead, he had his son Cyril make all the arrangements with Captain Charlie. This pub was a favorite meeting place, as the bartender seemed to know things well in advance of most people, and was willing to share ... for a price.

That evening, they were discussing new trade routes and ways of avoiding tariffs, when the bartender made his way over to Captain Charlie's table. Nodding toward the table on the far side of the tavern, he whispered, "Those officers spoke of treasure."

"What was that?" Cyril asked.

"See the gentlemen at that table over there?" Captain Charlie leaned back to look. "The officer at the head of the table has been blabbing about treasure he supposedly found on Robinson Island. He even produced pieces of it from his pocket."

Captain Charlie studied John's face.

"What exactly did you see?" Cyril prodded.

"Some gold coins and a fancy ring."

"Did they say how much of this so-called treasure was on the island?" Captain Charlie asked.

"He claims five chests."

"Hmmm." Captain Charlie gave the man a small bag of coins and said, "That will be all." Captain Charlie and Cyril put down their cards and quickly began planning.

Later that evening when John and his fellow officers were getting ready to leave, Captain Charlie called from the far dark corner of the bar.

"Is that my old shipmate from the HMS *Royal George*? Lieutenant John Bennett?"

John, in drunken good humor, called back, "It certainly is." He squinted, trying to identify the man in the low light. Walking closer, he recognized the voice, "Is that you Captain Charlie?"

"It is. Why don't you come over here and join us in a game of cards?"

Cyril, laughing loudly, mocked, "Don't bother. With his meager salary he can't afford to play."

John bristled at the insult. "Deal me in," he said defiantly, fingering the gold coins in his pocket.

John, drink in hand, dropped into a chair at the card table, his fellow officers standing behind him.

John was surprised to see his ex-commander, and it showed plainly on his face.

"You surprised to see me?"

"Well, I thought … "

"That I was in prison?"

"Yes," John said, scratching his head.

"It pays to have powerful friends," Captain Charlie said arrogantly as he turned and winked at Cyril. "I wasn't in but sixty-two days. Just long enough to work out my plans for the future," he said with a smile.

"Sixty-two days? I see you still have some luck in you, Captain."

Having just returned to England, John wasn't aware that Captain Charlie had become bitter and found work with a merchant company with a shady reputation.

Silence fell as the cards were dealt.

John won the first few hands, his fellow shipmates cheering on every victory. Then slowly John began losing more games than he won, his pile of coins quickly dwindling. Finally he was broke. He begged money off his shipmates so that he could keep in the game, feeling that his luck would soon change, but his cheering section slowly faded as the other men withdrew from the table and left the bar, not wanting to get involved. Soon it was only John, Captain Charlie, and Cyril at the table.

The big grin on Captain Charlie's face enraged John, especially when Cyril mocked, "Our poor officer has played beyond his means. He has no more money."

John had a competitive streak and often didn't know when to give in. Captain Charlie knew this and was using it to his advantage.

John reached into his pocket and recklessly pulled out the emerald ring. "How about this? This is worth more than enough to keep me in the game."

Captain Charlie examined the ring and then handed it to Cyril who studied it carefully. Giving it back to John, Cyril turned to Captain Charlie and said, "Even if that emerald is a complete fake, which I doubt, the band is solid gold and worth no small sum."

"Where did you get this?" Captain Charlie asked, as if he didn't already know.

"What difference does it make where I got it?" John slurred belligerently.

"We need to know that you came by this ring honestly and that it's yours to give away. We don't want to get involved with anything illegal," Cyril said.

"You think I stole it?" John laughed. "I found it myself on Robinson Island. It's mine, fair and square," he said, a defiant tone creeping into his voice.

"Is that so?" Captain Charlie asked.

"And there's much more where that came from," John boasted.

Captain Charlie grinned as he handed John a wad of money and the deck of cards. "I believe it's your turn to deal John."

The ring had brought John a new sense of confidence, but it didn't last long. Captain Charlie won hand after hand; always making sure that John's tankard was full. It didn't take long before John was completely out of money again. He stood, supporting himself against the table.

"Congratulations. It seems you still have your luck, Captain Charlie."

Captain Charlie scooped up his winnings and put the ring on his little finger.

"So tell us about Robinson Island," Cyril said. "You said there is more where that ring came from?"

John fell silent, realizing his mistake. "I have nothing more to say," he said as he turned to leave.

"Ah, but we're not through with you," murmured Cyril menacingly.

Ignoring them, John left the tavern and staggered off into the night.

The bartender came over to wipe down the table.

"I saw one officer take a coin and bite on it. He said it was over a hundred years old."

"Hmmm," mumbled Captain Charlie, thinking.

"You saw the ring?" the bartender asked.

"Oh, we saw it," Cyril smirked. Captain Charlie held up his hand, the ring gleaming on his finger.

Captain Charlie took a sip of his drink. "Mr. Bennett needs to be questioned further."

"Yes," Cyril said, raising his glass.

"I'll get back to you later," Captain Charlie said as he stood and straightened his coat. He reached into his pocket to pay the tab but Cyril stopped him.

"I'll take care of this; just as I know you'll take care of me later."

Captain Charlie looked into Cyril's eyes, reading the implied threat. He laughed as they walked out of the bar.

"I'll be sure to relay this information to my father," Cyril said as he entered his waiting carriage.

Captain Charlie nodded, swinging up onto his horse.

On the way home, Cyril caught sight of John as he was staggering back to the barracks. *No time like the present to set the hook,* he thought to himself. He had the driver pull alongside John.

"What's this about?" John asked, angry.

"Get in," Cyril demanded.

John hesitated, but didn't want to risk offending the son of Lord Wallace. Once inside, Cyril tapped the ceiling of the carriage with the brass knob of his walking stick. "Turn around and take us to Charlie at once."

From up above the driver called, "Yes, sir!"

The carriage turned and they were now heading back to the waterfront where Captain Charlie rented a room.

"What do you want?" John asked.

"Don't be a fool. You know exactly what I want. The treasure."

John felt uneasy as the carriage clattered down the cobbled streets. When they arrived at their destination the driver stepped down and opened the carriage door, but rather than getting out Cyril told the driver to fetch Captain Charlie.

Captain Charlie had just arrived a few minutes earlier and had already taken off his coat. He bristled at the sound of the door pounding and yanked it open demanding, "What is it?"

"My master would like to see you, sir," the groom said a bit reluctantly.

Grumbling, Captain Charlie grabbed his coat and followed the man back to the carriage.

"Get in."

Climbing up, Captain Charlie noticed John sitting in the corner. "Good to see you again, Lieutenant Bennett," he said, taking a seat next to Cyril.

"I have nothing to say to either of you about the treasure," John raged.

"Come now, Lieutenant," Captain Charlie soothed, "we're mates. We've sailed together. Don't lie to your old captain. The bartender at the Hook and Eye saw the treasure you flashed, and I have the ring that you could never have afforded on your own. You can't deny it."

John sat in silence.

"Maybe, you stole the ring from the Robinson family? I'll be sure to let Lieutenant Robinson know."

"I didn't take anything from the Robinsons," John said, defensively. "We found the treasure together."

"See, I was sure you knew more than you were letting on,"

Captain Charlie soothed.

John was still tipsy but sobering fast. His red eyes darted from Captain Charlie to Cyril.

"You know there are punishments for lying to a member of the Royal Family," Cyril threatened. "I can make things especially painful for you. Now tell us what you know."

John bristled at the man's tone. He looked at Charlie, who nodded. John knew he was defeated. "Yes, there is treasure."

"How much?" Captain Charlie asked

"A few chests."

"How many exactly?"

"Five."

"You will show us where it is!" Cyril demanded.

"I will not," John snapped. "The treasure is mine, and the Robinsons, of course. Even if I wanted to *share* it with you, which I don't, I could never find my way around that island on my own."

"Mr. Bennett, don't try our patience," Cyril sighed impatiently. "You will show us where the treasure is located. There are any number of unpleasant ways we can make you do it if you choose to not cooperate."

John turned to Captain Charlie. "Captain, you never cease to bring shame upon your name. You are a scoundrel."

"*I'm a scoundrel?*" Captain Charlie laughed, leaning forward. "And what about you? You have disclosed some very sensitive information and put the entire Robinson family in grave danger, and you did so in a public place for all to hear. And now, because of your indiscretion, rumors will spread and every profiteer and pirate from here to Spain will seek the treasure. You know where it is, and we have the means to go after it. Why not work together?"

"Take us to the treasure, and we will make you rich beyond your wildest imagination," Cyril added, his mouth smiling but his eyes as cold as a snake's.

John sat stone-faced.

"There may even be a peerage in it for you," Cyril tempted. "My father could arrange it."

John's drunken fog seemed to abruptly lift as he saw the two devils before him clearly. He suddenly felt sick. What had he done? Yes, he had nursed a strong resentment for what he assumed was betrayal on the part of Ernest and his father, but now in the presence of true evil, he recognized the sheer goodness of the Robinsons. They had accepted him as one of their family, and he had betrayed them. It was a truth that sat uncomfortably with him.

John now realized the wisdom of Father's decision to keep the treasure secret. They had trusted him to keep the family safe, and he had betrayed that trust.

"I will say no more," he whispered.

"Get out!" Cyril hissed. "This isn't the end of this."

John jumped from the carriage. He turned, looking directly at Captain Charlie. "For your information, Lieutenant Robinson is now *Captain* Robinson. He was promoted just this evening at the Royal Ball. Apparently there was an opening that needed to be filled. Just thought you'd like to know."

Captain Charlie fumed to think his position had been given to the man who condemned him with his testimony nearly a year earlier.

"Your loyalty to your friend is touching, Lieutenant Bennett, but it comes far too late. Tonight you have sealed his fate, and the fate of his family. Of course if you change your mind, you know where to find us."

The carriage lurched forward knocking John into the mud. He got to his feet and staggered to the barracks. As he lurched into the room he found his roommates and several other officers hanging about. "You look terrible," one of them said. "What happened to you?"

"Never mind that. Have any of you seen Ernest?"

"He went to Bristol."

"Why Bristol?" John wondered.

"To see Miss Cole's parents. It seems that our new captain has finally proposed marriage."

"Do you know when he'll be back?"

"In two days."

As the sun rose, John found that sleep eluded him completely, a symptom of the guilt and anxiety that plagued him. He desperately wanted to warn Ernest that he had disclosed the discovery of the treasure, and he desperately wanted to apologize and somehow right his wrong, but he couldn't face it yet. Now it seemed he would have to wait until Ernest returned. Not knowing what else to do, he got up and reported for duty.

Across town Captain Charlie and Cyril were meeting with Cyril's father, Lord Wallace, behind closed doors. They discussed in detail the conversation and evidence they had gathered regarding the treasure that was discovered on Robinson Island.

Lord Wallace, known for being greedy and unprincipled, jumped to his feet.

"Prepare your men and ship, Captain Charlie. I will arrange to have the necessary supplies and weapons loaded immediately. Once Robinson is in your custody, you will sail immediately."

"What about Lieutenant Bennett?"

"His weakness condemns him. We have no need of him. Robinson is the only person who can take us to the treasure. Bennett would only be a liability. Now, to your tasks! Speed is of the essence."

Chapter 18

For some time now the Cole family had looked forward to having Ernest as part of their family. He was respectful, kind, and confident. Strong, both physically and mentally, he had the qualifications of a good leader, and as far as they were concerned he possessed every attribute their daughter could want in a husband. And now that he had been promoted to captain, he would be able to provide well for their daughter.

Ernest, of course, assured Elizabeth's parents that he considered her to be the finest woman in England. She was more than beautiful; she was intelligent and determined. She could speak her mind and stand her ground when impressed to do so, but was soft, sweet, loving, and kind. Those qualities were perfect for Ernest and just what he wanted in a wife.

Elizabeth's father readily gave his blessing as Elizabeth and her mother started planning.

The following day, Ernest, Elizabeth, and Elizabeth's maid,

Jane, were once again in the carriage returning to Southampton. Elizabeth linked arms with Ernest, "You know, my parents couldn't be more thrilled to have you join our family."

"That's good to know," Ernest said with a grin. "I can't wait for my family to meet you. I had two months to tell them your every virtue, and they had two months to remind me how unworthy I am of you."

Elizabeth laughed. "Do you have any strong feelings about where we have the wedding?"

"Why not make it easy on everyone and elope?"

Elizabeth looked at Ernest with panic in her eyes, "Captain Robinson, now really! That would be most improper!"

Now it was Ernest's turn to laugh. "All right. No elopement. Where would you like to be married?"

"I wish we could have the wedding on Robinson Island, but with your naval duties and the time it would take to voyage back and forth …"

"It's not an option." Ernest completed her thought.

"And your family? What would they want?" asked Elizabeth.

"They have already given their blessings."

"Maybe we can arrange an extended visit with them in the future."

"You've obviously given this some thought."

Elizabeth smiled. "Maybe."

"So, you just assumed I would propose?"

"Not assumed." Elizabeth ducked her head, her cheeks flaming. "Hoped."

Ernest kissed her hand. "Your happiness is my life's mission." After a short pause, he continued, "We haven't time to waste. Let the planning begin, I say."

Elizabeth beamed.

It was true; Ernest and Elizabeth had little time to plan a wedding. Winter was only a couple months away and he was scheduled to report to duty as captain of the HSM *Royal George* in two weeks.

"Do you think a wedding could be organized before I report for duty?"

"Certainly. I believe my family is expecting it."

By the time they reached the outskirts of Southampton, dusk was setting in and they could see lights from the city winking to life.

When they pulled up to the front steps of the Crawford home it was fully dark. Ernest opened the door and helped the ladies down. The driver went to the back of the carriage and unhitched their small travel bags.

Ernest walked Elizabeth to the door and was saying goodnight when Rebecca bounced down the stairs.

"How was your trip?" Rebecca asked.

"Wonderful. Of course my parents are thrilled to have Ernest join the family," Elizabeth replied, looking at Ernest.

"I can't wait to hear all about it," Rebecca chirped.

"Well ladies, enjoy your evening," Ernest said. "I need to get back to the barracks."

As he stepped out the door Elizabeth reminded him, "Don't forget, you're having dinner here tomorrow night."

"I wouldn't miss it for the world," he said, taking Elizabeth's hand, kissing it gently.

"Good night, my love," she whispered.

Ernest turned and skipped down the cobblestone steps and into the street, his heart as light as a feather.

Chapter 19

Southampton, England, October 1816

Ernest walked down the well-lit cobblestone street barely suppressing the urge to click his heels together. Life was good, and getting better by the minute. He stopped momentarily to look through the front window of a jewelry store as it was closing up for the evening. Thinking of the recent discovery on the island, he thought to himself, *Soon I'll be able to get anything in this store for Elizabeth.*

In his distracted state Ernest was completely unaware that he had been followed ever since leaving the Crawford's house.

Tired from the long carriage ride, Ernest wanted to get home as soon as possible. He decided to take a shortcut down a dark, wide alley that was intersected by many smaller cross streets. This was a route routinely taken by him and his shipmates during the day, although even then they usually always carried a personal weapon for protection, as the area was somewhat rundown. Having just returned from Bristol, he wasn't carrying his pistol or knife but Ernest wasn't concerned; he could easily hold his own in a scuffle with two or three men, and it was unlikely he would encounter any trouble this early in the evening.

On the corner of the alley stood a newspaper stand that Ernest regularly bought from.

"Evening, Lieutenant Robinson. Paper tonight?"

"Not tonight, Mr. Fredrick, but I hope you had a successful day," Ernest replied.

"Indeed I did, and ye?"

"Mr. Fredrick, I am the happiest of men. I just got engaged to the most beautiful woman in the world."

"Well, now, that's right bonny! Congratulations."

"Thank you."

Ernest entered the alley whistling. He walked past women who called out to him, old men slumped in the gutters in drunken stupors, and younger men leaning against filthy walls, their eyes darting the street warily. Finally, Ernest's military training began to kick in. He noticed a man standing at a corner with his hat tipped forward. Farther along, three men and two women stood around a fire warming their hands. In the shadows beyond, two men seemed out of place, their dress and posture somehow distinguishing them from the others. Crossing another intersection, Ernest looked to his right and noticed the silhouette of a person keeping pace with him in the shadows. Senses coming alive, Ernest stayed calm and continued walking, looking for signs of trouble.

Occasionally he heard a shuffling of footsteps behind him, but when he stopped and turned, the sounds stopped and he

RETURN TO ROBINSON ISLAND

could see no one. Heart beating faster, he inwardly cursed himself for not carrying a weapon.

In an attempt to throw off his pursuers, he dashed down one of the cross alleys. A figure suddenly appeared out of the darkness ahead of him breathing heavily. Ernest stopped and placed his hand in the inside breast pocket of his tunic, hoping to fool his assailant into thinking that he was armed. He was surprised to hear a familiar voice.

"Ernest! Thank heavens I found you." It was John Bennett.

"John?" Ernest's quick breath matched his friend's. "What are you doing here?"

"I'm so glad I found you. You weren't at the Crawford's house, and then I ran into Mr. Fredrick while I was looking for you and he told me you had cut through the alley. Listen to me carefully … "

Ernest was puzzled hearing the alarm in John's voice.

"They know."

Ernest's face wrinkled in confusion. "Who knows what?"

They had come to the end of the alley, which was lit by a single lamp. Before John could respond, a large man silhouetted against the light called out.

"Mr. Robinson?"

Another voice, dripping with sarcasm, taunted, "Captain?" Ernest could hear laughing all around him.

The big man stepped forward.

"Do I know you? What's the meaning of this?" Ernest demanded.

John, his anxiety high, said, "We must get out of here!"

"You're not going anywhere," the big man said. "You're coming with us."

As Ernest and John turned to run, a group of men surrounded them from behind, blocking the way.

"What do you want?" Ernest asked.

The men inched closer.

"Take the few pounds I have in my wallet. You can have it all."

No response.

Finally, one man said, "Oh, we want more than that!"

Ernest whispered to John, "I'll take the ones on the left. You go for the others."

"Remember boys, we need Robinson alive," the big man instructed.

Believing that surprise was his best weapon, Ernest attacked the closest man, punching him in the face and twisting his arm around his back, breaking it. A loud scream of pain echoed through the alley as the man went down. Ernest then turned and hit the next man.

Meanwhile, John grappled with the man closest to him.

One of the thugs stepped up and swung a heavy stick at Ernest. Ernest saw the bludgeon and ducked. It whistled past him directly into the face of the man with whom he had just been trading blows, knocking him out cold. Without hesitation, Ernest kicked the man with the stick, breaking two ribs and bringing him to his knees. Ernest grabbed the stick as the man fell and hit him over the head, knocking him out cold.

Ducking a swing, John hit one man in the kidney and kicked another in the groin. Both men fell to the ground useless.

Five assailants were on the ground, but more stepped out of the shadows, drawing swords.

Screams echoed through the alley. Doors slammed and feet

pounded as onlookers ran to avoid the violence.

Using the stick, Ernest confronted two men at once, jabbing one in the chest and whacking the other over the head. From the corner of his eye, Ernest saw a fist coming at him. He dodged the blow, twisting, and brought both his arms down on the back of the big man's neck. The force of the blow should have brought down the man with ease, but the brute simply turned and smiled at Ernest.

John was holding his own until he was grabbed from behind. Without the use of his arms, he kicked the man directly in front of him and then threw his head back into the face of the man holding him, smashing his nose. The man let go of John as blood gushed down his face.

Ernest punched the big man a number of times but to no effect. Eventually the giant was able to get Ernest into a bear hug from behind and began squeezing the life out of him.

John rushed forward to assist Ernest when he was viciously stabbed in the side. Falling to the ground John yelled, "Ernest!" He lay helplessly on the ground as a pool of blood began pooling around his body.

Ernest managed to grab the big man's sausage-sized fingers, bending one back until it snapped. The man bellowed and let go, but by then his attackers had surrounded him, overpowering him by sheer numbers. One of them struck Ernest in the head with the hilt of a sword, knocking him unconscious.

"Bind and gag him," the big man ordered, holding his broken finger.

Ernest was lifted and hustled off to a waiting wagon at the end of the alley. The gang of thugs jumped aboard and the wagon clattered off into the night.

John lay bleeding and unconscious in the alley, left like a piece of trash.

In the sudden silence after the fight an old woman carefully opened a window and saw a man lying in the middle of the alley. Cautiously approaching the body, she found that he had been stabbed in the side just below the ribs. She ran back inside and grabbed a ragged blanket. She wrapped the tattered blanket tightly around the man's torso and then rummaged through his pockets. She found a single gold coin.

Compensation, she thought to herself. She doubted the lad would live through the night anyway.

She spread the remaining part of the blanket over him before disappearing back into her flat.

The wagon carrying Ernest wove through dark streets as it made its way to the docks. It eventually pulled up alongside a ship. In the nearby lamplight, the ship's name read *Independent*. From a carriage a discreet distance away, Lord Wallace and his son, Cyril, watched as the big man threw Ernest, who was bound at the wrists, over his shoulder.

Cyril opened the carriage door and stepped out.

"Make me proud, son," said Lord Wallace.

"I will." Cyril threw his duffle bag over his shoulder and walked toward the ship.

From aboard the ship a voice called out, "Hurry, we haven't much time."

On deck, Captain Charlie was issuing orders. As Cyril boarded the ship Captain Charlie noticed that John was not present. "Where's John Bennett?"

"He's dead," the big man said.

"Hmmm. You're sure?"

"Yeah. Barry stuck him good. He was laying in a pool of his own blood, and if he wasn't dead then, he will be by morning."

The rope tying the ship to the dock was released. The sails were raised and the *Independent* quietly drifted from the wharf into the quiet of the night. Once out at sea, tankards of ale were sloshed together as the men congratulated themselves on a successful night.

Chapter 20

Back in the alleyway a pickpocket passed by and heard John groaning. He searched John's pockets but came up empty.

"Help me," John whispered

"Sorry, mate," said the man walking away. "I ain't stickin' me neck out fer nowt."

The next morning, as the sun began to rise and the early fog was lifting, two naval officers walked through the alley on their way to their duties. They heard moaning and spotted John lying against a wall.

"Is that a naval officer?"

"Do you suppose he's sleeping one off?"

They drew closer. The blanket had fallen off of John and he was cold and shivering.

"We must help the poor devil."

Then, all at once, they realized who it was.

"It's Lieutenant Bennett!"

"Good Lord! Look at the blood. He's gravely wounded."

They carefully rolled John onto his back, trying to wake him. John came to, mumbling, "Ernest. Must...contact...Montrose."

"What's he saying?" asked one of the officers.

"I don't know," said the other as he inspected John's wound. "The bleeding's stopped, but he's lost a lot of blood. Lieutenant Bennett. Can you hear me?"

John's eyes fluttered but did not open.

"We've got to get him to a doctor."

"Stay here."

The officer ran to the end of the alley and flagged down a passing carriage. "We have an injured officer here. I need your help."

The driver ran back with the officer into the alley. The men carefully picked John up and carried him to the carriage, then jumped aboard and ordered the driver to take them to the nearest hospital.

Hours later, John woke lying in a hospital bed. A gash below his eye and a stab wound in his side had been cleaned, stitched, and properly bandaged. His eyes were slow to focus. As he regained consciousness and realized where he was, he began struggling to get out of bed. A nurse came running and forced him back to his pillow.

"Lie down. You'll tear your wound open."

John mumbled, "I can't. No time."

"Nonsense," she said. She offered him a piece of bread and a glass of water, which he pushed aside.

"No. Thank you. You have been very kind, but I must be on my way."

"You try to leave that bed, young man, and I will put

restraints on you."

John knew he was no match for the strong nurse in his current state, and the last thing he wanted right now was to be restrained. He lay back down and obediently ate the bread and drank the water. Satisfied that her patient was cooperating, the nurse left the room.

With the nurse gone, John found the energy to stumble out of bed. Stifling a groan and ignoring the pain, he donned his shirt, put on his breeches, and stumbled to the door just as the nurse was coming back in.

"Get back in bed, Lieutenant!"

She grabbed his shoulders, pushing him back in the room. John held desperately to the door. Looking into her eyes he pleaded, "I must go! My best friend's in danger!"

"Ridiculous."

"No! I'm telling you! I must get word to someone. My friend has been abducted."

Something in John's expression convinced the nurse that he was sincere. "Very well," she conceded. "I can see that you're determined. Take this, you'll need it," she said, giving him a bundle of extra bandages and medicine for the pain.

"Thank you."

Unsteady from loss of blood, John stumbled out into the street and headed for the harbor. He remembered that just before he had fallen unconscious in the alley, he heard the thugs speaking of getting Ernest to a ship. The Southampton Harbor had many docks and ships, both naval and merchant, as it was one of the busiest shipping ports in England. That's where he would look. Stopping to rest frequently, John finally made it to the waterfront and located the harbormaster's office.

"Were there any ships that departed this morning?" John asked.

"None this morning."

John wavered, nearly falling down. The harbormaster grabbed him and placed him in a chair.

"Easy there, man."

"My best friend was kidnapped last night and put aboard a ship in this harbor," John said.

"Well now, you didn't ask about last night. I came on this morning, but there was a ship that left at midnight."

John perked up. "What was the name of the ship?"

"The *Independent*."

"Oh my ... "

"Are you quite all right?" asked the harbormaster.

"Yes. Can you tell me the name on record?"

"I suppose, but you don't look well."

"Please," John whispered, exhausted. "It's a matter of life and death."

"Give me a moment then," he said, reaching down and opening his record book. "Let's see," he said to himself, drawing his finger down the page.

"It says here ... C.C.W."

John's heart sank. Captain Charles Williamson.

"Is her destination listed?"

Again, the harbormaster consulted his record book. "No. That's strange. It was left blank."

"Thank you, sir." John rose, coughing.

"Are you sure there's nothing I can do for you? You look decidedly unwell."

John clenched his fist over his mouth, lurching from the office and stumbling out into the street. He needed to get to Sir Montrose's merchant office, and it was a good half kilometer away in the heart of the harbor. Finding himself weaker with each step and with no time to waste, he began frantically waving down any passing carriages. Finally, a driver stopped.

"I need a lift to the Tisbury docks."

"Yes, sir," the driver said, noting John's physical condition.

John reached into his pocket to pay before he remembered that he had been robbed. "I can pay you when we get there," he said, confident that Sir Montrose would help.

"By the looks of it, ye've come on hard times," the driver noted. "I'll take you, and glad to help."

John's thoughts raged in the short time it took to reach Tisbury dock. He was torn, full of guilt and disgust. It was Ernest who had been promoted. Ernest had the intelligent and beautiful Elizabeth and a loving and supportive family. And, although no one knew it, Ernest was also very wealthy. Yes, it was difficult to admit, but John had been terribly envious of his best friend. And yet, despite all that, he had never wanted any harm to come to Ernest, or any of the Robinsons.

He was disgusted with himself. How could he have betrayed the trust the Robinsons had placed in him, treating him like one of their own? What would he say to Elizabeth?

It hit him like a thunderbolt: it was not Ernest, or his family, who was dishonest and greedy. He was. His childish suspicions and petty jealousy would have terrible consequences for a family who had never done him a bit of harm. He was a wretch! At that moment, he determined that no matter the cost, no matter the consequences, he would do all he could to help Ernest and his family. He would somehow make amends, or die trying.

The carriage arrived at Sir Montrose's office. John lurched out of the carriage and into the office.

"Where is Sir Montrose? I need him immediately," he said to the clerk sitting behind the counter.

"I'm sorry, he's in a meeting with one of his captains," the clerk responded suspiciously.

"I must speak with him at once."

"I'm afraid that's not possible," the clerk insisted, noting John's disheveled appearance.

John's knees buckled and he leaned on the counter for support. Gathering the last of his strength, he burst past the secretary and into Sir Montrose's office. Sir Montrose and Captain Briggs, who were in the middle of a discussion, jumped to their feet. Shocked to see the sickly looking, disheveled officer in front of them, Captain Briggs asked, "What is the meaning of this, Lieutenant Bennett?"

Sir Montrose came from around his desk. "What's happened to you, man? Here, sit." He helped John into the nearest chair.

"George!" he yelled to his secretary. "A cup of water please."

"They've taken Ernest," John gasped.

"Who?"

"Ernest Robinson."

"Ernest has been taken?" asked Sir Montrose. "By whom?"

"Captain Charlie and his men."

"Charles Williamson?" Captain Briggs asked.

"Yes."

"What do you mean? Why Ernest? Explain yourself man!" Sir Montrose demanded, handing John the water his secretary had just delivered.

"We were attacked last night while walking home."

"Why? Why Ernest?" Sir Montrose demanded.

"It's about the … the … " his eyes wandered to Captain Briggs.

"Briggs is a trustworthy man. Whatever you have to say, you can say to both of us."

John had already made the mistake of revealing the treasure once, and he was hesitant to mention it again in front of Captain Briggs, but he knew that time was of the essence, so he took a deep breath and said, "The treasure, Sir."

Sir Montrose blanched. "The treasure? You were sworn to secrecy."

"Treasure?" Captain Briggs asked, puzzled.

"I'll explain later," said Sir Montrose.

"You're right. I'm a fool," John cried, anguished. "It's all my fault. I was in a pub with friends, I drank too much, far too much, and … "

"Lieutenant Bennett!" Sir Montrose spat in disgust.

"My bragging was overheard and some pieces of the treasure were seen by the bartender, who I assume told Captain Charlie and Cyril Wallace who were in the back. I didn't know they were there."

"You said the bartender saw treasure?" Sir Montrose clarified.

"Yes. I had taken a few pieces from Ernest's duffel bag on our journey home."

Montrose's face grew red. "Blast you! Do you realize what you've done? And you're sure the Wallaces are involved?"

"Yes."

"This is disastrous. They are the most corrupt men I know."

"I'm sorry. I ... "

"There's no time to be sorry. We must act, and act fast," Sir Montrose said. "Do you know where Ernest is at this moment?"

"On a ship that left at midnight."

"What ship?"

"The *Independent*."

"That's Wallace's ship," Captain Briggs confirmed.

Sir Montrose yelled to his secretary, "Get my carriage at once."

Turning to John he said, "Know this. If they get to Robinson Island and harm my family, you will pay dearly! I suggest you get some rest. You're going to need it!"

"I need to return to my company."

"Who is your commander?"

"Admiral Weatherford."

"I'll make arrangements with him. He'll need to know what's happened to his newest captain at any rate. Briggs, get him back to the barracks. Lieutenant Bennett, prepare your things and get what rest you can. We'll fetch you once we're ready to depart."

"Yes, sir. Thank you. I'm grateful for the chance to make amends."

Montrose looked him squarely in the eyes, his anger barely suppressed. "Never mind that. I want you close. I want you where I can get my hands on you if anything goes wrong."

John looked down, ashamed. "I won't let you — or Ernest — down, Sir."

"Hmpfff!" snorted Montrose. "The word of a fool is worth little."

Turning to Captain Briggs, Sir Montrose said, "We have no time to waste. Get the *Conquest* stocked and prepared. We'll leave as soon as possible."

Captain Briggs followed Sir Montrose out to his carriage. "Where are you going, Sir Montrose?"

"To meet with an old friend."

And with that he was off, his carriage clattering rapidly over the cobblestone road.

Chapter 21

An hour later, Sir Montrose's carriage arrived at the gate of Lord Andrew Christopher's country estate in Westchester, on the outskirts of Southampton. The sky had turned an angry gray, rain pouring from the heavens. As the carriage traveled the quarter-mile drive leading up to the house, Sir Montrose's emotions raged. His fear for his loved ones chilled his blood. He couldn't shake the deep anxiety that settled over him like a heavy blanket, and it manifested itself when the doorman asked his business with Lord Christopher.

"Let me through immediately!" he roared. "Tell him Montrose is here."

Minutes later, coat dripping, he was standing in front of Lord Christopher, who sensed the desperation in his old friend's demeanor. Lord Christopher was a retired naval officer and a former lord of the Admiralty. He was very influential in naval and political circles and second cousin to King George III.

"Montrose, old friend. I'm so happy to see you, but tell me, what brings you out on such a miserable day?"

"It's a matter of great urgency, I'm afraid."

Lord Christopher took him by the arm and led him through to his study, eager to know how he might help his old friend. Several years earlier, Sir Montrose served as an officer under Lord Christopher. In the late 1780s, Sir Montrose risked his own life during a battle to save Lord Christopher from an oncoming saber. When he stepped in front of the blade, it struck Officer Montrose in the shoulder. It was an act of loyalty that Lord Christopher never forgot.

A servant closed the heavy wood doors behind them, while the butler poured two glasses of brandy. Lord Christopher reached for the drink, and Sir Montrose, who didn't drink, politely took the glass and set it down on the nearby table.

"One of the Royal Navy's finest officers, just promoted to captain, has been taken by force by Charles Williamson and his men."

"You don't mean court-martialed Charles Williamson, late of His Majesty's Navy?" Lord Christopher asked.

"The one and only."

"Why has he done this?"

"There is rumor treasure was found on Robinsons Island. I suspect they took Captain Robinson to help them locate the treasure. Lord Christopher, let me remind you that my granddaughter and three great-grandchildren live on that island. I fear the worst."

"I understand. How can I help?"

"They left on the *Independent* late last night."

"The *Independent?*"

"Yes. Lord Wallace's ship. Evidently, he and his son are involved."

"Scoundrels! The *Independent* is old, but fast in the water," Lord Christopher pointed out. He strolled to a nearby window and gazed out as rain rolled down the windowpane.

"I could use a skilled crew of navy men," Sir Montrose ventured.

Lord Christopher, his hands folded behind his back, paused before speaking.

"Has anyone spoken to Admiral Weatherford?"

"No. I believed due to the urgency of the matter I had to go directly to the top."

"You realize, Montrose, that I am retired and have no real authority to call out the navy."

"Yes, sir."

"However," said Lord Christopher, a glint in his eye, "I think I still have some influence with the admiral."

"I hoped as much," said Sir Montrose.

"It's the least I can do for a man who saved my life. When were you planning to leave?"

"Immediately. I am provisioning the *Conquest* as we speak."

"Understood. I will attend to it right away."

Sir Montrose reached out his hand. "Thank you, m'lord. I will forever be indebted to you." The old Scotsman was near tears with gratitude.

"No. I will always be indebted to you," Lord Christopher countered. "Besides, the Wallaces are a disgrace to the royal family. It's time they're dealt with."

John was escorted back to the barracks by Captain Briggs. During the carriage ride he submitted to a severe tongue-lashing. Once inside his room, he fell into a deep sleep. Hours later, he was roused by loud knocking. He slowly dragged himself out of bed and stumbled to the door, opening it. Elizabeth and her uncle stood on the stoop.

"John. I'm so sorry to disturb you at this hour. You know my uncle, Mr. Crawford?"

John bowed painfully and was about to speak but was interrupted by Elizabeth.

"Have you seen Ernest? We were due to have dinner with Rebecca and my uncle and aunt hours ago. It's not like Ernest to not show up."

"What's happened to you, man?" asked Mr. Crawford, alarmed by John's white face and stooped posture.

Elizabeth stopped speaking, noticing John's strained demeanor and the stitches and huge bruise under his eye.

John stood aside, his head lowered in shame.

"Please come in."

They followed him into the room, noticing the painful way he walked.

"I was meaning to come to you," John said.

"What do you mean?"

"Miss Cole. I … I … I don't know how to say this."

"What is it, John?" Her face was pale.

"Ernest has been taken. He's been abducted against his will."

"What!" Mr. Crawford jumped to his feet.

Elizabeth opened her mouth several times to say something but nothing came out. Finally she stammered, "What are you talking about?"

"He's being held on a ship heading to Robinsons Island as we speak."

"I don't believe you!" she cried.

"Explain yourself, sir," said Mr. Crawford.

"Did Ernest tell you about the treasure we found on the island?"

"Treasure? No."

John grabbed the nearest chair and eased himself down into it, burying his head in his hands. The physical pain he felt was nothing compared to the emotional anguish he was feeling.

"Tell me what you mean!" Elizabeth reached out and shook his shoulder.

The words began to tumble out of him. John told them about the treasure — how they had found it and agreed to keep it a secret until its disposition could be arranged.

"We all swore an oath of secrecy for the safety of the family," he said. Then, looking into Elizabeth's eyes, hoping that somehow she would understand, he continued, "One night I overheard Ernest and his father planning to take some of the treasure to Sir Montrose. I thought they were trying to … to … cheat me out of my share."

Elizabeth gasped. "Ernest would never do such a thing."

"I was blinded by greed," said John. "I admit it. And after

the Royal Ball, when Ernest was promoted to captain, and asked you to marry him, I was angry and jealous! I went with some officers to a tavern and had, oh, I don't know, far too much to drink, and I began talking about the treasure. Unfortunately I was overheard."

"Oh, John. How could you?" Elizabeth cried with tears in her eyes.

"How could I? Because I am a fool!"

"Who heard you?" demanded Mr. Crawford.

"Captain Charlie and Cyril Wallace. They were in the tavern and heard everything. They demanded that I take them to the island to show them where the treasure is hidden. I refused. So they went after Ernest."

"Oh!" gasped Elizabeth.

"How did you get into this condition?" asked Mr. Crawford.

"Last night I went to find Ernest. I had to warn him. After I left your house, I found him walking home through the alleys near the waterfront. We didn't realize he was being followed. We were attacked."

Stricken, Elizabeth collapsed into a nearby chair. She couldn't breathe.

John tried comforting her. "Please don't despair, Miss Cole. I was stabbed, but I made my way to Sir Montrose and told him everything. He is preparing his fastest ship. We're leaving as soon as we can get the *Conquest* provisioned. We'll catch up to them; they won't even make it to the island."

"I pray you're right," whispered Elizabeth, tears running freely down her face.

"Come. Let's get you home," said her uncle. "We must let your parents know immediately."

John escorted Elizabeth and Mr. Crawford to the carriage. As he was handing her up into her seat, Mr. Crawford turned to John and whispered, "You know if they get to that island and retrieve the treasure they won't let any of the Robinsons remain alive."

"Yes," John nodded. "I am keenly aware of that fact. I know firsthand how ruthless Williamson can be."

Mr. Crawford stepped into the carriage and it jolted away. John went back to his room, once again thinking of how he had proven himself an unworthy friend, and wondered at the flaws of his own character. He remembered how gracious and kind the Robinsons had been, yet he had given in to his lowest instincts, his greed and jealously, and in doing so his best friend and his family were in danger.

In agony he dropped to his knees, tears falling through his fingers as he pressed his fists into his eyes. He prayed that God would protect them.

Chapter 22

Aboard the Independent, *at Sea*

It was dark and muggy two levels down in the hold of the *Independent*. A rat scampered across Ernest's legs and woke him just as a small bowl of food slid through the opening in the bars of his cell. Ernest sat up and reeled from the pain in his head. He could feel the huge knot on the back of his head throbbing. He kicked at the rat and reached for the bowl. It was just as well the rat had wakened him; otherwise the filthy rodent would have eaten his dinner while he slept.

The crewman who had brought the food laughed and taunted, "Fighting rats for your food now, eh, Captain Robinson?"

Ernest stumbled to his feet and fell forward toward the bars. "What is this about? What is the meaning of this?"

The crewman said nothing as he moved off.

"Answer me!"

Still no answer. In a far corner a group of crewmen on the off-duty watch were playing cards. They were sitting under a single lantern as it swung over their heads in rhythm with the waves of the sea. The men were laughing and would periodically lean in toward each other and whisper. When they did, they looked in Ernest's direction. In the dim light Ernest recognized the voice of a man he had served with on the HMS *Royal George* under Captain Charlie. The man had two missing fingers on his left hand.

"Is that you, Erickson?"

"Aye it is," he said without looking up.

"What are you doing on this ship?"

"Well," he said, holding up his fingerless left hand, "It has to do with the old seaman's saying, 'One hand for the ship and one hand for yourself.' I figure I gave enough for the king. Now I'm working for Captain Charlie and meself."

Ernest could hear the bitterness in his voice.

"How long have I been here?"

"One day and many more to go." The men at the card table began to laugh.

"I demand to know where we're heading!"

"We're taking you home to Robinson Island."

"What? What interest do you have with the island?"

One man made a rude gesture and said, "Your mother!"

Ernest glared at the man, gripping the bars until his hands went white. The leader at the table slugged the seaman in the arm and looked at Ernest. "We're getting the treasure."

"Treasure?" Ernest said, feigning surprise. "You must be mistaken."

"Don't treat us like fools. We know all about the treasure

thanks to your friend Lieutenant Bennett."

They all looked at Ernest, now fuming and stunned. He sat on the floor. The small five-by-six-foot cell was covered with a thin layer of hay. Looking around he noticed a blanket, a slop bucket, and a candle. He leaned his back against the wall of the ship, the pain in his head intensifying as thoughts swirled through his mind. The bowl of food was far from his mind. *How could John betray him? Did the treasure mean more to him than his friendship? Was it John who led the men down the alley only to make it look like an accident?*

Dockside at Tisbury, Montrose's ship *Conquest* was almost ready for departure. The crew had been furiously making preparations for the past day and a half, which for a long voyage like this was no small feat. The rigging had to be inspected and sails repaired or replaced; and since the *Conquest* had just returned from sea, cleaning was necessary. Food had to be purchased and properly stored. Fresh meat was salted and stored in the meat cellar. Animals had to be brought on board; chickens for eggs, goats for milk, and cows for meat. The list went on and on. Through it all, Sir Montrose came and went, directing the ship's refitting. He moved with the energy of a man half his age.

A contingent of Royal Marines had arrived and was carrying boxes of guns and other munitions and supplies aboard. The ship was bustling as Sir Montrose boarded her.

Captain Briggs greeted him. "Sir."

"Gather the crew."

Briggs called the crew to the quarterdeck to hear Sir Montrose. They were already buzzing about the nature of this secretive voyage. Tension was high and there was a sense of urgency, although most of the men did not know why. Montrose, his hands on the rail of the quarterdeck, looked down at the expectant crew.

"Men, we don't have much time, so I'll make this brief. All of you know the Robinson family; they are my family."

"Aye." Nods came from those who made up Montrose's regular crew. They had been to Robinson Island, and many of them had become personally acquainted with the Robinson family.

"I have troubling news. The Robinsons are in terrible danger."

The crew leaned in, intent on hearing what came next.

"Most of you know Ernest Robinson who has recently been promoted to captain in the Royal Navy."

A collective murmur of agreement went up from the crew, then silence fell. Only the call of the seagulls and the slapping of the incoming tide on the hull of the *Conquest* could be heard. In the distance a bell clanged.

"Well, gentlemen, Captain Robinson has been kidnapped!"

Murmurs went through the crew.

"By whom, sir?" someone called out.

"Charles Williamson and his men on the *Independent*. They left two days ago to attack and take control of Robinson Island."

Murmurs of anger spread through the men. Shouts were heard.

"Captain Charlie? Why would he do that?"

"I thought he was in prison."

"What does he want with Robinson Island?"

"Quiet! Please!" Captain Briggs shouted. "I will have order on this ship!"

Not wanting to disclose information about the treasure, Sir Montrose said, "Men, I cannot tell you at this time of Williamson's motives. I can tell you that there is no justification for such an attack. What matters now is that my granddaughter and three great-grandchildren live on that island, and they are now in harm's way."

He continued. "I do not feel inclined to honor Williamson with the title of captain, and I will not hear of him being referred to as Captain Charlie again. He has lost that privilege. Williamson is a convicted criminal and has become nothing more than a pirate, thieving and plundering under the guise of running merchant ships for Lord Wallace and his son, Cyril, whom I also consider criminals. Williamson is especially bitter toward Captain Robinson for testifying against him at his trial. He and his crew plan to destroy the Robinsons and take possession of the island."

One of Montrose's most loyal men shouted, "How can we help, sir?"

Suddenly overcome by emotion, Sir Montrose looked up and took a deep breath. "I know that many of you have just returned from long voyages. I appreciate all your hard work, and I know you were looking forward to a much deserved leave and being with your families. Asking you to turn around at such short notice will be a great sacrifice for them; however, I need sixty men willing to head back to Robinson Island to protect my family."

Quiet murmuring among the crew suggested uncertainty among some of the men.

Sir Montrose continued. "This is a matter of life—and I'm afraid—death, for my loved ones. Allow me to be perfectly clear before I ask for volunteers. If you choose not to go, I will hold no ill will and your employment with me will not be in jeopardy. But for those of you who choose to join me, I want all of you to understand that the task before us will not be easy. There will be danger and the possibility of injury or death. Our mission is to sail to Robinson Island, confront Williamson and his men, and rescue Captain Robinson as well as the whole Robinson family if necessary. This no doubt will involve certain risks and some hard fighting. Williamson is a seasoned and capable commander. I don't want anyone going under false illusions. Our task will be difficult. It's possible that some of you may not return."

Sir Montrose paused, looking his men in the eyes. "I realize I am asking you to put your lives on the line, so any of you who choose to go along will be paid a double salary."

There was silence on the quarterdeck. Then breaking the silence, a man called out, "Aye. Count me in."

"Aye," came another voice as a man stepped forward.

"Aye. I'm with you," came yet another.

Soon, nearly all voices were raised saying "Aye." A few of the men, knowing they were unable to make the voyage, shook the hands of their mates and moved to the other side of the ship.

Then a man called out, "Sir, if I may?"

"Yes, what is it?" asked Sir Montrose.

"You have our loyalty, and there's enough of us to sail the ship, but we're not fighting men. How can we contend against the experience of Williamson and his men?"

Sir Montrose smiled. "Don't fear, gentlemen. We'll have the help of the Royal Marines, the very men you've seen carrying supplies onto this vessel."

"But sir, I count only twenty or so of them. Will that be enough?"

Sir Montrose continued, "There will be at least sixty marines and they are the finest the Royal Navy has to offer."

Sir Montrose was secretly pleased that so many of his men had volunteered before they knew that they would be assisted by the Royal Marines. "That will give us 120 men strong and true."

At this, a great shout erupted from the crew.

"And you will be led by one of the finest captains on the sea, Captain Briggs."

Another cheer went up in support for Briggs, once a respected commander in the Royal Navy, and now the most respected captain in Sir Montrose's employment.

The *Conquest* was the newest of the seven ships in Montrose's fleet. It was built strong and fast, but both Sir Montrose and Captain Briggs knew they would need to capitalize on every opportunity they could find if they were to have a chance at catching up to the *Independent,* already two days ahead. That, and a good deal of luck.

Sir Montrose went on. "I, too, will be joining you."

Age and the responsibilities of running a successful business meant that Sir Montrose rarely went to sea anymore. His presence on the ship signified to the crew the importance he placed on this mission. The crew cheered for Sir Montrose, their respect evident.

Sir Montrose was glowing with pride and gratitude. Unlike many men of wealth and privilege, Sir Montrose was a self-made man who believed in the principle of treating people fairly — a policy that was now paying off richly in the form of loyalty and respect.

"Thank you all from the bottom of my heart," he said. "For those of you that have decided to stay behind, I understand. For the rest of you, gather your belongings and say your good-byes. We'll be leaving with the tide. We haven't any time to waste."

"Aye aye, sir," the men chorused.

John had gathered his things and was heading to Tisbury Pier when he had the distinct impression to take a detour to the Crawford residence. A servant answered and conducted him to the sitting room.

"Lieutenant Bennett is here to see you, Miss Cole."

Elizabeth sat quietly in a chair, her needlework long abandoned on her lap. She lifted her head.

"Yes, Lieutenant Bennett. What is it?"

"I came to tell you that we're leaving —at dusk. I just thought you should know. Sir Montrose was able to arrange my leave to go, thanks to Lord Christopher. I wanted to let you know that I will be joining the crew and that I will do everything in my power …"

"Thank you," she interrupted, "that was kind."

"Miss Cole, we'll get him back. You'll see Ernest again."

"I pray that you're right."

An uncomfortable silence filled the room. Taking this as his cue to leave, John turned but Elizabeth stopped him. "Do you have time to gather some clothes for Captain Robinson? He is sure to need them … "

"Yes. I'll return to the barracks and pack some of his things."

John left the house and mounted his horse, as Elizabeth looked down from the sitting room window.

"I promise I won't return without Captain Robinson!" he shouted as he spurred his horse and galloped away.

Hours later the dock was crowded as families gathered to say good-bye to their husbands, fathers, and sons.

John stood alone on the deck of the ship watching.

"You understand, Lieutenant Bennett, that you will be expected to do ordinary seaman's duties on this voyage," Captain Briggs said, walking up beside him.

"Aye, sir. I understand. I'll do whatever I can to help."

Softening, Captain Briggs added, "John. I know you. I like you, you're a good man — in here," he said, pressing his finger to John's chest. "We'll need your expertise when we get to Robinson Island."

"Thank you, sir."

"I hope to see you once again in the good graces of Sir Montrose and the Robinsons."

"With all my soul, I hope so too."

Captain Briggs gave the command to sound the bell. Those on the dock said their final good-byes, while the last supplies were being carried on board. As the crew made their way onto the ship, so did two unfamiliar figures carrying boxes on their shoulders. In the chaos, no one noticed as the two figures set the boxes down and moved out of sight.

When all sailors were aboard and accounted for, the order was given to release the ropes that secured the ship to the dock. As the last rope was untied the ship began to slowly move away from the dock.

Captain Briggs called out, "Smooth sailing and God speed, men."

Once the *Conquest* was well underway in open water, Sir Montrose stepped down from the quarterdeck and made his way to his cabin when the two figures approached him from behind.

"Sir, I beg you for your forgiveness."

"Pardon me?" he said turning around. The voice was oddly familiar.

The figure removed its hat, releasing a mass of thick, long hair.

"What is the meaning of this?"

"I cannot sit idly by hoping to one day receive good news," she said looking down at the deck.

"Miss Cole?" Sir Montrose asked, the shock evident in his voice.

"Yes."

"What are you doing here? Don't you know this is no place for a woman?"

"I'm aware of that."

"And who is this?" he asked referring to the second figure.

"This is Jane. My maid."

"Miss Cole, I don't understand."

"I had no other choice, sir. Captain Robinson is my life, and I refuse to sit at home doing nothing. To go another year or more without him would be intolerable. I had to do *something*."

"But Elizabeth," he said, "this is highly irregular. I cannot guarantee your safety, or comfort for that matter, on my ship."

"I care little for my comfort, especially while Ernest is in grave danger."

"And your family?"

"I left a letter. They've probably found it by now."

Captain Briggs suddenly appeared standing at the quarterdeck rail above them. "Is everything okay, sir?"

"We have some unexpected visitors."

"Oh?"

"Miss Cole and her maid have decided to join us."

Captain Briggs looked down at Elizabeth, a look of pure shock on his face.

"I'm sorry, Captain Briggs. This was the only way. If I had asked, you would have had no choice but to deny me. I've thought carefully about this. As you may know, Captain Robinson and I became engaged just a few nights ago."

"Yes. We were all very pleased to hear of your happiness."

"That's very kind of you," Elizabeth said, bowing her head. "I know this isn't the proper thing for a lady to do, but I'm not concerned with etiquette. I'm concerned for my future husband and I am determined on this matter."

Sir Montrose knew they couldn't risk losing time by turning

back. For better or worse the ladies were there to stay.

"You won't have to worry about us," Elizabeth said.

"I may not have to, but I will nevertheless."

Elizabeth hugged Sir Montrose and looked up and thanked Captain Briggs.

Sir Montrose, spotting John nearby, snapped, "Mr. Bennett, take Miss Cole and her maid's bags to my quarters. I'll bunk in one of the other rooms."

"I can't take you from your quarters, sir."

"I insist. Besides, we'll be family soon," he said with a smile.

"Miss Cole? What are you doing here?" John asked.

"I had no choice. I either die at home waiting for word, or risk everything going to help save Ernest … "

John picked up the bags that the girls had hidden in the boxes they had carried onto the ship. He followed Sir Montrose as he led them down to his spacious, private stateroom.

"I think you'll find that life aboard ship is difficult and dangerous," John said.

"But I'll understand why my fiancé loves this life, won't I?"

John thought about this; the discipline and order of ship life, the call to duty, the glory of manning a beautiful sailing vessel. Yes, there was hard work and many dangers involved, but the call of the sea sang in his ears strongly. He knew it did for Ernest also.

"Yes, I suppose so. If you can grow your sea legs and hold your stomach, you just might grow to love it, too."

Elizabeth smiled.

When they reached the door of the spacious room, Sir Montrose opened it and stepped inside to gather his things. "Come in. I'll need only a few minutes, and then the room will be yours. You will find it to be very comfortable I think."

"Thank you, sir. You are very kind."

John set the bags down just inside the door and then turned to leave. "Miss Cole? I … " he started to speak but Elizabeth cut him off.

"Lieutenant Bennett. You made a terrible mistake, and I do not doubt you are suffering for it — we all are. Let's hope that with God's will, it will turn out well, shall we?"

"Yes," John said. "God willing."

When the men left the room, Elizabeth sat down on the bed and exhaled. "We made it."

"Indeed we did."

"Thank you, Jane, for coming with me. Your companionship will be a blessing."

"You have always been good to me, Miss Cole. I couldn't imagine you doing this on your own," Jane said.

"Now, how about we get out of these awful clothes?"

Jane opened a bag and pulled out two dresses.

"Yes," Elizabeth smiled. "Much better."

Chapter 23

Before Lord Christopher's carriage could come to a stop in front of the townhouse of Lord Basil Wallace, Lord Christopher had already stepped down and opened the front door. He brushed right past the startled butler and walked down the long hallway toward Sir Wallace's den, throwing the door open.

Lord Wallace sat leaning back in his chair enjoying a brandy and cigar, his feet propped up on the desk in front of him. He jumped to his feet the moment he recognized his distant and very influential cousin.

Lord Christopher spoke directly. "I know all about your scheme."

"To what are you referring?" Wallace quipped back snidely.

"Charles Williamson has kidnapped one of the navy's finest officers, and the finger points to you as the mastermind behind this crime."

"You must be mistaken. I know nothing of it," Lord Wallace lied smoothly. "May I ask how this is any concern of yours?"

"Don't lie to me, you weak-minded fool! Williamson has sailed with Captain Robinson as a prisoner on the *Independent* — one of your ships. Their destination is Robinson Island!"

Realizing that Lord Christopher knew more than he thought, Lord Wallace decided the wisest course of action was to drop the charade. "We are only retrieving what is already ours."

"*Ours?* Are you mad?"

"You and I are members of the ruling family of the most powerful country on Earth. What we don't already control, we should."

"Your arrogance is beyond the pale, Basil. This is England. The private property of the Robinsons is not ours to take, and it's certainly not your place to run your own mission, especially when you're putting lives in danger. Most galling of all, you are putting our family's reputation at risk. Do you know what this could do to King George if something goes awry?"

"I am well aware of it, and for that reason my name is not associated with Captain Williamson, his men, or the mission."

"You are a complete fool! Your name is, in fact, closely associated with this matter."

"And how is that?"

"Not only is it your ship, but your son was seen with Williamson the night before Robinson disappeared."

"And how do you know this?" Lord Wallace demanded.

"Lieutenant John Bennett is ready to testify to that fact. In fact, Bennett divulged everything to Sir Montrose two days ago," Lord Christopher said.

"Not possible," Lord Wallace blurted. "Lieutenant Bennett

is dead."

"And how would you *know* that, Basil?" Lord Christopher asked.

Wallace coughed uncomfortably, "Well ... "

"Basil. Enough! Stop the lies. Your involvement in this matter is completely transparent," Lord Christopher said. "Your men left Bennett to die in an alley. Unfortunately for you, two officers found him very much alive and anxious to report what had happened."

Wallace blanched, thinking he had indeed been a fool to trust Cyril's word on this matter. "What are you going to do about it?" he asked.

"Montrose's ship, the *Conquest*, is already in pursuit."

"When did the *Conquest* sail?"

"Last night."

"She's already two days behind," Wallace blurted, not even pretending to conceal his involvement at this point. "There is no way she can catch up to the *Independent*."

"You had better hope she does," growled Lord Christopher. "If Captain Robinson or his family are harmed in any way ... "

Lord Wallace shook his head. "This is unfortunate."

"Unfortunate? You're an idiot, Basil! As I was saying, if anything happens to Captain Robinson or his family, it will be on your head and I will see to it that both you and that fop of a son are held responsible, royal blood or not."

"You wouldn't do that," Wallace sputtered. "The scandal could ruin us!"

"Make no mistake, Basil. I can, and I will. Now, get Cyril in here. I want to speak to him."

"Ummm ... "

"What is it?"

"I'm afraid Cyril's not here."

"Then tell me where he is and I'll go to him."

"That will be difficult," Wallace said, pouring himself another drink and offering one to Lord Christopher.

"And why is that?"

"He is ... traveling. Abroad."

Lord Christopher placed the glass on a nearby table. His eyes narrowed as he approached Lord Wallace. "Please don't tell me he's on the *Independent!*"

"Cyril is overseeing business ... "

Now Lord Christopher was standing toe to toe with Wallace.

"Your loathsome son is on that ship with Williamson — completely in league with and party to kidnapping, robbery, and piracy?"

Wallace pulled himself to his full height, a look of pure disdain on his face. "My son is ensuring that our family's wealth is secure, and that it will be guaranteed in perpetuity."

"Your son is ensuring that your family will rot in prison!"

At that, Lord Christopher abruptly left the room and charged down the hallway. At the bottom of the front steps his driver was standing by the open door of the carriage. Lord Christopher stepped in, and the horses quickly carried him away.

Chapter 24

Aboard the Independent, at sea, January 1817

Ernest's mind was too wrought with apprehension to worry about the physical discomfort of his prison. He slept on the hard floor with only minimal straw for a bed and a slop bucket for a toilet. The food was either the leftovers of the crew, or else maggot infested. The water was stale and had a sour taste to it. Every few days he was taken above deck to empty his sewage and enjoy a few moments of fresh air. He had been a prisoner for six weeks before he was taken up to the main deck for a bath. The once clean-cut naval officer was now almost unrecognizable. The poor living conditions and lack of food had taken a toll on his weight, and his clothes were filthy and hung on him like a slack sail.

Throughout the long weeks of his captivity Ernest did all he could to maintain his strength and sanity. He did stretches, push-ups, sit-ups, and any other exercise he could manage in his cramped quarters. He did all this during the day when he would be least noticed, not wanting to attract any undue attention from the crew. Thus, his monotonous routine was set, and the days and weeks torturously moved along.

As there was no porthole in his cell he couldn't see the moon or stars, so he was never quite sure where the ship was. It was only through snatches of overheard conversations between the crew that he picked up clues on the ship's progress.

For the first time in his seafaring life, Ernest daily prayed for bad weather to slow the ship. Even better, he hoped for a complete cessation of wind. He knew in his heart that Sir Montrose would send help, but he also knew it would take time to provision a ship, and a large head start would give Captain Charlie an almost unbeatable advantage.

After two months of sailing, Ernest was securely bound by iron chains and taken on deck. The seas were running fast and the sun was shining bright and warm, but Ernest felt a cold dread enter his heart.

The men who were assigned to guard him as he washed himself were making snide comments and laughing at each other's vile jokes. Ernest usually ignored them, but today he had had enough. He turned to the men, looked into their eyes ,and warned, "You'll never live to tell about your experience on Robinson Island. Even if you are fortunate enough to make it off the island and return to England, you and Captain Charlie will suffer the same fate as the late Captain Kidd."

"And what fate is that?" one of the men asked.

"Execution by hanging."

"Oh, I doubt it," a voice interrupted.

Ernest looked up to the quarterdeck into the grinning face of Cyril Wallace.

"You!"

"Yes," said Cyril, holding a handkerchief to his nose. "What a stench! You really should be more attentive to your grooming."

The crew erupted into new rounds of laughter.

"Your lovely Elizabeth would be appalled."

Ernest lurched against his restraints. "Wallace, you dog!"

One of the guards punched Ernest in the back, knocking him to one knee.

Captain Charlie, hearing the commotion, stepped out of his cabin and onto the quarterdeck. He sauntered down the steps to the main deck and over to his men.

"You are not to talk to or listen to this man," he ordered.

It was the first time Ernest had seen Captain Charlie since he had testified against him in court. Their eyes met only briefly.

"Take him back to his cell."

"Aye, aye, sir," the guards said, jerking on the chain that secured Ernest.

The captain turned away.

After being dragged a few steps, Ernest suddenly resisted. He looked up at Captain Charlie.

"Sir! Could I have a word with you?"

"You are not to address the captain," a guard barked.

Captain Charlie stopped and turned.

Ernest called out a second time. "Captain, I'd like a word with you!"

A guard viciously jammed his rifle butt into Ernest's stomach, making him double over in pain. Captain Charlie moved to the quarterdeck rail. Each guard had his gun pointed at Ernest except one who, as Captain Charlie stepped forward, had his gun pointed in the direction of Captain Charlie. Captain Charlie hit the gun away.

"You bloody fool! You could have shot me."

"My apologies, sir. I wasn't thinking."

"Yes. That's obvious."

Everyone laughed nervously, except Ernest who was struggling to catch his breath.

"One of these days you're going to kill someone, if you don't kill yourself first," Captain Charlie warned the careless guard.

"Captain," said Ernest straightening. "You have illegally detained me. I demand my immediate release."

Captain Charlie sneered. "Detained you? Hardly. You are a guest on this vessel."

The men roared at this.

Ernest stood defiantly. "I am a prisoner."

"Then you must be a criminal. Take him to his cell," Captain Charlie ordered his men.

The guards grabbed Ernest, dragging him toward the hold.

Ernest made eye contact with Captain Charlie. "We both know who the criminal is here … sir!"

"Wait!" yelled Captain Charlie. "How dare you proclaim me a criminal — again! Because of you I lost my commission. I was disgraced!"

Ernest retorted, "You disgraced yourself — just as you do now!"

"Tie him to the mast," ordered Charlie. "This insolence stops now."

The men dragged Ernest and tied him facing the main mast. A man ripped his shirt to his waist. In the meantime, Cyril had come down from the quarterdeck. One of the crew handed a long leather whip to Captain Charlie, who turned to Cyril.

"Would you like the honor?"

Cyril recoiled. "Heavens, no. I'll leave that to you. I'm just here to enjoy the spectacle."

Whip in hand, Captain Charlie approached Ernest. "I think fifteen lashes should teach you some restraint."

He flung his arm back then snapped it forward, cutting

Ernest viciously across the back with the long lash. Ernest arched his head in pain.

Captain Charlie drew back and once again sent the lash flying with brutal force. Ernest groaned, gritting his teeth against the shock and pain.

Ten lashes flew against Ernest's raw and bleeding back before he mercifully lost consciousness, the remaining five lashes biting into his flesh. Finally it was over and he was taken down and carried back to his cell, where he was dropped on the floor.

He woke hours later, the intense, throbbing pain his constant companion. He lay on his stomach for days, feverish and in and out of delirium. He lapped at his food and water from his plate like a dog. Finally, when the swelling subsided a bit, he was able to sit up.

Thoughts of retribution filled his head. How he would love to get his hands on Cyril Wallace. What could he do to disrupt Captain Charlie's plans? How could he protect his family? At times he feared he would go mad with anger and desperation; but when such thoughts arose, he found solace in prayer and meditation. Ernest was a product of his family, who had many times relied on divine help to find resolution to their problems. He was also a disciplined man, and when discouraging thoughts entered his mind he forced them out.

He knew he couldn't physically overpower the men on the ship; he would have to outsmart them. He needed to devise a plan and take advantage of any sudden opportunity that might arise.

Many options ran through his mind. He knew he could mislead Captain Charlie and Wallace as to the location of the treasure, or he could tell them he wasn't with the others the day the treasure was found and therefore couldn't lead them to it. These were weak defenses and he knew it. They did nothing to ultimately protect his family.

As the days went by Ernest became increasingly frantic about his family. In frustration, he threw his head back against the ship siding. The force of the impact hurt, but it didn't hurt as much as it should have. Ernest realized that the sideboards of the ship were soft and rotting in places.

A plan began to form in his mind. The *Independent* was a fast but old vessel, badly in need of caulking. Ernest's cell was below the main deck but still above the water level. The sidewalls of the ship had small leaks that became more apparent during the occasional storm and high swells. These breaches made Ernest's prison even more miserable, as it was wet for days on end. Suddenly Ernest's plan became clear; he would cut a hole in the side of the ship and free himself when the opportunity arose.

Using his belt buckle, Ernest scraped at the hardened tar-like caulking made from pine sap used to seam the sidewall planks together, making the ship watertight. Unfortunately, when he removed the caulking it allowed light to shine in, which if noticed would ruin his plan. To remedy this, Ernest moistened straw with his drinking water and mixed it with the removed pine sap and then filled in the gaps. The mixture of straw and pine sap would easily pull away when the time came, but it would keep the old planks watertight in the meantime. Most importantly, it would keep the sunlight from shining through.

Hour after hour, day after day, Ernest worked to cut through the planking. At times he used his dinner fork, alternating with his belt buckle.

Although the crew wasn't always watching him, they would

periodically come by to provide a meal or drink. After weeks of being on the ship the routine was set and predictable. He knew what time of day was best to continue his labor, but even then he needed to proceed with extreme caution. If he were caught he would have no second chances for escape.

When they had first departed from England it was cold, and he had been issued a thin blanket. Now that they were in warmer climates sailing down the west side of Africa, he had less need for it so he hung it on the sidewall to cover his work.

One of the guards had asked about his reason for hanging the blanket.

"To air it out, of course. You don't expect me to sleep in a moldy blanket, do you?" Ernest answered.

This was a reasonable answer. Seamen were a superstitious lot and feared the spread of mold, particularly black mold, as it was known to cause death. Soon after that Ernest noticed the crew hanging up their own blankets in their sleeping quarters.

Ernest diligently worked on an area about three feet by three feet, just big enough for him to escape once they reached the island. However, it was one thing to loosen the caulking, but it was an entirely different challenge to cut the sidewall planks. This was the most difficult part of his strategy that he wasn't even sure would work.

It was a slow and monotonous task as he used his crude tools to scratch at the boards. Under the blanket during the day, or freely at night while everyone was asleep, he methodically chipped away at the wood, hiding the shavings in his slop bucket, until the planks were almost completely cut through on his side. When the time was right, he planned to kick through the weakened planks and make his escape.

Ernest figured that he would have to make a total of eight cuts vertically down four planks, two to each plank, in order to have enough space to fit through. It was a task that consumed him. Worried that he was running out of time, Ernest spent every moment possible working to secure his escape.

One day several weeks after the flogging, Captain Charlie and one of his guards were heard coming below deck. Captain Charlie had been wounded in battle years ago and had a distinct walk, and each thumping step announced his presence. Ernest had just enough time to cover his work and scoot out into the open.

"It stinks foully down here. I hope it's not unbearable," Captain Charlie said.

Ernest stood, gripping the bars. "You have just made it worse — you bastard!"

Captain Charlie smiled and signaled for the guardsmen to back away and give them space to talk in private.

"Now, now. Is that the language of a newly promoted captain?"

Ernest glared at Captain Charlie.

"Let me offer you my heartiest congratulations!" Captain Charlie said.

"Is there something I can help you with *Mr. Williamson?*" Ernest smiled.

Captain Charlie's anger flared. "*Captain*, to you."

"You will never be 'Captain' to me again."

"Robinson. I only came down here to ensure that you were still alive. That is the only courtesy you will receive from me until you lead us to the treasure."

"Treasure?" Ernest feigned.

"Oh come now, Robinson," Captain Charlie said with a sarcastic chuckle. "I remember you being much brighter than that."

"You overestimate me; I don't know what you are talking about."

Picking at his nails, Captain Charlie continued. "When you realize that your family's lives are at stake you will suddenly know exactly what I am talking about."

"You won't survive," Ernest said under his breath.

"Pardon me?"

"You won't make it off the island, no matter how many men you have under your command," Ernest said boldly.

Captain Charlie cleared his throat.

"Bravado! I admire that in a man, Robinson."

Ernest couldn't help but stare at this man under whom he had been tutored and once respected.

Captain Charlie saw Ernest's introspection and asked, "What? Do tell me what you're thinking."

"I was just wondering how a once-great man like you could have fallen so low."

"Once great?"

"At one time I thought so. Up until the incident on the *Royal George*. If I had any inkling that enemy ships were in the area, I would have left those sailors to drown too."

"Oh?" Captain Charlie said, as if to question Ernest's sincerity. "You would have committed a war crime?"

"If it had been true, it would not have been a war crime. Sometimes terrible things have to be done in time of war; to save your own men you sacrifice the enemy. That's the nature of warfare. But, in your case, you lied. We all know that there were no enemy ships in the area. You simply murdered those men."

"What do you know about the responsibilities of command? You've never had such responsibility."

"Time and again I backed your decisions. I learned from you and admired you, but in those last few months, I noticed a cruel, reckless streak developing in you."

"Years of war will do that to a man," Captain Charlie said.

"Not every man. The king saw fit to give me a captaincy. It is an honor and station to which I plan to stay true. I will honor the men who serve under me, my conscience, and my God. I will never succumb to the depths of selfishness and greed into which you have fallen."

"How very noble of you. Unfortunately, you'll never have the opportunity to practice your high-minded principles. Do you really think we're going to let you live after we recover the treasure? Don't be a fool!"

"Why, Charlie? Why?"

"Excuse me?"

"How could a man, a good man, who served the king for thirty years, go bad?" Ernest asked. "The bitter man I see before me is not the Captain Charlie I knew; under whom I respectfully served."

"You would never understand," Captain Charlie said.

"Try me."

"I was twelve years old when my parents indentured me as a cabin boy on one of the king's ships. She was the frigate *Indomitable*; a mighty three-masted ship. We saw action in the Caribbean fighting the pirates off the coast of South America and against the Spanish."

Ernest could see the pride in his eyes, and in his voice, as the grizzled veteran spoke of his old ship.

"Back then the king's navy was a much tougher proposition than it is now. A man could be flogged for a lot of offenses that slip by today."

"So I've heard—and felt!" Ernest said.

Captain Charlie smiled. "Back then, even keelhauling was legal. A man could die serving his king, and I don't mean in battle. As a young boy, I endured beatings and abuse of the most vicious kind. I worked like a man in the rigging. I learned to shoot and use a saber and helped run the cannon shot and powder during the most terrifying battles."

Ernest remained silent.

"I wanted to be a sailor. It was the only life I knew, and I loved serving in His Majesty's Royal Navy. I gave my life to King George, and what did the navy do for me? I make a decision that I thought benefited my ship, my crew, and my king; and I'm cast aside. I'm out. After thirty years of service there is nothing to show for it. They threw me to the wolves."

"A purely metaphorical punishment I would say for a man who literally threw two hundred men to the sharks," Ernest said. "You condemned yourself when you turned your back on honor."

Captain Charlie's eyes narrowed. "You had the nerve to testify against me, Robinson, and for that you'll pay. Your family will pay with the treasure — and their lives — thanks to your friend John Bennett."

Captain Charlie extended his hand to show Ernest the ring he had won from John the night of the Royal Ball.

"Does this look familiar?"

Ernest's heart stopped for a moment. He recognized the ring but said nothing. There before him was the evidence of John's betrayal, and it was on Captain Charlie's finger. Ernest looked at Captain Charlie, knowing there was nothing he could say or do to cause Captain Charlie to soften or change course.

Captain Charlie abruptly turned and walked away.

"Tell your men to say their prayers. They'll need it," Ernest yelled after him.

Ernest went weak. Dropping to his knees, he began to pray to God for deliverance. He knew God's hand would have to stretch over his family at home if they were to have any chance of survival. Defending themselves against at least a hundred men under the leadership of Captain Charlie would put all their skills, learning, fortitude, will, and faith to the test like never before.

Ernest's thoughts turned to John. He was as angry as he was dismayed that greed could cause such weakness in a man. He prayed that in time he would be able to forgive his friend.

Then he rose and went back to work on the sidewall planks with a fierce determination. He had made good progress but had so much more to do before reaching the island.

Chapter 25

Robinson Island, January 1817

It was a beautiful, sunny day on Robinson Island, and the family was on the beach relaxing. Father, Mother, and Jenny lounged under a bamboo leaf umbrella watching Fritz and the boys play in the surf. Anne, now a toddler, sat next to Mother, playing in the sand.

Father had brought a book along and was reading it while Jenny began preparing lunch. He loved hearing the voices of his sons and grandsons drifting in the wind.

"Let me jump off your back."

"Okay."

"My turn, Pa."

They had been out in the water for some time when Jenny stood and called to them. "Come out and have some lunch!"

As Fritz and the boys were making their way ashore, she

noticed movement and unusual shapes in the distance. "It looks like we have some visitors," she called.

Father lowered his book. He and Mother stood, their hands shading their eyes from the glaring sun. Floating on the ocean swells were six hand-carved outrigger canoes carrying three to four people each.

"The Baraourou have come."

"How nice," Mother said.

"Yes," Father agreed.

The family all stood on the beach waving at the oncoming boats, welcoming them to their home. Although the Baraourou were a cannibal tribe from an island approximately fifteen nautical miles to the east, they were friendly to the Robinsons.

Not long after the family had shipwrecked, Father, Fritz, Ernest, Jack, and Turk — Sunshine's father — were out hunting when they heard women screaming. Father immediately grabbed the dog by his muzzle, commanded him to silence, and motioned to his sons to lie on their bellies. Inching up over the ridge they could see down to the beach. Two young native women were being dragged out of a cockboat by a small group of sailors, while a small merchant ship rested two hundred yards off the coast.

Father took out his spyglass to get a better view. It was obvious by their struggles, and the cords binding their hands, that the women were being held against their will. The boys each asked to look through the glass. They had never seen indigenous people before.

"What are they?" Fritz, always curious, had asked.

Before father could respond, Ernest whispered, "They're the savages we've read about, right Father?"

"Yes. I'm certain they are." Father paused then continued,

"They must live on one of the islands nearby."

"What shall we do?" Fritz asked.

"We must help them," Father said as he scanned from the beach to the merchant ship sitting in the harbor.

"How many men do you see?" Fritz whispered.

"Twenty or so in the ship and four on the beach."

"What are they doing here?" Ernest asked.

"Probably looking for provisions."

"But what will they do with the savage women?" asked Jack innocently.

Laughing, the men on the beach untied their captives. A man slapped one of the women.

"Take them as slaves," Father answered Jack. "They are not good men, and they don't belong here."

"What can we do?" Fritz asked. "There are too many men for us to handle on our own. Maybe we should just let them be."

"Those women are children of God, and the Lord expects us to do our part. We must free them."

"Are you sure, Father?" a nervous fourteen-year-old Ernest asked.

"Yes. I'm sure. Jack, you stay here with Turk. Keep him quiet until I call for you. Fritz, Ernest, and I will move in closer and give them a warning to leave the women alone. If they refuse, we will respond decisively."

"Yes, Father," the boys nodded, showing they understood and trusted their father.

They quietly made their way down the ridge toward the edge of the beach and hid behind a large boulder. Fritz and Ernest had their rifles ready and aimed at the beach. Once in position, Father stood up, exposing his head and upper chest.

"You! On the beach! Leave the savages and depart!"

Surprised to see Europeans on the island, the men turned toward the demanding voice, drawing their guns.

"I'd put those guns away if I were you," Father warned.

"Who are you? What do you want?" one of the men yelled.

"Put your guns down, and let the women go," Father repeated.

One of the men fired. Father ducked behind the boulder, his back slumped against the boulder next to his sons. Another man yelled, "These is cannibals! Ain't worth gettin' yourselves killed over."

"That's not what my God teaches me," Father yelled back as he prepared his rifle. He offered one more chance. "Leave the savages, and you can depart in peace."

To his sons he said, "I don't suppose they are going to leave without a fight. We'll need to act fast while there are only four of them, while we have the advantage."

"What advantage?" Fritz asked.

"We have the protection of the boulder and a surprise. You two."

Just then another shot ricocheted off the boulder near Fritz's head. At Father's nod, they stood and fired. Father and Fritz hit two of the men. Ernest missed. The third man, fearing for his life, rushed to the boat and pushed off into the water, rowing toward the ship and leaving his shipmate behind. The Robinsons ducked back behind the boulder and reloaded their rifles. The last man jumped behind the women, using them as shields.

"You haven't a chance. Save yourself while you can," Father yelled

The man was shaking, obviously terrified. Knowing he was

in the right, Father stood and slowly walked toward the man, his rifle aimed and loaded. The man pushed the women aside and fired at Father but missed. Father, calm and steady, pulled the trigger and shot the man. He fell backwards onto the sandy beach.

The man who had escaped in the cockboat rowed as fast as he could back to the merchant ship. The men on the merchant ship were spooked, and not knowing how many more men were on the island, quickly raised anchor. Once the man made it back to the ship, they stowed the cockboat, raised sail, and sailed away.

When the danger had passed, Father whistled and Jack and the dog came running. It was a solemn sight to see the three dead men lying in the sand. It was a sober lesson for the Robinson boys.

"To protect yourself or your family there are times when it is appropriate to kill a man," Father said. "However, it is only an option after all other solutions have been tried. Remember that, boys."

"Yes, Father," the boys chorused.

Father turned to check on the two women, who had not moved for fear of the dog. Terrified, they cowered at Father's feet, crying in their native tongue, obviously begging for mercy.

Father set his gun aside and leaned down, taking each woman by the hand. He looked directly into their eyes and smiled, raising them to their feet.

Ernest and Fritz watched from a short distance, suddenly frozen with embarrassment. They had never seen a woman undressed before.

Father smiled, and motioning to himself and his sons, he said, "Friends."

The women cowered.

"Friends," Father repeated and motioned to the boys to do the same.

"Friends," they repeated, smiling, tucking their guns behind their legs. Fritz uncorked his canteen and offered it to the women. One grabbed it and drank greedily, then gave it to her companion who did the same.

Ernest dug into his pack and produced the bread and dried meat Mother had packed for him. The women cautiously took the food, and then devoured it as if they were starving. When they had eaten, Father motioned for the women to follow him, which at first they were afraid to do.

Father whistled to Turk. The dog was off exploring a nearby tide pool. When he came running, the women cowered again in fear. Jack, only ten years old, said, "Don't be afraid." He patted Turk on the head. "See. He won't hurt you."

The women relaxed somewhat, soothed by Jack's innocent, friendly demeanor.

"All right," Ernest said, smiling. "Let's go meet Mother."

Something in his easy manner calmed the women.

"What about the dead men?" Fritz asked Father. "What do we do? Bury them?"

"No. They were sailors, so I think they would have wanted to be committed to the sea."

They hauled the men out into the breakers, where they washed out to their final resting place.

When it was finally time to leave, the women cautiously followed as Father, Fritz, Jack, and Ernest led them into the jungle and eventually to Falconhurst, where they were lovingly and efficiently cared for by Mother.

Two weeks later, the family and their native guests were on the beach when they noticed a group of outrigger canoes coming toward the island. The women became very excited, jumping up and down, waving their arms and shouting.

Father cautioned his family to stand quietly.

"It's very possible they will be hostile. They don't know it wasn't us who kidnapped their women."

Five canoes, each with four men, came ashore.

The women, who had been standing on the shore yelling and pointing to the family, suddenly dropped to their knees and bowed their heads. The men piled out of the canoes, which were formed from large, hollowed-out trees with bamboo outriggers. They were all dressed simply in loincloths, each man carrying a spear. They formed a line on the beach as an older man, the only one wearing a headpiece and several beaded necklaces, stepped forward. He spoke quietly to the women, who rose and led him to the Robinsons.

It was obvious from their smiles and gestures they were describing their miraculous rescue by the hands of the Robinsons.

"Evidently," said Father, "this man is the chief." Father stepped forward and nodded his head, offering his hand.

"William," he said, introducing himself.

The chief frowned at Father's proffered hand. "Baraourou," he said placing his hand on his own chest."

Father turned to his family, "I think his name is 'Baraourou.'"

After a few more gestures and interpretations of meaning, the whole group of natives seemed to relax.

Father introduced his sons, pronouncing each name clearly, as Mother came forward and bowed her head. The chief was extremely surprised by this and returned the gesture by shaking his hand above his head and bowing.

Mother put her fingers to her lips and said "food" in the language she had learned from the native women.

The afternoon wore into evening as the two groups ate and celebrated a most unusual alliance. The Robinson boys entertained their new friends with hilarious pantomimes, and as the fire died down, the savages sang and danced.

Mother invited the men to sleep in the tree houses but they declined, making rudimentary beds out in the open below the trees.

The next day their new friends left, their canoes filled with preserved meat, fruit jams, and dried grains. The chief, whose name they learned was King Baraourou, which meant "strong warrior," gave Father a beautifully carved wooden mask of a monkey. King Baraourou was a wise and revered leader, and with time the Robinsons began referring to the tribe as the Baraourou as a tribute to their chief.

Over the course of the following months and years, the Baraourou visited Robinson Island often. With time, both groups taught one another the important elements of their languages. Both knew valuable survival skills. The Baraourou were extremely skilled with hunting and trapping. The Robinsons were able engineers and practitioners of herbal medicine. Over the years, the Robinsons took all this learning and coupled it with the knowledge they had brought with them to the island. With the help of the Baraourou, the Robinsons didn't just survive on the island, they thrived there.

One year an event occurred that greatly benefited both the Robinsons and the Baraourou. A sperm whale was discovered floating just offshore of Robinson Island. Sperm whales were rarely seen in that part of the world, but occasionally one would drift into the warm waters of the Indian Ocean.

The Baraourou were just as excited as the Robinsons to discover the giant whale, and preparations were quickly made to try and harpoon it. This would not be an easy task, but the Baraourou were skilled in the water, and it was only possible because the whale was close to shore.

"Father," Ernest said, full of excitement. "I've been reading about sperm whales. Did you know they have a cavity in their head that contains a liquid wax called spermaceti, which is how they get their name? Spermaceti is a valuable type of oil used for lubricants, oil lamps, and candles. There can be as much as three hundred to five hundred gallons in a single whale."

"Wonderful," said Father, straining against the oars of their longboat.

"I've never seen a creature this big before," Fritz said, also rowing with all his might. "If we can catch it, it'll provide food for us and the Baraourou for more than a year."

"It can weigh as much as fifteen to twenty tons … "

"Thank you, Ernest," Fritz said impatiently.

"… and be as long as sixty or seventy feet."

"Pray God she doesn't dive," said Father.

"Yes," said Ernest. "If she doesn't it's because she's sick or dying."

The Robinsons and the Baraourou surrounded the whale with their boats and on the Baraourou's command, they threw their harpoons as one. The whale emitted a horrible, keening wail so loud it felt as though their eardrums would burst. Then, rolling onto its side, it whipped its tail up, cracking one of the canoes and knocking the native men into the water. As the warriors were climbing into the other canoes the whale rolled over onto its other side, let out another wail, and then went silent. The whale was dead. Ropes were slung across the carcass. The men pulled with all their strength as they slowly made their way to shore, the giant whale trailing behind them. The men caught a break as the incoming surf lifted the carcass up and into the shallows where its weight finally came to rest.

The Robinsons and the Baraourou worked for days hacking and carving at the giant beast. The spermaceti was collected in large wooden barrels salvaged long ago from the shipwreck. The blubber was cut, rendered over huge open fires, and was later used to make soap. The tough hide was shaved from the carcass, scraped, and preserved. It could be used for a thousand purposes where a watertight, flexible material was needed. The meat was cut into thin strips and smoked over green-willow fires and hung to dry. The natives cut and hollowed every bone. They considered the bone marrow and the whale's eyes to be a special delicacy.

When the work was finally done, the Baraourou conducted a special ceremony, thanking the whale for giving its life and the great God for sending this animal to them.

As the years passed, the bond between the Baraourou and the Robinson family had developed into a strong and meaningful friendship. They were friends and allies in the struggle to survive in such an isolated area of the world.

Now, more than fifteen years later, the Baraourou, both women and men, exited the boats and dragged them further up shore to ensure they wouldn't be swept away by the rising tide.

The Robinsons gathered their belongings and met the natives on the beach.

Twenty-four Baraourou had come this day. The two groups

greeted each other warmly. This visit did not include King Baraourou who was now eighty years old and too fragile to make the long journey to Robinson Island. Instead, his oldest son, Zartuk, was the leader of this visit. Father and Zartuk embraced each other.

"How is the king?" Father asked.

"He is getting old but sends his regards," Zartuk replied in his native tongue.

The Baraourou had come just before the rainy season set in. Each of their visits was a time to feast, share stories, and reminisce. It was also a time when Father, Fritz, Francis, Nicholas, and Jacob would seek to learn more survival skills.

Over the years the Baraourou had taught them how to construct primitive, yet effective, weapons. It was the Baraourou who had taught the Robinsons how to build a blowgun using poisonous darts that could be used to take down a bird or a monkey. The poison was taken from the milky extract of a toad, obtained by rubbing the dart against the anal glands of the frog, a job no one relished.

That evening at Falconhurst they were eating a shared meal of both traditional island food made by the Baraourou and also European food prepared by the Robinsons. Francis entertained the group recounting the first time he had seen a native catch a lizard and, without cooking it, toss it into his mouth and eat it.

As the evening wore on Zartuk spoke to Father and Fritz alone, as they lounged on the porch.

"My father speaks about a worrisome dream," Zartuk said. "What is it?"

"He fears your son Ernest may be in danger."

A sudden breeze blew through Falconhurst as if to portend

that what Zartuk was saying was true. King Baraourou was like a prophet to his people. He would often have premonitions or visions of things that invariably came to pass. His people believed that his powers came from their god.

"Three nights ago my father awoke, sweating, and speaking of a dream. In it harm has come upon Ernest," Zartuk said.

Father and Fritz looked at one another. They had come to respect the old man's abilities, having seen the accuracy of them for themselves.

"He spoke of a ship," Zartuk continued. "I know nothing more. It is all my father shared with me."

"Thank you, Zartuk, and thank your father."

Zartuk grasped Father's shoulder. "You must prepare for trouble."

"Again, thank you my good friend. Send your father our wishes for his continued good health."

Zartuk joined his tribe to sleep for the night. Before they left the following morning they performed an unusual ritual chant around the fire to encourage the spirits to protect Robinson Island.

"What was that all about?" Mother asked as she waved goodbye to the canoes vanishing toward the horizon.

Father and Fritz looked at one another and shrugged. They had decided not to mention the king's dream to Mother or the others. They didn't want to cause them any unnecessary distress.

"Perhaps King Baraourou is deteriorating with age," Father whispered to Fritz. "God willing it was only a dream."

"I don't know, Father. It seems that his intuition only increases with age."

Father put his hand on Fritz's shoulder and smiled. "Well, it won't hurt for us to increase our own prayers."

"Yes," Fritz agreed.

"And make an inspection of the island's defenses just in case," Father added.

"Right."

Chapter 26

Aboard the Conquest, *January 1817*

The dinner bell rang five times. The officer's mess typically included Sir Montrose; Captain Briggs; Lieutenant Patterson, the ship's first mate; Kenneth Spangler, the surgeon; Officer Moore, the ranking marine on board; Elizabeth; and her maid, Jane. There was a joke among the officers that the food always tasted better when the ladies were at the table.

This night's dinner was vegetables and sea turtle steaks, which was a favorite of the crew. Sea turtles weighed anywhere between eighty and four hundred pounds and were a convenient meat source. Turtles were known to live up to a year without needing to eat. They simply wandered around licking the deck until fresh meat was required. Sea turtles could also yield many pounds of fat to be used as oil for lanterns or cooking.

Elizabeth had never eaten turtle meat, but was always open

to adventure, so Captain Briggs ordered it for dinner. Elizabeth took her first bite. While she let it settle in her mouth and savored the taste, the others at the table looked on and waited for her response.

"This is delicious and richly tender."

Sometimes when the meal was over, they would remain in the captain's quarters to share stories, philosophize, and drink a little wine. The men would often speak of strategies to find and rescue Captain Robinson; however, these conversations took place outside of Elizabeth's presence so as not to worry her.

Having women on board any ship during a long sea voyage was generally discouraged, and for good reason. Women on board often attract unwanted attention from crewmen, but not on this ship. Most members of the crew had worked for Sir Montrose for quite some time and knew Ernest and the entire Robinson Family well. The men liked and respected Ernest, and that respect easily transferred to Elizabeth and Jane. The women had only been on board a short time before the crew recognized their kind and gentle natures, and now, after weeks at sea, there wasn't anything the men wouldn't do to protect the ladies. In fact, having the ladies on board reminded the crew daily of their important mission and rekindled in them the desire to stand up for all that is good and lovely in the world.

Knowing the journey would be long, Elizabeth had brought her drawing kit. She spent many days on deck sketching the ship and the various activities that constituted ship life. At times, when duties weren't demanding, she would sketch portraits of the crew to send home to their families. In the evenings, after dinner, Elizabeth met the men in the mess area to read to them from the books Sir Montrose kept in his cabin. The crew looked forward to these evenings as it provided a welcome break to the monotonous routine of ship life, and many of the men couldn't read themselves.

One late night when most of the crew had retired, Elizabeth was lying in bed unable to sleep. While her lantern swayed to the rhythm of the ocean, she listened to the ship creaking. She got out of bed, put on her robe, and walked out to the quarterdeck to gaze into the night sky.

Sir Montrose was in his cramped quarters reading, but he too was unable to sleep. He rolled out of bed, put on his coat, and stepped out onto the deck for some fresh air. He noticed Elizabeth quietly standing on the quarterdeck.

Sir Montrose climbed up to the quarterdeck and stood next to her, leaning against the rail.

"How are you holding up, my dear?"

"Very well, thank you," she said smiling. After a moment she continued, "How do you think Ernest is doing?"

"I'm sure he's fine. After all, they need him alive." The last thing he wanted to do was alarm her with his suspicions of how Ernest was really being treated by Williamson and his crew.

"Do you honestly think we'll make it in time to help?"

"We are making excellent headway. Let's keep our hopes high."

Elizabeth turned to this kind and generous man standing resolute, his lined face looking out to sea. Impulsively, she put her arm through his.

Sir Montrose was like a father to all. *It's easy to confide in him,* Elizabeth thought. *He listens to people and respects them.*

"Tell me, what happened to your son? Ernest tells me he was a fine man."

"Indeed, he was. He was a navy captain and well respected by his men." Sir Montrose bowed his head looking down at the swift current below. "He was also a wonderful son and father. His name was William. He was married to Claire, a delightful woman. Sadly, she died giving birth to their only child."

"I'm so sorry to hear that," said Elizabeth. "I'm sorry if my curiosity has caused you pain."

"No, no," Sir Montrose said, gently patting her hand. "Of course, it was devastating for all of us, but for years after her death William couldn't bear to be without Jenny. She lived in India with him. When she was seventeen, war broke out and my son returned to navy life. He didn't want to leave Jenny alone in India, so he put her on a merchant ship bound for England."

Sir Montrose paused, looking up at the night sky.

"On that voyage, her ship encountered a storm that carried it off course. The ship was damaged and began to take on water. The crew was forced to abandon ship and board longboats. They were tossed in the storm for days. The boats were separated and, presumably, lost. Jenny told us that someone in her boat spotted land in the distance and they headed for it. The boat capsized in the breakers offshore and Jenny, miraculously, was the only person to make it to shore alive. That landfall was Robinson Island."

"What a harrowing story, Sir Montrose. Your Jenny was quite a woman to survive it."

"That's not all," Sir Montrose chuckled. "After reaching shore, not knowing where she was or what kind of inhabitants might be on the island, she relieved one of the drowned men of his clothing and dressed herself in them, disguising herself as a boy. That's the condition in which the Robinsons found her.

They thought she was a cabin boy."

Elizabeth laughed.

"Eventually, they discovered her true nature. The family took her in and treated her with all of the tenderness and kindness for which they are known. Soon after that, one of my merchant ships landed on Robinson Island searching for survivors. It was with immense joy that they brought back news to my wife and me that Jenny was alive."

"How wonderful that must have been for you."

"Yes. It helped ease our sadness. You see, Jenny's father was killed in battle."

"Oh," Elizabeth said.

"Yes. Well ... ," Sir Montrose cleared the emotion from his throat. "I set sail for Robinson Island to find Jenny safe and in love with their oldest son. I happily gave my consent for them to marry. You may not know this, but Ernest's father, William, was a clergyman in Switzerland, and he married them. Of course by then Jenny had not just fallen in love with Fritz but with the island too. She refused to leave."

Again, Elizabeth laughed. There was a sudden chill as the wind increased and filled the sails. "What does your wife think about this voyage to rescue Ernest?"

"She couldn't get me out of the house fast enough," Sir Montrose laughed. "She was so relieved when our ship finally set sail. It would devastate her to lose Jenny and the rest of the Robinsons. We're family. You know, she couldn't be more pleased with Ernest's choice to marry you. You're the perfect match for Ernest and will be a wonderful addition to the family."

"You're very kind. I feel so blessed to have Ernest in my life. I pray for his safety every day."

"Try not to spend too much time worrying about it," Sir Montrose soothed, patting her arm. "Ernest is a bright man and very ingenious. If anyone can make the best of this difficult situation it'll be Ernest."

"Thank you for all you're doing."

"Stuff and nonsense," said Montrose, blushing. "Come, it's time to get some sleep," he said gently.

Sir Montrose walked Elizabeth back to her room. He had just turned toward his cabin when a yell rang out from the crow's nest.

"Sail off the starboard bow! Sail off the starboard bow!"

Feet clattered onto the quarterdeck. The helmsman repeated the call, "Sail off the starboard bow."

First mate Patterson yelled for the bell to be rung. The crewmen jumped from their cots and rushed above deck.

Sir Montrose joined Patterson and Captain Briggs at the helm. Patterson had his spyglass pressed to his eye to get a better view of the ship in the distance.

"What do you see?" Captain Briggs asked.

"Not quite sure. I can only make out the vague shape of the ship. If there were more moon, perhaps ... "

Elizabeth, having heard the call, joined them. "Could it be the *Independent*?" she asked.

"Stay on her. Lights out. Silence on board. We'll follow her until morning," Captain Briggs ordered.

With the order given, Captain Briggs turned to go below. Elizabeth touched his arm. "Captain Briggs. Do you think it's the *Independent*?"

"I doubt it," he said.

Elizabeth sighed.

"We'll know for sure in the morning. Get some rest, we've a long night ahead of us," Captain Briggs said.

"Good night," Elizabeth responded to no one in particular, as she retired to her cabin.

Sleep eluded her until she finally dozed off in the early morning only to be awakened at light's first break with the sounds of crewmen hustling on deck. Pulling on her robe, she hurried to the quarterdeck.

"Pull the stay," one midshipman yelled.

The *Conquest* was at full sail with the mystery ship much closer in front of them.

A yell sounded from the quarterdeck. "Captain on deck."

"Let me see the glass," Captain Briggs commanded.

He studied the ship ahead of them then lowered his glass, shaking his head.

"She's not the *Independent*. It looks to be a Brazilian merchant ship."

Elizabeth and Sir Montrose nodded. Elizabeth smiled weakly and turned away.

"Stay in the wind," Captain Briggs ordered. "Four points port side."

"Aye, aye sir."

"Four points port side. Stay in the wind." First mate Patterson relayed the command to the helmsman.

Soon the merchant ship disappeared into the distance.

Chapter 27

Aboard the Independent, *January 1817*

Ernest sat in his dark, muggy cell aboard the *Independent*. Above deck he could hear the unmistakable sounds of someone being flogged. He shuddered at each snap of the whip and resulting scream.

Confined below deck, Ernest spent most of his time alone working to cut through the side timbers. He had just stopped to rest when he heard steps shuffling slowly in his direction. He quickly covered the evidence of his activities.

A young sailor stopped outside his cell, looking sick and frightened.

"You look a little green about the gills, sailor," Ernest said. "How old are you?"

"Sixteen, sir."

"You're not a day over Fourteen."

The young boy nodded.

"I just … I never … I didn't think it would be like this," he stammered.

Ernest felt a rush of sympathy for the boy, and looking at him it wasn't hard to imagine Captain Charlie as a young boy growing up in the harsh seafaring world.

"What are you doing here?" Ernest asked. "Shouldn't you be on deck?"

"I just … wanted to say … I … remember when you were flogged … and, I'm sorry."

"Do you have a family, young man?"

"Yes, sir. I guess. I don't hear from 'em anymore."

Tender memories of his own family flooded Ernest's thoughts. He loved them deeply and longed for the day they would see each other again. He thought if he were blessed to reunite with them he would make a stronger effort to value them more … to express his love more openly … to be more caring and affectionate.

"You should write to them," Ernest said.

Above them, the whipping and screams abruptly stopped.

"You'd better get up there before you're missed. All hands witness punishment, right?"

"Yes, sir," the boy said as he turned and ran.

Alone once again, Ernest suppressed the urge to yell at the circumstances he found himself in. He could almost bear it if he didn't think about Elizabeth. He took small comfort knowing that although Elizabeth had a gentle countenance and loving heart, she could be as fierce as a lion. Ernest knew that if there was any woman who could make it through this trying time, it would be her.

Ernest got to his knees and began praying, just as his mother and father had taught him to do as a child. Thoughts of John entered his mind and he resolved to stay on his knees until forgiveness entered his heart. It befuddled him that his best friend could betray him. How could he do such a thing? Then his thoughts turned to the young boy he had just met. John could very well have been that boy. John, like Captain Charlie, had been indentured young into a man's world. It was because of their determination that both John and Captain Charlie had become fine officers in the Royal Navy. Perhaps it was inevitable that John would turn to greed, just like Captain Charlie. *I can't judge him too harshly,* Ernest realized.

"Help John turn from a life that will undoubtedly lead to his destruction," he prayed.

Ernest looked up and stared at the wood planking above his head. *I wonder what Elizabeth is doing right now? Will we ever be together again?*

A strange feeling of peace came over him, as if he could feel her spirit close. Feeling comforted, he moved toward the wall, pulled back the blanket hanging there, and went back to his task with renewed energy.

Chapter 28

Aboard the Independent, *February 1817*

A few weeks later, after scraping away at the sidewall for hours, an exhausted Ernest found escape in a deep sleep. He dreamed of Elizabeth, seeing a vivid panorama of their future life together. He envisioned a little boy and girl running through waves and collecting seashells while he held Elizabeth in his arms. He felt strands of her hair blowing against his face as he held her. He gently caressed her face, trailing whisper soft kisses down her jawline. Elizabeth giggled and tried pushing him away, but he picked her up and ran into the surf pretending to throw her in. Elizabeth screamed for the children to save her. Ernest saw their children laughing and running to free their mother, yelling, "Mama, we'll save you! We'll save you!"

He saw Elizabeth taking care of and nurturing their children. Most importantly, he saw himself holding his beloved

Elizabeth in his arms and gazing into her soft blue eyes. It was all a dream, but the love was real. It was a much-needed respite from reality. After months of imprisonment, Ernest was wasting away. His muscles and joints burned from malnutrition. The work he had been doing scratching and clawing at the wooden boards blistered, gouged, and bloodied his hands. But in this brief moment in sleep, however, he felt at peace. In his dreams he was able to experience the safety and hope he was desperately yearning for.

Ernest was ripped from sleep when the first mate came down the stairs and yelled, "Everyone up! Robinson Island is dead ahead. We've got work to do before sunrise."

The crew rolled out of their swaying hammocks, stretching and yawning. Ernest's heart swelled knowing that he was so close to his family, but he was also filled with dread knowing the danger that they were in. It was time to escape and warn his family.

Once he knew everyone was above deck, Ernest sat on the floor with his back against the cell bars. He pushed aside the blanket that was covering his work and kicked as hard as he could against the planks. He had cut through enough of the siding that two planks fell into the water below, but there wasn't enough space to squeeze his body through. He kicked like a mad man at the third plank but to no avail. The timber held stubbornly. He had only been able to cut through one side of the third plank. He punched at it again and again with his feet, but the planking held fast.

Deeply frustrated, Ernest kneeled in front of the opening created by the two missing planks and looked out. Although it was dark, he was able to see the shape of the island in the moonlight.

It was about three o'clock in the morning and still dark outside. Above him Ernest could hear the sounds of the men as they prepared to disembark the ship at sunrise. In his mind, he could see men racing among the rigging, adjusting and stowing the sails.

"Ease up the main sail!" yelled Hicks, the first mate, as Captain Charlie walked out onto the quarterdeck.

"Ease up the fore sail!" This second directive was given to slow the ship down.

"Steady," Captain Charlie cautioned the helmsman.

The *Independent* slowed as it approached the island.

"Drop anchor," Captain Charlie ordered.

The ship came to a stop in the main cove of the island — Safety Bay.

Ernest knew he had to come up with another escape plan fast. He could hear the shuffling and clunking of feet on the hard oak deck above. Suddenly he heard footsteps coming down the stairs toward the brig. He had just enough time to cover the hole with his blanket before two men appeared at the door of his cell.

"You're coming with us," the first man said.

Ernest knew all too well the men who had been assigned to guard him. The first was Knowles who, like Ernest, had a full mustache and beard. The second was a scrawny man named Russell. The two men unlocked and opened the iron doors. Stepping inside, they hauled Ernest roughly to his feet and bound his hands together in front of his body with iron cuffs. Once secure, they led Ernest above deck to Captain Charlie.

"Does this look familiar?" Captain Charlie said with satisfaction as he waved toward the shore.

Ernest looked. "No," he said.

Knowles punched Ernest in the back, knocking him to his knees.

"You've got the wrong island, Charlie," Ernest gasped

Knowles landed another blow.

"Your theatrics are amusing, Robinson, but I know this is the place," Captain Charlie said. "I can smell the treasure."

Struggling to his feet, Ernest stared squarely into Captain Charlie's eyes and spit in his face.

Captain Charlie's mood instantly changed as he wiped his sleeve across his face. He moved close, his fury barely suppressed. Ernest could smell rum on his breath. "You'll pay for this insolence, Robinson."

Ernest stood defiantly.

"Is this the right cove to dock this ship or not?"

Again, Ernest stared but said nothing.

First Mate Hicks was standing by Captain Charlie. "Don't worry, he'll talk," he said. We'll have his family soon. Robinson will see them die, one at a time, until his tongue loosens."

Captain Charlie ordered Knowles and Russell to escort Ernest back to his holding cell. "Take him down. He's of no use to us now."

As they dragged Ernest away, Captain Charlie called, "Let me remind you, we have a hundred men aboard this ship. What can your family do against those odds?"

You'll see soon enough, Ernest thought to himself.

Captain Charlie turned to his men. "Now get back to work. Do your jobs well, men, and we'll all have ourselves some treasure."

"Aye, aye!" they all yelled.

Ernest looked back over his shoulder as Knowles and Russell

pushed him below deck. Descending the stairs, he could hear Captain Charlie laughing and shouting orders. Ernest was chagrined at this twist of bad luck for his family. Captain Charlie had landed in the very cove that merchant ships used to anchor and come ashore. It was the main cove, and the path through the trees led directly to Falconhurst.

The smell of rum on Captain Charlie's breath made Ernest realize that the crew were either drunk or close to it, including the two imbeciles behind him. Without warning, Ernest attacked. Training and instinct took over. He shoved Knowles up against the wall, knocking the gun out of his hands. He buried his elbows into Knowles's ribs, knocking the breath out of him. Knowles slumped over in pain, and Ernest, hands bound together, slammed the iron cuffs down on the back of his neck, knocking him out cold.

Out of the corner of his eye Ernest saw Russell reach for the pistol that Knowles had dropped. Ernest kicked the gun out of Russell's reach. Russell took a step back and reached for his knife. The thin, wiry man danced with the knife in his hand, taunting Ernest. Time and movement slowed down. The waving of the knife became hypnotic as Ernest focused on its every movement.

After what seemed like an eternity, Russell lunged forward, wildly thrusting the knife. Ernest ducked, and grabbing Russell's arm, slammed him into the wall. Ernest kicked his feet out from beneath him, and as Russell dropped, Ernest threw his bound hands over Russell's head and squeezed as tight as he could until the breathing stopped.

The dead man's hand released the knife and Ernest took it. Moving quickly, Ernest rummaged through Knowles's pockets until he found the key to unlock the iron cuffs. Once free, he dragged Russell by the ankles and dumped his body behind two wooden barrels. He took off his own shredded clothes and threw them into the cell. Looking behind him to make sure he was still alone, Ernest dragged Knowles into the cell, gagged him with his own underpants, and then put on Knowles's rancid clothes.

Stepping over Knowles's body, Ernest closed the cell door and locked it, throwing the keys into the opposite corner of the ship. On the way to the stairs he noticed a leftover bowl of soup on the nearby table. Knowing that he needed all the energy he could get, he quickly gulped it down then made his way up to the deck.

It wasn't difficult to disguise himself as Knowles. They had similar body frames and were roughly the same height. They both had long, scraggly beards and similar hair color.

Ernest reached the top of the stairs and looked out. He straightened his clothes, put the knife through his belt, and walked out onto the main deck. Hicks was walking straight toward him. At that same moment a yell came from the forward bow.

"Knowles!"

It took Ernest a moment to realize the yell was directed at him. In the dark, thirty feet away, the boatswain barked, "Get your sorry bones up that mast!"

"Aye, sir," Ernest mumbled, disguising his voice. The second mate paused for a moment, then went about his business.

Ernest knew as long as he kept his face down he probably wouldn't be recognized in the dark. He hurried toward the rope ladder leading up the main mast. Several of the crew were above on the spars working the rigging.

Ernest was almost to the main mast when an officer yelled,

"Howard! Johnny! Where's Russell? Go down and fetch that lazy good-for-nothing. We need help up here."

"Yes, sir," they called.

"Be quick about it!"

Making his way below deck, Howard passed Ernest. Howard was the first below deck and heard frantic mumbling sounds. Curious, he moved toward the sound and found Knowles inside the brig with no clothes on. Howard reached his hand through the bars and pulled the gag from Knowles's mouth. Knowles took a deep breath before yelling, "Robinson's escaped! Get me out of here!"

Johnny tried to open the brig door.

"It's locked."

"Where's the key?" Knowles screamed, grabbing the bars.

"I don't know," Howard yelled.

"Just get up there and let everyone know Robinson's escaped!"

"Where's Russell?" Johnny asked. "They need him atop the foremast."

"I haven't seen him since Robinson ambushed us," Knowles spat.

Howard looked around and saw a boot poking out from behind the barrels. Grabbing a lantern, he made his way into the dark, shadowy storage area and discovered Russell's body lying there. He put his finger under Russell's nose, then looked at Knowles, who was putting on Ernest's discarded trousers.

"He's dead."

"Well, get moving!" Knowles snapped. "Tell the others. We haven't time to waste."

"You!" Knowles growled at Johnny. Get up to the captain's

quarters and get the second set of keys to this hellhole!"

Above, the cry went out. "Robinson's escaped! Robinson's gone!"

Chaos immediately erupted on board. A man looked up in the rigging and noticed Ernest, "There he is! Up there!"

"No. That's Knowles!" another man said.

"No! It's Robinson in Knowles's clothes!"

Men began climbing the mast after Ernest.

Ernest reached the spar, the two men close behind.

Captain Charlie came flying out of his quarters. "Where is he?"

"Up there, sir!" a man said, pointing up into the rigging.

The men on the spars were inching closer.

"Kingston, Bailey, remember we need him alive," Captain Charlie yelled.

The men lunged. Ernest crouched down and kicked the ankle of the first man, causing him to lose his footing. He reached back to grab the rigging, but there was nothing there. He fell, hitting another man who was making his way up the ropes. The two men fell to the deck with a sickening thud, dying instantly.

The second man reached Ernest and managed to land a couple of punches before Ernest swept the man's legs off the spar, but he managed to grab hold of the spar with his hands. Captain Charlie and the crew watched in dismay as Ernest walked over to the man and stepped on his hand. He fell screaming to his death.

Chapter 29

Standing on deck, a crewman raised his rifle and aimed at Ernest. Captain Charlie hit the muzzle of the gun just as it fired, the sound of the gunshot reverberating through the cove.

At Falconhurst, Fritz woke up. He turned to Jenny, nudging her. "Did you hear that?"

"Hear what?"

"Gunshot."

"How many?"

"One."

"Go," Jenny said.

On the ship, Captain Charlie was yelling at Wickham. "What were you thinking? We need him alive you fool!"

Fritz jumped out of bed and threw on his clothes. Through the bedroom window he could see a candle burning in his parents' house. He ran over the suspended bridge and into the living room just as Father and Francis were tying their shoes.

"You heard it too?" Fritz asked.

"Yes. One shot."

"I'll go to the beach," Fritz said.

"Okay, we'll check the traps along the main trail," Father responded as he grabbed two rifles standing in the corner of the living room and began loading them.

On the ship, more crewmen were ordered to climb the mast. Ernest saw a rope tied to both sides of the beam. Calculating the length of the rope, he moved to one end of the rope and started cutting it with Russell's knife. One of the men reached the beam just as the final cut was made. Ernest grabbed the rope, twisting it around his wrist, and jumped, his body swinging down and around the mast. The men in the rigging reached for him in a desperate attempt to stop him, but he was moving too fast.

The momentum of the swing flung Ernest up and over the water at which point he let go, landing in the dark water.

The sea was calm and inky black in the cove. The crew rushed to the rails, scanning the water below. They saw nothing.

"Where is he?"

"There goes our treasure!"

A sliver of light from the partial moon caught an object floating in the water thirty yards away.

"I see him. That's him! Over there!" several men shouted, pointing.

Captain Charlie ordered a longboat to be lowered. "Get to him quickly!"

The men worked the pulleys to lower the longboat down the side of the ship. When the boat hit the water, six armed men slid down the ropes and jumped in. Second Mate Tucker sat in the front of the boat with a lantern in one hand and a pistol in the other.

"Row, boys. Row!" Tucker ordered.

The boat began moving quickly through the water. All was silent except the sound of the oars slapping the water.

One man whispered to the others, "Don't it seem kind of quiet out here?"

Looking around, another responded, "Yeah, I was thinking the same thing."

"Shut yer yaps, ya fools!" Tucker snapped.

All talking ceased as they pulled alongside the body floating in the water.

"He's drowned."

"I don't think so," Tucker said. "Hand me an oar." Tucker handed the lantern to the man next to him, and taking the oar he jabbed at the coat floating in the water. The air trapped in the coat gave way and it quickly slipped below the water. The men looked around the sides of the boat, half expecting Ernest to attack them at any moment. Tucker yelled back to the ship, "We've been fooled! He's not here."

Captain Charlie trained the telescope toward the island. One of his men noticed something swimming close to the shore.

"There he is!"

The men in the longboat rowed frantically toward shore, but Ernest had already stumbled out of the water and was running across the beach toward the tree line.

Aboard the ship Hicks had his rifle loaded and ready. "Captain, do you want me to take the shot?"

"Yes! We must not let him get to the others!" the captain yelled. "But aim low. We need him alive."

Hicks had Ernest in his sights, tracking him as his dark

shape, contrasted against the white sand, ran toward the jungle. He squeezed the trigger. *Click!* The gun jammed.

Captain Charlie and his crew watched in frustration as Ernest disappeared into the trees.

Ernest ran for a little-used path on the south side of the cove. It meant he would have to run exposed on the sand for a long stretch, but it was a risk he was willing to take. He didn't want to lead Captain Charlie and the crew to the path that would take them directly to Falconhurst. The path opening was difficult to find in the predawn light, and it took longer to find it than he wanted. As he entered the path he slowed himself down. There were traps set periodically along the trail, and accidentally setting one off could be deadly.

The longboat reached the beach shortly after Ernest had disappeared into the jungle. The men jumped out of the boat and ran to the place they had seen Ernest entering the trees. With pistols and rifles in hand, the six men discovered the well-worn path.

"You two come with me," Tucker ordered, motioning for two men to follow him into the trees. "You three stay here and keep watch."

"Pratt. You take the lead. I'll be right behind you. Here's the lantern," Tucker said, shoving the lantern at Pratt. "Johnny, you bring up the rear."

The three men slowly walked into the dark jungle, as the

three guards watched uneasily.

Fools, Captain Charlie thought to himself, standing on the quarterdeck of the ship watching the men through his telescope.

In the jungle, Tucker and the other two men could barely see each other, despite the light coming from the lantern.

Swoosh! A blood-curdling scream split the air.

Pratt, in the lead, had suddenly disappeared. He had been caught by his ankles and had flipped up and hit his head on a rock. Now, moments later, he was hanging lifeless upside down in the air. The lantern had fallen from his hands, and the flame immediately went out as it hit the ground.

The other two men stopped, their blood turning cold. Spooked, Johnny spun around and ran out of the trees to the safety of the beach.

"What happened?" the guards asked.

"Pratt's gone."

Alone in the jungle, Tucker whispered, "Pratt? Pratt, you there?" There was no answer, just the unnatural stillness of the jungle. Tucker ran back to the beach.

"Did you find him?" one of the men on the beach asked.

"No," Tucker gasped, breathless.

"Something ain't right in there."

"You ever leave me standing alone again, I'll have you flogged," Tucker warned.

"Aye, sir. It's just … "

"There's little we can do until it's light," Tucker interrupted, not wanting the other men to see how afraid he was. "Let's get back to the ship."

They pushed the longboat out and boarded it, one person short. When they reached the ship, Captain Charlie and Hicks looked down at them.

"Where's Pratt?"

"He disappeared in the jungle."

There was a hush among the crew as the men climbed aboard. Captain Charlie paced back and forth, fuming.

"Idiots!" he snapped, his voice tight with anger. "There was only one man among the lot of you, and he's escaped! Prepare a landing party. We leave at first light."

Ernest raced along the path about halfway to Falconhurst. The effort of running in his weakened condition was exhausting, and he paused, bent over, to catch his breath. Without warning the barrel of a gun touched the back of his head. Feelings of frustration and dismay filled him. He had to get to Falconhurst and warn his family; their lives depended on it. He couldn't understand how the crew could have possibly caught up to him. Then he realized it couldn't be Captain Charlie's men.

"Don't move!" a voice said.

Still bent over and breathing hard, Ernest calmly said, "Fritz. It's me, Ernest. We haven't much time."

Uncertain, Fritz moved to face the intruder. All he could see in the weak predawn light was a wasted man with a full beard. If he looked hard enough he could almost see his brother in the man in front of him.

"Ernest? Is that you?"

"It is."

"What's the name of the savage king?"

"King Baraourou, and you have three children — Nicholas, Jacob, and Anne."

Fritz lowered the gun. "I'm sorry Ernest. I didn't recognize you in this light … the beard."

The brothers hugged. Although he was relieved to see his brother, Ernest knew there was little time before the sun rose.

"Fritz. We are all in terrible danger. We need to get to the others quickly."

The brothers raced to Falconhurst. Father and Francis had just returned from inspecting the surrounding trails, and had to do a double take when Fritz and Ernest ascended the stairwell and walked into the living room.

Noticing their uncertainty, Fritz explained, "It's Ernest."

Father leaned his rifle against the wall and embraced his son. Mother was in the kitchen preparing hot drinks when she heard the men talking. Going into the living room she saw the bearded stranger and was startled. "What's going on?" she asked nervously.

"It's Ernest," Francis said, his voice full of excitement.

Mother looked to Father who nodded.

"Mother, it's me. Truly it is," Ernest soothed.

Mother recognized his voice and gasped. She rushed to him and held his bearded face in her hands. "Son! What's happened to you? You're so thin."

"Never mind," said Ernest. "I'm fine now." He turned to the others. "We have to move quickly. Get Jenny and the children. Our lives are in grave danger!"

"You must eat," Mother said as she went to the kitchen to make porridge.

"Make enough for everyone. We're going to need it today."

"Hicks!" Captain Charlie roared. "Bring me the scum who was supposed to be guarding Robinson."

Captain Charlie was pacing the foredeck when Knowles was brought to him. Knowles, quaking, twisted his cap in his hands. Captain Charlie turned and thundered, "So you think you're good enough to sail with me? You think you're worthy of the treasure? I gave you a simple task, and you let a bound man escape!"

Knowles lowered his eyes in shame.

Captain Charlie unsheathed his broadsword and took a step toward the cowering Knowles. The crew stepped back, not wanting to expose themselves to Charlie's wrath. Captain Charlie raised his sword and then slammed it home into its sheath.

"If I didn't need every one of you … " he warned, looking at the crew, and then again at Knowles, "… you would be feeding the sharks. Now get out of my sight."

Knowles scurried away, grateful to still be alive. The other members of the crew turned back to their work, not wanting to attract attention.

Captain Charlie knew it would be difficult to get the treasure without Ernest. Frustrated, he started giving orders to his first mate.

"Prepare the boats. Load guns, ammunition, food, and water for two days. Pick a few good men to guard the ship. Tell them the signal for trouble is two cannon shots."

"Aye, sir," Hicks said as he set about his task.

The men lowered the longboats. They were instructed to row the boats to shore, unload the provisions on the beach, then return to the ship to load up again. Several trips would be required before they disembarked the ship.

The men were constantly alert, scanning the tree line. The crew had heard rumors of how pirates were unsuccessful in taking the island from the Robinsons, and now they had already lost one of their crew to the jungle. They all knew that with Ernest having escaped, it would be more difficult to find the treasure than they had planned. They also knew that Ernest was a skilled strategist who had proved himself in battle many times.

The men reassured themselves that they had a superior force, with ten times the manpower of the Robinsons. They took comfort knowing that they were being led by one of the most skilled captains in the world — Captain "Lucky" Charlie. He was the captain who had trained Ernest Robinson, and if anyone could outsmart the Robinsons, they reasoned, it was Captain Charlie.

Chapter 30

Francis, Ernest, and Father sat at the table eating porridge, bananas, strips of ham, with guava juice as fast as they could.

Fritz was heading out the door to get Jenny when she rushed into the main tree house.

"Jenny! I'm glad you're here. We must move quickly."

"What is it? What's wrong?" Jenny asked, the panic rising in her voice. Just then she noticed the stranger at the table.

"It's Ernest," said Fritz.

Ernest looked up and winked at her.

"What? How?"

"He was kidnapped."

"Why?" Jenny stepped forward and placed her hand on Ernest's shoulder.

"John Bennett got drunk and bragged about the treasure, and word of it reached the wrong people. They kidnapped Ernest and brought him here. They wanted him to lead them to the treasure. Lucky for us he escaped. There's an army in Safety Bay planning to come ashore at first light. We must get the children dressed and to the Grotto quickly."

Jenny ran back across the bridge to wake up the children as Mother went upstairs to get clean clothes for Ernest and gather a few things for herself. The men were all at the table eating — it would be a long day and they didn't know when they would get another chance to eat so well.

When the hurried breakfast was over, the men got up and started gathering supplies. Father retrieved several pistols and rifles and inspected them, ensuring they were ready for use. He then sat down at the table and began loading them.

"Francis, run as fast as you can and assess the situation on the beach," Father instructed. "They haven't had enough time to all be on shore yet, but be careful."

"Okay," Francis said, grabbing his crossbow.

"Wait, son. Take this," Father said, handing him a small barrel of gunpowder. "You know what to do with it."

"Be quick," Ernest said.

"And be extra cautious," Fritz added.

Francis raced down the stairwell and ran soundlessly into the forest.

Ernest moved to the end of the room and tore off the shirt and pants he had taken from Knowles. Not worried about convention, or modesty, at this point, he put on the clean clothes Mother had brought him.

Father, Mother, and Fritz gasped at his thin, wasted body and the vicious scars that crisscrossed his back.

"Oh, Ernest," Mother cried.

"Looks like you've lost a pound or two," Fritz said quietly.

"Yes, well ... they weren't very accommodating," Ernest said gently as he lifted his head and looking into Mother's eyes.

Mother rose and placed her hand gently on his back, running her fingers lightly over the red angry scars. "What did they do to you?"

Ernest turned to her and grinned. "I said something the captain didn't like. You always said I should learn to bridle my tongue."

Tears ran silently down her cheeks.

"Please, Mother. I'm fine. I've had plenty of time to heal, and I did my very best to stay strong. Fortunately, there was a young man that would bring me extra water so that I could keep the wounds clean until I healed," he assured her, kissing her gently on the forehead. "This is what you taught us to do when we were young, Mother." She nodded and wiped the tears from her face. She straightened and gathered her thoughts, saying,

"We must get out of here."

Nicholas and Jacob appeared in the doorway.

"Where's Uncle Ernest? Mother said he was here."

"I'm over here," Ernest said, pulling his shirt over his head.

They raced to greet him, but stopped when Ernest's head popped through the neck of the shirt. They didn't recognize the grizzled stranger looking at them. Ernest laughed at their confusion and assured them he was, in fact, Uncle Ernest.

The boys studied his face and looked over to their father, who nodded.

Ernest stepped toward the boys and embraced them heartily. He held them at arm's length so he could look in their eyes. "Are you ready to be men today?"

The boys' eyes got very large.

"There are men in the cove who want to hurt us," Ernest explained.

"Why?" Nicholas asked.

"I'll explain when Anne and your ma are here."

Mother set bowls of porridge and strips of ham on the table. "Eat up quickly, children."

Jenny arrived with Anne, now a robust toddler of two, and sat her down with the boys to eat. "Fill your bellies, children. We'll be away from home for some time," Jenny informed them.

"Where are we going?" Nicholas asked.

"The Grotto," Father said.

Mother and Jenny gathered food that could be carried easily.

"Father, will you please pack us some meat?" Mother called from the kitchen.

Father ran down the trunk stairwell and to the smokehouse

to get meat to take to the cave. Meat would help satisfy hunger longer than fruits and vegetables. He packed plenty, not knowing how long they would need to stay hidden. The Grotto was already well stocked with provisions: dried food, oil for lamps, bedding, medicines, and other necessities that made living on the remote island possible. There was also a small spring of pure water nearby. The family could survive comfortably in the Grotto for quite some time if needed. Father placed the bag full of meat at the base of the tree and ascended once more.

With everyone present, Ernest stood at the head of the table and cleared his voice. "We don't have much time, but let me give you the short version of how I ended up here and what to expect in the future."

Everyone's attention turned to him. Mother and Jenny, still in the kitchen, paused from their preparations to listen. All was silent, except the chirping of birds in the trees.

"John Bennett, our friend, has betrayed our trust."

Father and Fritz looked at each other knowingly. They remembered John's reluctance on the night Father had committed everyone to silence.

"John shared information about the treasure, and it reached the ears of my former commanding officer, Charles Williamson. As you well know, Captain Charlie was dishonorably discharged from His Majesty's Royal Navy and holds me personally responsible for his discharge. He's grown bitter and vengeful. He attacked me in England, and has brought me here against my will. He was hoping I'd lead them to the treasure. They will do anything to find the treasure. He and his men won't be easy to defeat."

Mother and Jenny looked at each other.

Father leveled his eyes at Ernest. "How many men does he have?"

"About a hundred."

A stunned silence fell on the group.

"What would the Lord do? Can't we just give them the treasure?" Mother suggested. "Maybe then they'll leave us alone."

"Yes," Jenny agreed. "That treasure's not worth the lives of our children, or our home."

Father naturally agreed, but said nothing. He knew that the Lord had sustained them many times in the past, but he was practical. He knew deep down they would need to lean on the Lord like never before but would also have to take matters into their own hands, just as King David or Gideon of old.

Speaking to everyone, Ernest continued, "I wish it were that simple, but it's extremely unlikely that they'll leave us here alive. Captain Charlie has a personal grudge against me. He'll hurt our family in any way he can. Besides, tyrants don't want to leave evidence of their crimes, especially when it comes to a member of the Royal Navy who is in good standing."

"Is there any other way?" Mother asked.

"No," Father answered with certainty.

"I wish I could tell you otherwise, but these men are evil. They're neither rational nor reasonable. They have one goal — get the treasure and leave without implicating themselves."

Fritz stood. "He's right."

"Captain Charlie's mission is backed by powerful men, including members of the royal family," Ernest continued.

"The only way to ensure the freedom we have worked so hard for is to defend this island, our home, our lives at all costs,"

Father agreed.

"Appeasing evil never works," Fritz agreed.

"It's time to get moving," Ernest said, bringing the conversation to a close.

Father turned to Mother and Jenny. "Take the children to the Grotto."

"Alone?" Mother asked.

"Yes," he said, reaching for her hand. "This island's going to become a dangerous place, and the boys and I can't defend our home if we're worrying about you and the children. Captain Charlie and his men won't be close to the cave anytime soon. You should be safe getting there on your own. For now we need to slow them down."

"Pa, I'm not a child," Nicholas said, stepping forward. "I want to go with you."

"Nicholas, I need you to get everyone to the Grotto safely. You have the most important job of all — safeguarding the family. You protect the family and we'll defend the island," Father said.

"But ... "

"Yes, Nicholas," Fritz interrupted, putting his hand on his son's shoulder. "You are nearly a man. You can hunt and trap and shoot almost as well as any of us. I'm depending on you to protect what's most precious to me in this world. Can you do that?"

"Yes, Father," Nicholas beamed, standing tall. "You can depend on me."

"Thank you, son," Fritz said. "I knew I could count on you to be a leader."

Turning to the family, Father continued. "This is our home, and we have the Lord on our side. With Him, all things are possible. He has promised us that we can move mountains. Now let's pray for his strength and guidance."

The family gathered in a circle holding hands. Father asked Mother to pray, "But quickly," he said smiling.

Mother nodded. "Dear God. We thank Thee for every blessing we have received at Thy hands, and now we ask Thee to help us defeat the evil that has come to our home. Lord, we have filled our lamps with oil. May thou strengthen our sons and my husband. May thou give them ears that hear and eyes that see. May thou quicken their minds and sharpen their movements. Please protect the rest of us as we make our way to the Grotto. We have faith in thee and thy goodness. In Jesus name, Amen."

The family continued holding hands for a moment after the prayer was finished, gathering strength from each other. The calm and reverent feeling was interrupted by the sound of Francis running up the stairs. He stumbled into the living room and fell to his knees, breathing hard.

"What's happened to you?" Mother cried. His arms and shirt were drenched in blood.

"Where are you hurt?" Father asked moving to inspect Francis's wounds.

Francis put his hand up and gasped through his ragged breath, "I'm fine. It's not my blood."

"What do you mean? What happened?" Mother asked.

"I left a warning," Francis said under his breath.

"A warning?"

"I was running to place the powder at the base of the cannon and I noticed a man, dead, caught in the trap at the riverside trail head. He was hanging upside down."

"And ... ?" Father prompted.

"I cut off his head."

"Oh, Francis! You didn't!" Mother cried.

"I did. I cut it off and put it on a stick in the ground next to his body that was still hanging upside down."

"Son, how could you? That's not what we are about," said Father.

At which point, Francis glanced over to Ernest, who said, "Father, I believe the Lord would understand. These men will stop at nothing."

"That should slow them down a little," Fritz said.

The family quickly came to the understanding of the severity of the situation. They did not delight in the shedding of blood. Being a God-loving people, the shedding of blood was the furthest thing from their mind and even the thought of it caused indescribable pain. It was contrary to their very nature. However, in their hearts the Robinsons knew this peaceful island would become violent, and they couldn't stand by hoping things would work out— they would need to take matters into their own hands to protect each other.

"What did you see in the cove?" asked Father.

"From what I can tell, they are still aboard ship making preparations."

"Anything else?"

"They were lowering provisions into longboats."

"Time is running out," Ernest said. "They'll be coming inland soon."

Francis dashed upstairs to change his shirt. A gentle dawn was beginning to flush over the jungle.

The parrot, Friend, flew into the room, and landed on Fritz's shoulder. The mood was tense and somber.

Father turned to Mother, "Don't waste any time."

Ernest kissed Mother on the cheek. "I love you, Mother. Try not to worry."

"Please be careful," Mother whispered

"It's time," said Father gently

Fritz kissed Jenny and picked Anne up for a hug. He kissed Mother and then transferred Friend to Nicholas's shoulder.

"Stay," he said, as he knelt before the boys who were visibly afraid. "Keep Friend with you. We don't need him distracting us. Be strong. Protect your mother and grandmother. We'll be seeing you soon, all right?"

The boys stood taller and nodded courageously.

Turning to Jenny he said, "When you get to the Grotto, stay there. Don't leave for any reason." Handing her a three-chamber pistol, he said, "Take this, and hide it in your dress."

Their eyes locked, communicating the love and concern they felt toward each other. "I love you," Fritz murmured, his voice full of emotion.

"I love you, too," she whispered.

"Now go."

Father turned to Mother, "We'll check in on you as soon as we're able." He kissed her and said to all of them, "Go now and hurry."

Mother and Jenny gathered the provisions and the children and departed by the stairs in the tree trunk. Mother grabbed the bag of meat by the door, while Father and the men followed them with rifles in hand, blowing out the stairway candles on their way down.

"Hurry!" Fritz called. "With the sun up, there may already be men on the island."

The little group started running. Jenny whistled for Sunshine, who raced to catch up to them. About twenty yards away, Nicholas turned back and waved to his father. Fritz raised his fist in the air and tapped his bicep, encouraging Nicholas to be strong.

When the women and children were safely on their way, Ernest said, "Fritz and I will go straightway to the cannon. We can get a few shots off to slow them down. They'll likely split up into groups. Father, you and Francis should get to the north trail and make sure that trap is set."

Francis touched the pistol in his belt, hefted his rifle, and threw his crossbow and arrows over his shoulder.

"God be with you, sons," Father said as he slung his rifle over his shoulder.

The men took as many weapons as they could, stashing them along the trail on their way to Safety Bay.

Chapter 31

Halfway to The Grotto, Mother realized she had forgotten her Bible on the dining room table.

"Wait," she cried, stopping. "We must go back."

"What is it, Mother?" Jenny asked.

"I forgot the Bible. It's on the table in the dining room. We must go back."

"Are you sure?" Jenny asked.

"Yes," Mother insisted. "We have no idea how long we'll be at the Grotto, or what will happen to our family. It will help give us peace while we wait out the storm."

Jenny nodded. "You wait here with the children, and I'll be right back," she said, taking the bag off her shoulder and racing back to Falconhurst.

Squawking, Friend jumped from Nicholas's shoulder and flew after her.

Anne began crying. Mother sat down and cuddled Anne,

quietly singing her a song. Jacob sat down beside them, nuzzling into Mother's side, drawing comfort from the song as well, while Nicholas kept watch.

By the time the Robinson men arrived at the cove, the sun had already been up for thirty minutes. To their surprise, almost all of Captain Charlie's men were standing on shore. Their provisions of food and weapons had been transported from the ship to the beach and the last two boatloads of men were preparing to launch from the ship.

The Robinsons knew that sooner or later they would have to engage Captain Charlie and his men, but now was not the time. There was no way they could engage a group that size all at once and be successful. Instead, they would have to use their knowledge of the jungle and the skills they had learned from the Baraourou and deal with Captain Charlie's crew one at a time. One resource that was immediately available to them was the animal traps along the trails, and their first order of business was to set them.

Father and Francis started with the main trailhead. They went to the trap, which was ten yards inland from the beach. The crew was busy dividing up the provisions and receiving their instructions. They weren't paying close attention to the jungle, but Father and Francis moved cautiously anyway, keeping themselves concealed as they moved toward the trap.

After seeing how risky it would be to set the trap, Father

suggested they move on to the next, but Francis was determined. He knew that they would need to use every available resource if they were going to successfully defend their home.

"It's too risky, Francis. They'll spot us," Father reasoned.

"Father, I can set it."

Father nodded. He and Francis quietly crept forward. While Francis worked with the trap, Father watched the last two boats rowing away from the ship. Staying as low as possible, Francis reached to bend the young tree and set it into the locking mechanism.

"Francis, hurry! More men are coming to shore," Father whispered.

"I'm having trouble locking the trap," Francis panted, the physical exertion taking a toll.

Just then one man on the beach turned and walked toward them.

"Be still," Father whispered. The man stopped eight feet from where Francis was lying. Francis grit his teeth, sweat pouring down his face. It was all he could do to hold the unlocked trap without moving. If he let go of the tree, it would catapult back to its original position and they would be discovered for sure. They would lose the island without even putting up a fight. He wouldn't let that happen.

The man opened his trousers and began to relieve himself. As he did, he leaned in to examine the opening of the main trail. Father and Francis held their breath. Fortunately, the man didn't see them, or the rope covered by palm fronds just feet from where he was standing.

When the man finished, he buttoned up his pants and walked back to join the others.

"All clear, son. Set the thing, and let's get out of here."

Francis drew on all his reserve strength, set the trap in place, and then crawled to where Father was waiting.

"That was close," Father whispered.

"Too close," breathed Francis, rubbing the muscles in his arms.

They were able to set several more traps as they moved inland along the trail. At the south side of the cove they met up with Fritz and Ernest on a ridge concealed by trees, where they were preparing the cannon. They poured a portion of the gunpowder Francis had delivered earlier into the fuse hole and lowered a ball into the barrel. They then ran a cotton fuse through the hole until it reached the gunpowder.

Looking down from the ridge they could see Captain Charlie on the beach, Cyril Wallace by his side, gathering his men together.

"Everyone fall in," First Mate Hicks yelled. "It's time to get ourselves some treasure!"

The men erupted in wild cheers as they surrounded Captain Charlie.

"We don't have any time to waste," Captain Charlie began. "I want Hicks's group to enter in through that trail over there," he said, pointing to the same trail Ernest had escaped through earlier.

"Knowles, I want you and two others to scout that small trailhead up there," Charlie said, pointing to an overgrown trail at the far end of the cove.

"Aye, aye, sir."

Knowles pointed at two men, and the three disappeared into the trees.

"The rest of you will follow Cyril and me through that trail opening over there. The Robinsons could be anywhere," he warned, "so keep your wits about you. Let's head out."

Up on the ridge Ernest and Fritz were ready with the loaded cannon.

"What do you think?" asked Fritz

"I say we take out one of those boats before they make it to shore."

As the crew was receiving their instructions, the brothers moved the cannon to face the boat. Ernest relaxed, letting his breathing slow as he took his time to level the cannon perfectly. There were small swells in the cove, which meant Ernest would have to time his shot perfectly. They only had one ball for the cannon, so it was very important he got it right.

Boom!

The cannon blast ricocheted through the cove. Charlie's men dove to the ground. Everyone turned to the sound of the shot, the smoke floating in the air.

Seconds later, Captain Charlie and the crew heard the scream of the cannon ball through the air, followed by a crash and splintering of wood behind them. The ball split the boat in half, killing one man instantly and catapulting two others into the sea. Watching from the shore, there was little they could do to help as they heard the cries of the men drowning in the water. The second boat moved to rescue the men, but only four survived, and they were wounded and badly shaken.

The men on the beach looked to Captain Charlie for direction, but he said nothing, his eyes flashing as he scanned the tree line around the cove for any sign of the Robinsons. He knew that the Robinsons would make this mission difficult but didn't express his concern to his men.

"Let's get moving!" he barked.

The men split into their groups. The group led by Hicks was the first to enter the jungle through the south trailhead. Captain Charlie and the other half of the men waited until the last boat came ashore. Just as it hit the shore, a bloodcurdling scream echoed through the cove. Moments later a man from Hicks's group ran frantically from the jungle and back onto the beach.

"I'm not going in there," he yelled, obviously terrified.

The men gathered around him. "What is it?" Cyril Wallace asked.

"It's Pratt!" the man gasped.

"Pratt?" one of the other men asked. "You found him?"

"Where?" asked another.

"He's ... he's ... dead. Hangin' from a tree."

The crew began to lose interest when the man added, "They cut his head off..."

"They what?" someone yelled.

"...and put it on a stake," the man finally finished.

At this, the crew began backing away, led by Cyril who was deathly pale.

"Stand still, you cowards!" Captain Charlie snarled. "Take another step and I'll keelhaul the lot of you."

The men froze. "I'll see this with my own eyes," Captain Charlie hissed walking toward the south trail.

He took a few steps and turned to his men standing still on the beach. "Follow me!" he yelled. "Idiots!" he mumbled to himself as he turned back around and pushed through the trees. He had only been on the trail a moment before he came upon Hicks and his men staring up in the trees. Pratt's corpse was slowly turning in the breeze, blood and coagulated gore oozing from his headless neck.

"Cut him down," Captain Charlie ordered.

A man climbed the tree to release the body. It landed with a sickening thud, and the men quickly worked to pull the body to the side of the trail. Captain Charlie pulled the stake out of the ground, the head still attached, and dumped it with the body.

"Don't let this scare you, *milksops*," Captain Charlie mocked.

The men ducked their heads, ashamed of their fear.

"Don't forget why we're here! Treasure! The Robinsons have to resort to tricks like this because they haven't got a chance against all of us."

"But Captain … "

"Shut your trap!" Captain Charlie thundered. "Mark my words, we'll get that treasure. No matter what happens! They can't hold out against us forever. We've got plenty of provisions and ammunition. We'll wait them out if we have to, but either way, the treasure will be ours!"

Captain Charlie turned and signaled for his men to follow him back out to the beach. Hicks and his group continued along the south trail, every man scanning the trees.

Captain Charlie, Cyril, and their men picked up their provisions and headed for the main trail. Just inside the jungle, two men in the front stepped into the trap Francis had set and were pulled off their feet and dragged, screaming, into the undergrowth of the jungle.

The man who had discovered Pratt's headless body started to shake uncontrollably. "This place is cursed!" he screamed, wild-eyed.

Captain Charlie cut the men free from the rope. They were

not severely wounded, but they were unnerved and shaking as they stumbled out of the jungle overgrowth. Captain Charlie turned and faced his group.

"You! Come here!" Captain Charlie said to the screaming sailor.

The man stumbled forward. Captain Charlie grabbed his throat, hissing, "If I hear you utter another word, I will cut out your tongue." He continued to squeeze until the man finally nodded. Captain Charlie let go, barking, "Move on!"

Another hundred yards along the trail, a man named Nickerson came across the statue of the carved monkey. Curious, he went over to get a closer look.

A scream filled the morning quiet. Every man clutched his weapon and looked frantically about. Captain Charlie elbowed his way to the front. Nickerson had disappeared.

Captain Charlie saw the carved monkey and, being far more experienced in combat, eased his way toward it. As he suspected, a pit opened up directly below the carving. Nickerson was splayed on his back, impaled by sharp bamboo stakes. Blood was streaming from the wounds on his chest, his eyes staring lifelessly toward the sky.

A shock went through the group as the men gathered around Captain Charlie to see Nickerson for themselves. Cyril turned and vomited.

"Should we go on down and see about him, sir?" one of the men asked.

"No, you fool. He's dead. Let's move on, but stay on the trail and keep an eye out! Let this man's death serve as a warning to all of you," Captain Charlie cautioned. "Be careful!"

They skirted the pit, each man taking a last furtive look at their dead comrade.

Hicks and his men were hiking on the south trail, winding alongside the river, when they reached the Family Bridge. The river flowed gently from the island's center mountain past Falconhurst and out to the ocean. The Robinsons had built the bridge a few feet above the waterline.

"Once they're on the bridge, take your shots," Ernest said.

"We should have time to reload and fire again before Fritz reaches the dam," Father added.

A year and a half earlier, the Robinsons had dammed the river to harvest fish, creating a large pool of water upriver.

"Spread out and take aim," Father instructed.

Father and his three sons positioned themselves, with Fritz nearest the bend in the river.

Hicks and his men moved out onto the bridge. Without warning, balls whistled through the air, hitting two men and knocking them into the river.

A third ball hit the pistol of a man, taking off his finger.

"My hand!" he screamed.

Hicks's men fired back, running for the safety of the shore. A barrage of balls whizzed around the Robinsons, chipping away at the rocky ridge.

After the first shot, Fritz had dropped out of sight. He made his way around the bend, heading upriver.

Hicks's men began to reload, but the Robinsons were ready

and fired a second time, killing two more men and wounding another.

Fritz reached the fishpond, pulled out his long-blade knife, and began cutting the leather straps holding the logs together, weakening the structure. Moving out of the way, Fritz pulled the final long leather strap with all his might and the dam gave way, a violent flood of water rushing around the bend. With no time to react, the men standing on the bridge were swept up into the roiling water filled with logs and debris. In a matter of moments the bridge had disappeared entirely.

When the flood dissipated, Hicks ordered the men standing on either side of the bank to help the men in the water.

The crew hesitated, unsure what to do.

"Grab this," a man yelled as he extended his rifle toward a man in the water, pulling him out.

The spell broken, several men locked arms, with the last stepping into the river and reaching for survivors, pulling them to the shore. Of the twenty-one men standing on the bridge, eleven were now dead, carried downstream where they would eventually end up snagged in the shallows or washed out to sea.

"Let's go," whispered Ernest.

Before leaving, Francis aimed his crossbow and fired an arrow, hitting Hicks in the shoulder.

"I've been hit," Hicks cried as he dropped to the ground.

Two men came to his aid, while the others fired their rifles upward toward the ridge, but the Robinsons were nowhere in sight, already racing ahead to the glen.

A man pulled the arrow from Hicks' shoulder and bandaged the wound with a filthy strip of material torn from his shirt. Bleeding and weakened, Hicks slowly rose to his feet.

"Let's go," he rasped.

The water level had fallen so that the men on the opposite side of the shore could ford the river. Once on the other side, they walked slowly along the trail, wary of being ambushed. There was complete silence other than a gentle breeze making its way through the trees. The men were wet and weary; many were low on powder and shot, and others had lost their weapons entirely to the river.

"This is a dangerous place," a man said to nobody in particular.

"Keep your eyes peeled," Hicks growled.

Chapter 32

Mother and the children were waiting anxiously for Jenny to return. They had heard the cannon blast earlier and, more recently, gunfire. When Mother saw Jenny running toward them, she felt such a strong sense of relief she almost started to cry.

"We must hurry," Jenny panted, bending forward to catch her breath.

Friend landed in a nearby tree, refusing to obey Nicholas's signal to come when he stuck out his arm.

"Father will be angry with me if we don't take him with us," Nicholas said.

"No," Jenny reassured her son. "Friend is a wild creature with a mind of his own. He'll be fine. Let's go."

They continued their hike toward the Grotto.

"Did you see anyone?" Mother asked.

"No. It was quiet … almost too quiet. Even the animals

seemed subdued."

"I'm sure they can sense the danger around us," Mother reflected

Jacob became tired of carrying his load and sank to the ground to rest. "We can't stop now Jacob, we're almost there," Jenny cajoled them.

Aware of his little brother's struggle, Nicholas shouldered his pack and took his hand. He pulled Jacob to his feet and they started walking again.

The cave was in sight when Sunshine suddenly stopped and growled, her belly low to the ground. There was no threat in sight and Sunshine would only behave in such a way if she felt threatened. Mother and Jenny were looking for the danger when Knowles suddenly jumped out from behind a thicket of trees and snatched Jacob.

Mother and Jenny froze when they heard Jacob's screams and Sunshine's frantic barking.

"Where'd you think you're going?" Knowles taunted Jacob, as Howard and Wickham stepped out of the trees laughing.

Without warning, Friend flew at Wickham, clawing his face with his razor-sharp talons, screeching loudly. At the same time, Sunshine, her teeth bared, darted toward Knowles. Howard jumped in front, and as he did, Sunshine bit down on his lower leg. He screamed in pain, trying to shake the dog, but Sunshine refused to let go. Howard grabbed his rifle and hit Sunshine on the head, but she still refused to let go. Knowles, still holding on to Jacob, kicked Sunshine in the belly, hurling her several feet away. Sunshine immediately twisted back to her feet, growling as she prepared to attack again.

Anne started to cry.

"Take your hands off my boy!" Jenny yelled, rushing at Knowles.

Knowles, startled by her boldness, shoved Jacob at his mother.

"Give me the gun," Wickham snarled as he yanked the rifle slung on her back.

"Sit down! All of you," Knowles ordered.

Sunshine continued to growl and bark, saliva dripping from her mouth, and she suddenly lunged again.

Knowles drew his pistol and shot the dog. Sunshine yelped and fell to her side. Nicholas threw himself over his dog, but it was too late. Sunshine was dead. Friend let out a keening cry, and landed on Sunshine's head. Furious, Nicholas jumped to his feet and lunged at Knowles who thrust the muzzle of his gun into his chest, sending him sprawling on the ground. Mother cried out and went to him. Anne was now howling hysterically and gasping for breath.

The children had never experienced such cruelty.

"I said, sit! All of you sit!" Knowles yelled, waving his gun.

Jacob and Anne immediately sat on the ground, Jenny slowly sinking down next to them. Other than having a bruised chest, Nicholas was not seriously hurt. He sat up and glared at the men, Friend flying to his shoulder. Mother moved over and took Anne in her arms, trying to soothe her screams.

Mother and Jenny looked at each other. They knew the location of every animal trap on the island, and one was very close to them.

"Shut that kid up or I will!" Wickham shouted at Mother.

Mother spoke gently to Anne, and after a few minutes she settled down. Jacob was trying mightily to hold back his tears.

Nicholas watched for an opportunity to do something.

"Jacob, you're being brave and strong," Jenny whispered to her son.

"Now, ladies, where are the others?" Knowles asked.

"I don't know," Jenny said defiantly.

"Don't play games with us," Knowles warned, moving toward Mother. "Tell us where the treasure is!" he snarled.

"I don't know what you're talking about," Mother said innocently.

"Where were you going? Do you always go out walking with a rifle?" Howard asked Jenny.

"Actually, yes," Mother said with a quick laugh. "There're wild animals on this island — it can be a very dangerous place."

"Where's the treasure?" Knowles asked, looking directly at Jenny.

"I told you, we don't know what you are talking about," Mother insisted.

Knowles slapped Mother across the face. Again, the parrot flew into Knowles's face, clawing at his eyes. Knowles batted it away viciously, sending the bird screeching to the nearest tree.

Jenny jumped up, but was roughly pushed back by one of the men. Nicholas rushed to his grandmother, but Wickham stopped him with a kick. Jacob flew at Wickham and managed to hit him in the belly before he, too, was thrown down to the ground. Anne burst into a fresh round of hysterical crying.

"I'm not going to ask again," Knowles barked.

Mother wiped the blood from her lip and smiled. "I'll say it one more time. I don't know what you are talking about."

Knowles pointed his gun to her head.

"Please, let us be," Jenny begged. "We don't know anything."

Knowles sighed, tired of the charade. "You'll tell us, or I will kill her."

"If you want the treasure," Jenny said, thinking fast, "You'll need us alive. Killing us won't do you any good."

Turning to Jenny, Knowles said, "We'll let *you* live. Grandma would just slow us down."

Another look passed between Jenny and Mother. "I'll only go with you if you don't harm any of the others," Jenny finally said.

As the men turned away to discuss the offer Jenny began slowly scooting backward, whispering, "Stay where you are," to Nicholas and Jacob.

Knowles noticed the movement. "What're you doing?" he demanded.

"What do you mean?" Jenny asked.

"Why were you moving?"

"I was sitting on a rock and it was uncomfortable," she replied.

"Well, stay where you are," he demanded.

The men turned back to each other, and, as they did, Jenny slipped her hand into the underbrush searching for a release trigger.

"I know how to handle a wench like her," Howard laughed, standing next to Knowles.

Her fingers finally found what they were looking for. Taking a breath, Jenny yanked the mechanism.

A bamboo tree that was bent back and covered with jungle foliage violently shot forward.

With no time to react, Knowles and Howard were struck by a series of sharpened stakes embedded into the tree. The stakes struck them both in the midsection killing them instantly.

Reacting to the surprise, Mother and the children screamed.

Wickham, mesmerized by the scene, hesitated. Jenny reached under her skirt, pulled out the pistol Fritz had given to her, and fired. Wickham dropped at her feet with an amazed look on his dying face.

Friend flew in a circle overhead squawking, "Good Jenny," before disappearing into the jungle.

Jenny rose and straightened her skirt with shaking hands. "Mother, please take Jacob and Anne to the Grotto." Then turning to Nicholas she said, "We can't leave the bodies out here. Others will soon come."

While Mother walked Jacob and Anne up the trail to the entrance to the Grotto, Jenny and Nicholas set about the dirty work of releasing the two men from the spikes. When the bodies had fallen to the ground they collected their weapons and dragged them into the underbrush.

"Mother," Nicholas said as they worked. "I can't believe you killed that man."

"I took no pleasure in it, son," Jenny sighed, "but I'd do it again to keep you children safe from men like that. Now let's hurry up. We can't afford to get caught out in the open again."

Chapter 33

Captain Charlie and his group were the first to arrive at Falconhurst. As the men approached, they were stunned by the elegance, ingenuity, and size of the tree houses and the surrounding buildings on the ground.

The tree houses were like castles in the air. The trees themselves were larger than anything they had ever seen before. From the ground they could see several rooms nestled above the main living area like birds' nests. At the highest point of the tree there was a lookout post much like the crow's nest on a ship. They also saw the pulley system that delivered water and the bridge that connected the two houses. There was even a swing on a lowest branch of the tree.

"Search every room, every hole!" Captain Charlie roared, standing below the main tree house. "I want every piece of treasure on this island!"

"How do we get up there?"

The men looked up at the tree houses suspended thirty feet in the air. There didn't appear to be any way of reaching the structures from the ground.

The men circled the tree, amazed at the size and girth of the trunk. "I think I found it," a man called, pulling on the bark-covered door that opened to the inside of the tree.

"Yes! This is it!" the man exclaimed, seeing stairs inside. The crew rushed to the door, reaching their heads in and looking up. All they could see in the dim light was a staircase circling a pillar in the center.

Captain Charlie and Cyril Wallace shoved their way through the group to get a closer look.

"Get up there!" Captain Charlie ordered. Crewmen rushed past him and scurried up the stairs like a pack of rats.

First they made their way into the living room and kitchen. They threw out pots and pans and went through every drawer in their lust to find treasure. Other men made their way to the upper rooms, searching and ransacking both tree houses.

"Captain," a man standing near the stove called out, "the coals in the stove are still warm. They can't be far."

"Of course they can't be far, you fool! We're on an island, and we'll search every inch of it until we get what we've come for!" Captain Charlie stepped out onto the balcony, scanning the jungle. "They're out there somewhere," he muttered to himself.

Captain Charlie's men went through the smokehouse and the blacksmith shop to be sure the Robinsons hadn't stowed any of the treasure there. They found nothing. In reality, the treasure hadn't been moved from where it had been found. It had little use or value on the island. It was safe in its original hiding place.

Still on the winding trail, the group led by Hicks was pushing through a small glen not far from Falconhurst, unaware that the Robinsons were on the high ground watching them. Ernest and Father were on one side of the glen, with Fritz and Francis on the other. They were hiding in a thicket of trees interspersed with large boulders, which provided good cover.

A net suddenly snatched up two men. The Robinsons began shooting arrows from both sides of the glen. The men in the net were the first to die, their blood falling on the men below. The men on the ground spun around looking for the shooters, but not surprisingly, they found none. Unsure what to do, the crew let loose a volley of gun shots in random directions hoping to draw the Robinsons into a gun fight so their location could be discovered. The Robinsons held back until the crew had fired all of their guns and then fired, killing three more men.

The shots echoing through the trees drew the attention of the group at Falconhurst. Captain Charlie and Cyril, standing on the balcony, looked toward the direction of the gunfight. "You men! Go see what's happening," Captain Charlie yelled to several men standing below.

The men reluctantly made their way along the trail toward the sound of the gunshots.

Meanwhile, Hicks ordered his men, "Climb the ridge after them!" Several men set out after the Robinsons in the direction they believed the shots came from but soon returned having found no one. Immediately after firing their guns, the Robinsons had withdrawn, disappearing into the jungle.

"They'll be regrouping at Falconhurst soon," Ernest said to Father.

"I think I ought to check on Mother and the children while I can." Father said.

"I'll go with you," Ernest said.

"No. I'll be fine. Go meet up with your brothers. I'll meet you all at The Rock in two hours."

"Are you sure you should go alone?"

Father nodded. "The Rock. Two hours."

Father slipped silently into the jungle, while Ernest began making his way toward his brothers.

Captain Charlie's men reached Hicks and his contingent.

"We're glad to see you," Hicks said, obviously relieved.

The newly arrived men observed blood pooling beneath Hicks's shirt.

"He was shot with an arrow," one of Hicks's men explained.

"Where are the rest of your men?"

"They're dead," said Hicks. "We lost them in the river."

"How?"

"The Robinsons flooded the river," Hicks explained impatiently "It took out a bridge and half my men with it."

"How many were lost?"

"We've lost sixteen since leaving shore," one of Hicks's men said, his eyes darting around nervously.

"We lost five just now," another said, pointing to the three dead men on the ground then pointing up into the tree to the two corpses hanging upside down, slowly twisting in the breeze. A chill went through the group as another man mused, "The

Robinsons strike like phantoms."

Ernest crossed over the river to meet up with Fritz and Francis. He gave a distinct whistle as he approached. An answering whistle greeted him. He found his brothers sitting on the ground, reloading their weapons.

"Where's Father?" Fritz asked.

"He's checking on Mother and the children."

"Alone?"

"I tried to talk him out of it, but he insisted," Ernest explained. "Don't worry, Father can take care of himself. Let's go to Falconhurst, and see what they're up to. Father will meet us at The Rock in two hours."

"Falconhurst? What'll we do there?" Francis asked. "There's no way we can take on that many men at once."

"You're right," Fritz agreed, "but hopefully we can hear what their plan is before meeting back up with Father."

The three quietly made their way toward Falconhurst, collecting the weapons and ammunition they had scattered along the trail.

Hicks and his men finally arrived at Falconhurst, bedraggled and dirty.

"Get the surgeon," Second Mate Tucker ordered when he saw Hicks bleeding heavily down the right side of his body.

The ship's surgeon arrived as they were passing the smokehouse and instructed Hicks to lie on the table for examination.

Captain Charlie saw the men stumbling into Falconhurst, their numbers greatly reduced.

"Where are the others?" he demanded, yelling from the balcony.

The exhausted man closest to the tree house responded, "Dead. Butchered by those foul Robinsons."

"One second they were there, and the next ... gone," another responded.

"Nonsense!" Captain Charlie fumed. "The Robinsons aren't gods!" Then, calming himself down, he said, "We *will* defeat them. We'll get our treasure! You can be sure of that."

At the smokehouse, the surgeon ripped open Hicks's shirt to inspect his wound. "What hit you?" he asked.

"An arrow," Hicks rasped, exhausted from pain and loss of blood.

The wound was deep.

"Get him a drink," the surgeon ordered his assistant. "He's going to need it."

The surgeon was washing the wound with water, when his assistant came back with wine. Hicks gulped down half the bottle then slumped back down on the table.

The surgeon wrapped a cloth around a strong stick.

"Put this in your mouth and bite hard," he said. Expertly wielding a needle and thread, he poked through the deep layers of flesh. Hicks bit down hard and groaned. The surgeon kept at his task, sewing together the muscles and flesh until the wound was finally closed.

"Keep pressure against the stitches until the bleeding stops," he instructed his assistant.

When the bleeding had stopped and the wound was dressed, a couple of men helped Hicks up the winding staircase to join Captain Charlie in the living room.

"Tough going was it?" Captain Charlie asked.

Hicks said nothing as he fell heavily into a chair.

"How many men did you lose?"

"Sixteen," Hicks whispered, his eyes closed.

"Unbelievable! Those Robinsons will pay!" Captain Charlie said, slamming his fists down onto the table.

Father made his way safely to Mother and the children at the Grotto. Knocking at the door of the cave, he gave the password they had decided on earlier that morning, *Gideon.*

The story of Gideon was one of the family's favorites. Gideon was a young prophet who, with his small army of 300, was able to defeat an army of 134,000. They had chosen that particular password to give the family courage.

"The password is Gideon," Father whispered again.

Mother opened the door slowly. "Oh, Father! Come in," she said, hugging him fiercely. "How are the boys?" she asked.

"Fine. Fine. They're doing a remarkable job. I came to check on you and the children and get a lantern for tonight."

"What's your plan?"

"We're not quite sure, yet. The boys are tracking the movements of the crew, and we should have a better idea of what to do soon. No matter what happens though, no one leaves this cave." He looked at Mother, Jenny, and children, all of whom nodded their understanding.

"I noticed the trap was triggered. How did that happen?" he asked.

"Three men came upon us just as we were approaching the Grotto," Mother explained.

"What? Were any of you hurt?" he asked, looking around the room.

"No. Everyone is fine," Mother said, looking at Jenny. "Your clever daughter-in-law lured them into the trap."

Father looked at Jenny, who was holding Anne, and smiled.

"Grandfather, they shot Sunshine," Jacob sobbed, unable to hold his feelings in any longer.

Father took the young boy in his arms and held him as he cried. "I'm sorry, Jacob," said Father gently. "These are bad men. Sunshine was just trying to protect you. With her gone now, you must obey your mother and grandmother. Do you understand?"

"Yes, sir."

"What happened to the men?" Father asked.

"The trap killed two of them, and Jenny shot the other," Mother said.

"Where are the bodies?"

"Nicholas and I dragged them into the ravine," Jenny answered. "We covered them well with leaves."

"Good man," Father said, ruffling Nicholas's hair.

Nicholas beamed with pleasure.

"We couldn't reset the trap," Mother said.

"Don't worry, I'll do it. It looks like we'll have rain tonight. This may work in our favor."

He gave each member of the family a hug. "I love you all," he said simply, as Mother handed him a lantern.

"We love you, Grandfather," the boys said.

"When you see my pa, please tell him that I'm praying for him," said Jacob.

"Indeed, I will," he said, lifting his eyes to Mother.

"We're praying for all of you," Mother said.

Father slipped out of the Grotto and reset the trap. It was a difficult task to do alone, as one slip could send the bamboo cane swinging forward with deadly consequences. Father positioned himself behind the tree pulling it back into the locked position. After a few minutes, the trap was reset; and Father placed jungle debris all around to hide it.

With his task complete, Father picked up the lantern and headed toward The Rock. The Rock was a large, flat rock formation several hundred yards from both Falconhurst and the Grotto. Situated on a hill near the ocean, it was a special place where the children often gathered to play games. Surrounded by boulders, it had the feel of a secret fort, which is exactly what it would be today.

Shortly after leaving the Grotto on his way to the Rock, Father heard the unmistakable sound of someone struggling through the underbrush. He paused to listen, taking cover behind a large tree. He was so intent on finding the hiker that he failed to notice the man creeping up behind him, gun in hand. Without warning he was struck in the back of the head, dropping unconscious to the jungle floor.

"I got one!"

Several men came running and looked at Father as he lay sprawled on the ground.

"Must be the father," a man said.

"Captain Charlie will be glad about this," said another man.

"Let's get him back to camp."

Two men hoisted Father up, pulling his arms around each man's shoulder; another man picking up the lantern. The group hiked back to Falconhurst and dropped the unconscious body on the ground under the main tree house. A man ran upstairs, interrupting a conversation between Captain Charlie, Hicks, and Cyril.

"What is it?" Captain Charlie growled.

"We have one of the Robinsons."

"Where is he?" Captain Charlie asked, jumping up.

"Down below."

By the time Captain Charlie and Cyril reached the ground, a group of men had gathered to see the hostage. A feeling of excitement and hope was spreading among the men. Perhaps their luck was finally changing.

From a short distance, concealed in the jungle, Francis, Ernest, and Fritz were watching the scene unfold.

"They have Father," Ernest whispered. "It looks like he's unconscious."

One of Charlie's men slapped Father, trying to wake him up.

Francis started forward, but Ernest held him back.

"Not yet," he whispered.

"Get some water," Captain Charlie ordered.

A man ran upstairs and filled a pail with water. When he came back, Captain Charlie took the pail and doused Father. He woke, gasping for air.

Charlie's men bound him with strong cords then roughly sat him on the ground against the trunk of the enormous tree.

Father closed his eyes, the pain in his head overwhelming. After a time he slowly opened his eyes and looked around, trying to focus his thoughts. His gaze finally rested on Captain Charlie, who stood over him, Cyril by his side.

"Well, who do we have here?" Captain Charlie said grinning. "You must be Ernest Robinson's father."

Father stared past them, saying nothing.

"Where's the treasure?" Cyril demanded.

Father continued to stare.

Captain Charlie pulled a knife from its sheath and held it to Father's throat.

At this, Fritz gave a distinctive whistle letting Father know he wasn't alone. Father grinned.

"Look, Robinson, I'm in no mood for games. You've already given me enough trouble. Now you will lead us to the treasure."

Father looked Captain Charlie in the eye. His eyes were cold and dead. They were the eyes of a man capable of anything. In that moment, Father knew that if he pushed Captain Charlie too much he would most likely kill him and then hunt his family down. He also knew his sons had a better chance of defeating Captain Charlie's men if they were moving through the treacherous and unfamiliar jungle rather than in an open setting like Falconhurst. After weighing the options, Father decided it was best if he drew the men away from Falconhurst.

"It's inland," he finally answered.

"How far?" Cyril asked.

"The mountain. A full day's hike; and a treacherous hike, I

might add," Father conceded.

"Where are the others?" Captain Charlie wanted to know.

"I'm not sure," Father answered honestly.

"Where are they? Where's Ernest?" Captain Charlie demanded.

"Dead for all I know. I haven't seen them for hours. We split up."

Captain Charlie studied Father's face for a moment.

"You were out there all by yourself?" he asked.

"Yes. I was."

Captain Charlie looked at his men for confirmation. They nodded. "We saw no one else, sir," the leader of the group said.

Captain Charlie considered himself a good judge of men. It was obvious that the old man was telling the truth, but he couldn't understand why he was cooperating so easily. *Perhaps he wants to keep his family safe, and he thinks cooperation is the best way to do that, Captain Charlie thought to himself. Little does he know we'll leave no one alive after the treasure is found. Still, he must be watched carefully. If he is even half as clever as his son, he's dangerous, in spite of his age.*

His mind made up, he turned to his men and announced, "We have ourselves a guide."

Chapter 34

⁓⁓⁕⁓⁓

Fritz, Ernest, and Francis watched from a distance as Captain Charlie's men prepared to hike inland. The scene was busy as men gathered supplies at the base of the giant tree. Most interestingly, five wooden chests were brought to the tree for inspection.

Father noticed the lightness of the chests as they were lowered to the ground. Realizing they were probably empty, he asked, "What are the chests for?"

"We were told there were five chests of treasure, but the chests themselves were rotting and probably wouldn't make it down the mountain in one piece."

Father took a deep breath. This was the first real evidence that the intruders had concrete knowledge that the treasure existed. How else would they know that there were five chests specifically?

"Does that align with your recollection, Mr. Robinson?"

Captain Charlie asked sarcastically.

"I suppose it does," Father replied honestly.

Turning, Captain Charlie called, "Gather around, gentlemen!" The men came from all parts of Falconhurst — some from Fritz and Jenny's home, others from the garden and the enclosures of nearby livestock. Some, by assignment, stood guard, scanning the tree line. A few leaned over the balcony above, anticipating their orders.

Captain Charlie spoke privately to Hicks, who had slowly made his way down the stairwell, carefully holding his arm. "Given the state your shoulder is in, you'll be staying here. Keep an eye out for visitors."

"Sir. Are you sure about this?" Hicks asked, not wanting to be left behind.

"Yes. I'm sure. You're no use to us hiking up a mountain with your shoulder in that condition."

Hicks and some of the other men had begun doubting their safety having seen for themselves exactly what the Robinsons were capable of. The last thing Hicks wanted was to be left alone at Falconhurst. Sensing his apprehension, Captain Charlie added, "Cyril Wallace will be joining you, with a small contingent of men."

Captain Charlie then turned to the gathered men. "Gentlemen, Mr. Robinson has kindly agreed to lead us to the treasure."

The crew erupted in wild cheering. A man from the balcony above spit down on Father, who was sitting on the ground with his hands bound in front of him. Father lifted his arms to wipe the spittle from his face. The men laughed.

A distance away, the Robinson sons observed the despicable

treatment toward their Father. Francis lunged forward impulsively but was held back once again by Ernest.

"Sit down, Francis," Fritz said. "We must think rationally. Father would expect that of us."

"Yes," Ernest agreed. "It's going to get much worse than that. We must show restraint. We must outthink them."

Captain Charlie named the fifteen men that would stay behind with Cyril and Hicks to protect Falconhurst from intruders. At least half of the men chosen were wounded and weak.

"Aye, sir," they responded.

"The rest of you will be joining me to retrieve the treasure. Finish gathering the provisions. We leave immediately."

"The weather will be in our favor tonight," Ernest said, looking up at the sky. Ever since he was a young boy, Ernest had the ability to read the skies. The Robinson brothers quietly rose to their feet, hefting their powder, guns, and crossbows.

"Leaving now means that they'll only hike for a few hours before they'll need to camp for the night," whispered Fritz. "Father will take them to the little valley at the base of the mountain. It's what I would do."

"Yes," said Francis. "That's what I would do, too.

"Agreed," said Ernest. "Our best chance is to attack in the early morning hours before dawn, when they least expect it. Until then we should head to the Grotto to check on the family and get some rest."

Fritz sent the secret birdcall echoing through the valley. Father delicately and slowly adjusted his head acknowledging the sound. Trusting that Father would be safe for the time being, the brothers started to the Grotto.

The mood in the cave was somber. Mother, Jenny, and the children were making do, although worried and nervous. The waiting was agony.

"When's Pa coming back?" Jacob asked for what seemed like the thousandth time.

"He'll be back as soon as he can," Jenny soothed. "I expect it will be a while yet. Now, let's eat dinner." Jenny and Mother had set the table and prepared a meal of smoked meat, papaya, and a fresh loaf of bread baked early that morning while the men were investigating the rifle shot. The events of the morning seemed like a lifetime ago to the family waiting in the cave.

"Come children. Let's pray," said Mother, gathering the children to the table.

They knelt in a circle to thank God for the food for which they were about to partake and to ask safety for their family members who were in harm's way.

"Our Father who art in heaven … "

Knock. Knock.

The prayer was abandoned as the knocks echoed through the cave.

"Shhh." Mother and Jenny gestured to the children to stay where they were. The knocking sounded again. Jenny, pistol in hand, moved close to the door and listened. To her relief she heard, "It's Fritz. The password is Gideon."

Jenny released the hammer on the gun and threw open the

door. Seeing her husband, the normally stoic Jenny threw herself into his arms. Before she could speak, her emotions took over and she began crying.

"Jenny! Is everything okay?" Fritz asked, looking around the Grotto frantically. "What is it?"

"We were attacked!"

"What?" Fritz gently moved his wife into the room so Ernest and Francis could close and bar the door behind them.

"We were stopped by three men just as we were approaching the Grotto," Jenny sobbed.

"What about the other two men? Do they know you're here?" Ernest asked anxiously.

"No. They're dead too."

"The trap got them," Nicholas interjected, rushing forward to greet his pa.

"I'm sorry … Is everyone okay?" Fritz began.

"Yes. Everyon is fine. It's wonderful to see you," Jenny said, pulling herself together.

Nicholas and Jacob both wrapped their arms around their pa's waist. "Pa, Pa. We were worried about you," said Jacob.

Fritz smiled down at his boys. "I'm fine. Are you two being strong? Yes? You've been a help to your Ma and Grandmother?"

"Yes, sir, we have," said Nicholas.

Mother, who was holding Anne's hand, came forward from the rear of the Grotto. "Where's your father?"

"They have him, Mother," Ernest said plainly.

"Oh no," she cried, overcome with distress.

"Don't worry, Mother," Ernest quickly added. "He'll be fine."

"How can you know that?"

Fritz took Anne into his arms and said, "Father is leading them to the mountain. They're not going to hurt him until they get the treasure, and by then we'll have freed him."

"How did this happen?" Jenny asked.

"We don't know. He never made it to The Rock," Francis explained.

"Did he come here to see you?" Ernest wanted to know.

"Yes. Hours ago," Jenny responded.

"Then they must have captured him on his way to The Rock," said Ernest. "We were checking on conditions at Falconhurst when they brought him in as their prisoner."

"How're they treating him?" asked Mother.

"Just roughly enough to make him good and angry," Fritz said, grinning. "When we left Falconhurst they were preparing to leave."

"What's your plan?" Mother asked.

"Based on how much sun is left in the day, we know about where Father will have them set up camp for the night. That's where we'll free him," Ernest calmly explained.

"For now, let's get some food in our bellies," said Fritz. "Where's Friend?"

"He flew away," said Nicholas. "I'm sorry, Father."

Fritz sighed. "Don't worry." He looked around again. "And Sunshine?"

"They shot her," Jacob whispered.

"Who did?" Fritz, Ernest, and Francis all asked at the same time.

"The man Ma shot," Nicholas said.

Fritz turned to Jenny. Ernest and Francis looked at her as well, amazed.

"It's a good story," Jenny grinned. "I'll tell you about it later, but first let me get you some food."

The men standing near Father grabbed him under the arms and hoisted him up to his feet. They pushed him toward the front of the group, and the hike began.

Father knew how quickly the sun would drop below the horizon, bringing darkness to the island. His goal was to get Captain Charlie and his men to a certain valley, well known to his sons, to camp for the night.

The valley was on their way toward the base of the mountain. It was an open, grassy clearing in the middle of the jungle. Woods and big boulders surrounded three sides of the clearing. From the valley there were small game trails leading off in various directions.

Knowing my sons, he thought, *I'll be leading Captain Charlie's men directly into a trap.*

Chapter 35

Father led Captain Charlie and his men through the jungle to the center of the island. They hiked for hours. The men, already nervous, were occasionally spooked by rustling in the trees and strange animal calls. When they looked toward the direction of the sounds, with rifles pointed, they could only see monkeys in the distance swinging from tree to tree and birds flapping their wings as they took flight. One bird in particular, a brightly colored parrot, seemed to be following them.

Father's goal was to move as slowly as possible to give his sons time to plan their next move and get some rest. Moving slow wasn't difficult for Father whose hands were still bound in front of his body. Occasionally Captain Charlie deemed their pace to be too slow and would shove Father forward growling, "Pick up the pace!"

"Keep a sharp watch for the Robinson boys," Captain Charlie reminded his men from time to time. It was an unnecessary reminder. The men had seen with their own eyes exactly what the Robinsons were capable of, and no one wanted to be caught in an ambush. Other than having to negotiate the terrain, however, it had been an uneventful hike. The Robinsons were nowhere in sight.

As a professional seaman, Captain Charlie was always aware of the weather and was keeping a watchful eye on the thunderheads building in the south.

"Weather, Captain?" a man asked.

"It'll be a wet one tonight."

Just then the sound of thunder echoed through the sky.

Hours earlier, before leaving Falconhurst, Captain Charlie suspected it might rain, and had ordered his men to gather dry wood and sail cloth so that when the rain did come, they would be able to have some shelter and enjoy the comfort of a warm fire.

Safe in the Grotto, the family had eaten and were now resting, waiting for night.

"How will you free your father?" Mother asked.

"Hard to say now but, rest assured, we *will* free him," Ernest replied with a confidence that calmed his mother's nerves.

"How're you boys holding up?" Fritz asked Nicholas and Jacob. "You can endure a few more days of camping out, can't you?"

"Yes, Pa," the boys answered, glad to have their pa with them.

Ernest rolled a blanket to form a pillow. "There's little we can do right now. The best way we can help Father right now is by getting some sleep," he said as he tossed out a second blanket next to Francis who was already fast asleep. He stretched his body down on his bed and was asleep in a matter of seconds.

"He must be exhausted," said Mother.

"Yes. He's been through quite a lot in the past few months," Fritz said, making a bed for himself on the floor next to Ernest. "Try not to worry too much, Mother. Father will be fine. They won't have him much longer … I promise." He handed his pocket watch to Jenny. "Please wake us up in two hours."

Outside, the rain was beating down and lightning flashed across the sky. As the men were sleeping, Mother, Jenny, and Nicholas filled flasks with fresh rainwater. Years earlier, the family had devised a system for collecting water, similar to the one at Falconhurst. With an opening in the cave ceiling and a piece of sailcloth, they directed water through an array of bamboo piping to an open halfbarrel that rested on the floor at the side of the cave.

When the barrel began to overflow, the water was channeled to a small opening at the base of the door where it drained out, keeping the cave dry.

Once the flasks were filled, Mother and Jenny kept the children from waking the men.

"Come children, let's let the men sleep. They'll need their strength tonight," Jenny said as she gathered the children around a lantern on the other side of the cave. There they played games, and Mother and Jenny read to them.

Anne was getting restless, so Jenny made a bed out of blankets and lay down with her until she fell asleep.

Many of Captain Charlie's men had never hiked in such heavy rainfall and they were miserable. To make maters worse, their pace slowed considerably when they came upon a series of rocky hills full of boulders. It was wet, slippery, and treacherous.

"Robinson. Are you certain this is the way?"

"It is," Father replied.

"If you're leading us on a merry chase, I promise, I will cut your throat myself," Second Mate Tucker threatened.

Father said nothing.

They stopped at dusk to light several lanterns to help light the way. They finally reached the end of the trail, which opened to a grassy clearing.

"We'll camp here tonight, men," Captain Charlie announced. "Set up over there against those boulders."

The men placed provisions under tarps, thankful for the break. "Other than being soaked to the bone, we made it here in one piece," a man said, lowering a chest.

"I wonder where the Robinsons are," said another, scanning the tree line.

"Take Robinson over there and tie him to a tree," Captain Charlie ordered, pointing to a tree on the outskirts of camp. "You," he barked, pointing to the men carrying the sailcloth, "Set up my tent."

The men chose a suitable spot on the flat ground to set up a canopy of sorts for Captain Charlie, while other men set about trying to start a fire. It was a difficult task with so much rain, but after a time they managed to get a blazing fire going. The cook cut the potatoes, carrots, and meat they had taken from Falconhurst and, adding spices, he placed the food in a large cast iron pot filled with water over the fire. Every man had an assignment, and after forty minutes, dinner was served. The men sat under their canopies with bowl and spoon in hand, as the rain poured down. "Nothing like a warm bowl of soup on a night like this," a man mused.

Father sat tied to a tree with no protection from the rain. He was given a small bowl with the burnt remains of the soup.

"Thank you," Father said, always gracious.

"Eat up while you can," the man sneered. "Who knows? This may be your last meal."

Father quietly ate the soup. With his hands bound he was unable to use a spoon, so he brought the bowl to his mouth. When he had finished, he handed it back to the man.

"Do you have a family back home?"

"Maybe I do."

"Would you like to see them again?" Father asked.

"What's that to you?"

"Tell your friends that your days, even hours, are numbered on this island if you don't turn back now," Father warned.

The man tried not to show his worry, but the working of his throat betrayed him.

"How many men have you lost so far?"

"Shut your mouth," the man hissed as he turned and stalked away.

Captain Charlie stood. "Tucker, you have first shift. Pick a few men and spread around camp." To the remaining crew he said, "Keep your powder and shot dry. You'll need it."

As Tucker organized his men around the camp perimeter, the rest of the crew arranged their bedrolls, packing themselves tight under the canopies in an attempt to stay dry and warm.

"When'll this bloody rain stop?" the men grumbled.

Cyril and Hicks were sitting in the tree house playing a game of cards while the men were taking shifts walking the balconies and keeping an eye on the dark compound below.

"It's fortunate for us to be here out of the rain," Cyril said, as the storm thundered all around them.

"Aye, it is," Hicks murmured.

"It'll be a long night for the captain and the men."

"Captain Charlie can handle it," Hicks answered matter of factly, laying down his cards.

"True. England turned on a good man, but in the end he —we — will triumph."

"What do you plan to do with your portion of the treasure?" asked Hicks.

"Let's just say I won't ever have to answer to my family again," Cyril said, shuffling the deck.

"I'm surprised to hear you say that," Hicks responded. "I thought life as a member of the royal family was a dream come true."

"It's not all you think it is," Cyril laughed. "There're too many rules to live by. It'll be nice not to answer to anybody. Not even King George."

"Oh? How do you plan on doing that?"

"I'm not returning to England."

"Where'll you go?" Hicks wondered.

"Possibly Spain or even Brazil."

The conversation was cut short by one of the men on the balcony. "There's something out there."

"What is it?" asked Cyril, pushing his chair back and getting to his feet.

"I'm not sure, but there's something in the tree, and it's moving closer."

Hicks and Cyril dropped behind the sofa while the man took aim and fired. He missed. He was reloading his rifle when the object suddenly dropped from the roof onto the balcony rail.

The man shrieked and fired wildly into the night.

"It's a monkey, you idiot!" Hicks yelled, as he and Cyril popped their heads up over the living room sofa.

"Get rid of it!" Cyril ordered, his high and shaky voice betraying his fear.

The man tried to shoo the monkey away, but the animal slapped him in the face. The other men on guard laughed uproariously. Embarrassed, the man took a swing at the monkey, but it leapt up to the branches of the tree and was soon out of sight.

"I've never been that close to a monkey before," the man said.

"You're lucky the beast didn't bite you," Hicks said sarcastically.

"I must say, this place is everything I'd heard it was … and more," said the would-be monkey catcher.

"A paradise — with teeth!" another man laughed.

"Shut your traps and get back to your duties," Hicks snapped.

He and Cyril returned to their game. "Do you think you could live here?" Cyril asked.

"I believe I could under one condition."

"What's that?"

"Women. 'It's not good that man should to be alone.' I read that somewhere," he said chuckling. With that they lifted their glasses of wine and toasted.

"It's getting late," Cyril said, standing up. "Let's get some rest."

"Yes," Hicks agreed. Turning to the men on watch, he ordered, "Stay alert! The rest of you get some sleep."

"Aye, sir," they said as one.

Meanwhile, in the valley, all was peaceful. As it grew darker, Captain Charlie reminded his men again to keep their powder dry. One by one, the men began falling asleep under their canopies.

Father, on the other hand, was unable to sleep, exposed as he was to the relentless rain. Captain Charlie assigned a man to stand watch over him.

At the Grotto, Nicholas, Jacob, and Anne were sleeping peacefully when Mother and Jenny woke Fritz, Ernest, and Francis.

"It's time," Jenny said.

"Thank you," said Fritz, standing and stretching his arms. Jenny hugged him. He held her and whispered, "I love you" in her ear.

"I love you too," she whispered back.

Francis rubbed his eyes, while Ernest rolled over onto his stomach and began doing push-ups and stretches. Soon the three brothers were awake and enjoying a warm drink of hickory tea with bread and jam.

"Thank you, Mother," Ernest said, giving her hand a squeeze.

They gathered powder, bows, and all the arrows that were stored in the cave. They wrapped their rifles in oiled animal hide to protect them from the rain. They put on hide ponchos that dropped over their heads and covered them from their shoulders all the way down past their knees.

The brothers stepped out of the cave and into the wet weather to begin their hike toward the valley where they hoped Father would be.

Jenny closed the door. "I'm expecting another baby," she whispered to Mother.

"Oh, my dear. How wonderful!"

"Do you think I should've told Fritz?"

"No," she said, hugging her daughter-in-law. "It will be a wonderful surprise when this is all over."

Chapter 36

The Robinson men reached the edge of the valley. "There they are," Francis whispered, seeing the fire.

The brothers weaved their way in and out of the wet boulders, taking care not to slip. It was still raining, which helped to conceal their movements. When they finally made it to the tree line, they crouched down to inspect the camp.

Captain Charlie and his men were sleeping in close quarters under canopies, the campfire sputtering in the rain. Lanterns glowed on the faces of the men on watch as they played a wet game of cards on a rock. They were easy targets.

"I see three on watch," Ernest whispered, pointing to the big boulder on the left.

"We need to get closer," said Fritz, melting back into the trees.

They slipped silently along the edge of the woods, creeping up to the perimeter of the camp. "There're four. See?" Fritz pointed. "Over there." A man was pacing alone in the rain.

"And there's Father," Francis whispered excitedly.

"Where?"

"He's tied to the tree near the last man."

"I see him," Ernest breathed.

While they were watching, the four guards suddenly left their posts. Ernest took the opportunity to whistle the family's secret call. Father's head jerked up. He looked toward the edge of the forest, and although he could see nothing, he knew his sons were there. Ernest gave an answering call, and Father smiled, dropping his head again as if asleep.

Under the canopies, the wet and exhausted guards were waking up their replacements.

"Wake up. It's your shift. Wake up," they said roughly, kicking the sleeping men.

"It's time already?" a man grumbled, wiping the sleep from his eyes.

Another sat up, scratching his head, "Still raining?"

"Shut up, you fool!" a man growled, annoyed that his sleep was being disturbed.

From the trees, the Robinsons watched.

"Stoke the fire on your way out," the cook called. "If you want a hot breakfast, that is," he added when the men grumbled.

The replacement guard nearest Father tugged on the rope binding him to the tree, making sure they were secure.

"Sir, please," said Father in agony.

"What is it?"

"My shoulders can't bear the entire evening in this position. Any way you could bind my hands in front of my body? With my ankle secured to the tree, I'm not going anywhere."

The man thought for a moment and didn't see any harm in it, so he proceeded to loosen Father's hands from behind the tree. He then quickly and securely bound his wrists in front of his body without saying a word.

"Thank you for your kindness," Father said to the guard.

At which point the guard mumbled under his breath and sat down ten feet away, leaning up against a boulder. Tipping his hat forward, he soon fell back asleep. He was twenty yards away from the other three men, who had picked up the card game where the previous group had left off.

"Did you hear that?" a guard asked, putting down the cards.

"I did."

"Go check it out. Keep your eyes open."

The man took the lantern and held it high, cautiously walking toward the sound coming from behind the large boulder. Lightning pitch forked across the black sky and lit up the area, revealing a mongoose scampering across the ground. The guard sighed with relief and returned to the campfire.

"What was it?"

"I dunno. Some kind of animal!" he said, picking up his cards.

The brothers looked at one another and grinned. It was time to put their plan into action.

Minutes later, the guards heard another unfamiliar noise behind the boulder.

"It's your turn," the first guard said.

"It's probably just another animal," the other guard complained.

"Get out there and be sure."

Irritated, the man put down his cards, grabbed a lantern, and casually walked over to inspect behind the boulder. Taking advantage of the break in the game, one of the other men left to fill his cup with coffee from the kettle on the fire, leaving one man at the rock post.

The first man went behind the boulder, glanced around, and seeing nothing, put down his lantern, unbuttoned his trousers, and began to relieve himself. Quiet as a whisper, Ernest came from behind and cut his throat. He extinguished the lantern and dragged the body out of sight.

After several minutes, the guard at the rock whispered, "Perkins?" It was dark and the rain had quickened, beating on the rocks and making it difficult to hear. Hearing no response, he went to check behind the boulder.

"Perkins. Where are you?" he called a little louder.

As he walked behind the boulder, he kicked the unlit lantern. As he bent to pick it up, he, too, dropped to the ground without a sound. This time it was Fritz who dragged the body out of sight.

When the third man returned with his cup of coffee, neither of the other guards was present. The cards were still resting face down on the rock.

"Perkins? Daniel?" he whispered, his voice edged with panic.

The sky thundered. Slowly he edged behind the boulder.

"Perkins? Daniel?"

Lightning briefly lit up the sky. He saw the lantern lying on its side. He quickly pulled the pistol from his belt, wiped the rainwater from his eyes, and moved forward to inspect.

"Perkins? Daniel? Where are you? Come on … quit fooling around."

Without warning, Fritz was behind him. The knife gleamed briefly in another flash of lightning, and the man crumpled to the ground suffering the same fate as his friends.

Ernest and Fritz ran back to the trees to join Francis. They watched the camp for several minutes. All was quiet.

"Looks like the guard sitting next to Father is asleep," Francis observed.

"He's out cold," Francis agreed.

"What're you thinking?" asked Fritz.

"Father is closer to camp and more exposed than the other guards were. It'll be risky getting too close to him. I say before we hit them, let's gather whatever weapons we can," Ernest offered.

"Some of the rifles will be useless because of the rain," said Fritz.

"Wet rifles go in the fire," Ernest clarified.

"Fine," said Fritz.

"Francis. You stay here and cover us," Ernest instructed.

"While we are down there, I'll give Father my knife," said Fritz.

"Good idea."

Leaving their guns behind, Ernest and Fritz silently made their way into the camp. Ernest began collecting rifles while Fritz ran toward Father, the rain dampening the sound of his steps. He positioned himself behind Father, in the tree line, and out of view.

"Father," Fritz breathed

Father, still feigning sleep, nodded.

"How're you holding up?"

"I'm managing. How're your mother and the others?" Father whispered.

"Everyone's fine."

The guard sitting next to Father shifted. Fritz put his hand on his knife, ready to strike, but the man merely sighed and settled back to sleep.

"We'll be attacking from the tree line," Fritz said. "That'll be your chance to escape. Take my knife."

The guard stirred again.

"Go, son," said Father, slipping the knife under his leg. "I'll take care of myself. He'll be waking up soon. Go help your brother with the guns."

Ernest had gathered three rifles and placed them quietly at the edge of the fire, not wanting them to explode prematurely.

He had retrieved two dry rifles that he took to the tree line, waiting for Fritz.

Fritz was still moving about the camp when one of the rifles fell from his arms.

Clank!

A member of the crew woke up. "Did you hear that?" he asked, nudging the man on the bedroll next to him.

"Hear what?" the man answered, irritated. "Go back to sleep."

Fritz picked up the dropped rifle and returned to the tree line with his brothers. "How many do we have?" he asked, breathless.

"Including our own, we have a total of nine," said Francis.

"Okay. Make sure they're all loaded and ready to fire. We'll go and get more," Ernest said.

"How's Father?" Francis asked, loading the rifles.

"A little bruised, but otherwise fine. He'll cut himself free and meet us up here," said Fritz.

Ernest and Fritz returned to camp and were able to secure two more dry rifles and dispose of three wet ones.

Father was sawing at the rope binding his wrists, when the guard next to him woke with a start. Father lowered his head to his chest, pretending to sleep, and Ernest dropped flat on the ground, blending in with the sleeping men. Fritz hid behind the chests.

The guard looked over at the rock where the other guards were assigned, but saw no one. Curious, he stood, tugging on the rope binding Father's legs to make sure it was holding firm, then walked over to where the men were supposed to be.

"Daniel? Perkins? Moody?" He looked down at the cards resting on the rock then pulled out his pistol and edged toward the boulder.

As soon as the guard was out of sight, Father positioned the handle of the knife between his knees and frantically ran the thick rope that bound his wrists up and down the sharp blade. It was difficult to firmly secure the knife's handle in the rain, but he continued, knowing that he was almost out of time.

Ernest jumped to his feet, racing to place all of the wet guns into the fire. Fritz ran to the trees with two rifles in hand.

The guard came back around the boulder to see Fritz's silhouette running out of camp. Francis aimed his crossbow and pulled the trigger. An arrow split the air and hit the guard in the chest, but not before he yelled and fired his pistol. He took a final shuddering breath before dropping to his knees and falling forward, face down, in the mud. At the same time, several of the rifles that Ernest had thrown in the fire exploded.

Startled from sleep, Captain Charlie's men reached for their guns but in most cases, found nothing. From the trees, the Robinsons began firing at the men below.

The scene was pure chaos. Captain Charlie dove behind a boulder, musket balls whizzing past his head. With the guns that were still in the camp, Charlie's men fired back at the flashes winking at them from the trees.

Realizing he was unable to cut through the rope in time, Father hid the knife in his boot and twisted his body behind the tree to avoid being hit by stray bullets.

Finally, when their powder and shot ran out, Fritz, Ernest, and Francis switched to crossbows, hitting several more men.

"Time to go," Ernest said, seeing that the men in the camp were getting more organized in their movements. "Take whatever you can and fall back. Captain Charlie will be sending men after us any minute."

As the brothers stood to leave, Captain Charlie, who had been letting his eyes adjust to the darkness, carefully aimed and fired. Francis caught the musket ball in his side, nicking his ribs, and fell to the ground.

"After them!" Captain Charlie ordered. His men hesitated only a moment before setting out in pursuit.

Fritz dropped down next to Francis who was clutching his side, moaning. He wrapped Francis's arm around his shoulder saying, "Come on. Just keep your feet moving."

The two limped off into the jungle as Ernest covered their retreat. He was able to hit the man in the lead, which brought the group to a halt.

"We'll never find anyone in the dark," one of Captain Charlie's men reasoned as they turned back.

"Did you get them?" Captain Charlie roared as the men stumbled back into camp.

"No, sir. They got away, but I think we winged one," a man said, carrying three rifles he had retrieved from the woods.

Captain Charlie stormed over to Father. "You'll pay for this!"

"No. You will. You chose the wrong family to mess with," Father replied calmly.

Captain Charlie bristled. He backhanded Father across the face and said, "Once we have possession of the treasure, you're a dead man, and then I'll track down the rest of your family and kill them one by one."

Captain Charlie turned toward the dark jungle. "Shall I kill your father now?" he yelled, holding a pistol to Father's head. "What's he worth to you?"

The brothers could hear Captain Charlie yelling, but they

kept their silence. "Charlie won't be foolish enough to kill his only guide to the treasure," Ernest reassured his brothers.

After a few minutes, Captain Charlie knew his bluff had been called. He lowered his pistol. Scanning the surrounding tree line, he told his men, "No more sleep tonight. Clean up this mess."

The men gathered their dead, stacking the bodies to await burial in the morning.

"How many have we lost?" Captain Charlie asked.

After discovering the bodies of the three men behind the boulder the count was given. "Twelve, sir. Several more wounded!"

Fuming, Captain Charlie shook with rage. He looked to the sky and let out a frustrated bellow. He stalked over to the fire and stared into the flames, seeing that the Robinsons had stoked the fire with their own weapons.

Brilliant, he thought. He turned to his men. "Anyone missing a gun?"

Several stood with their heads down.

"If your gun is missing, take one from your fallen comrades. You'll need it."

Chapter 37

By 3:00 a.m. the rain had stopped. Fritz, Ernest, and Francis had moved forward along the trail where Father would lead Captain Charlie and his men later that morning.

Ernest quickly lit a fire in the damp and examined Francis's wound.

"It's not too bad," he said, cleaning the area. "The ball went straight through. Looks like it nicked your rib."

Ernest placed direct pressure on the wound while Fritz searched the nearby jungle for a particular leaf that would help stop the bleeding. The plant would help the wound scab over and heal without infection. Fritz chewed on the leaf, making a poultice of it, and smeared the paste on the wound. Ernest wrapped Francis's torso tightly with a piece of his clean shirt, then, drawing strength and comfort from the fire, the brothers rested.

At first light, Captain Charlie and his men, with Father again in the lead, left the valley and began the long, steep hike up the mountain. The hiking conditions were slippery and muddy from the previous night's rain, and a thick fog had settled over the jungle making it difficult to see. Men were tired and anxious from the attack in the night, making them jumpy and short with each other. Weapons in hand and heads swiveling, they continually scanned the jungle for a surprise attack.

Captain Charlie, trying to keep order, kept up a constant barrage of admonishments.

"Men, if you see the Robinsons, don't hesitate … Shoot to kill … I want them dead."

Crewmembers were mumbling, careful not to let Captain Charlie hear them. They had found nothing but misfortune in the island; death lashed out at them at every step.

"This place is bedeviled," one man whispered

"I agree," answered another. "Let's just get the treasure, and get away from this hellhole."

To make matters worse, Father continually voiced warnings.

"Watch your backs … My boys are like foxes. You'll never outwit them … Watch out for traps … You'll never see them coming."

"I see something," a call came from the front. Everyone dropped to the wet ground aiming his rifle forward.

The point men whispered a message back that quickly spread among the men. "It's them!"

Through the heavy fog the silhouettes of two men could vaguely be seen standing in the middle of the trail thirty yards ahead. A strange voice drifted toward them. *"Ahoy. Ahoy"* it said.

"What boldness," whispered the point man. "To stand there

bold as brass sayin' ahoy."

A gentle breeze sent ripples through the fog making the silhouettes visible one moment and then gone the next.

Again, they heard the strange voice, *"Ahoy. Ahoy."*

Several men in the front of the group fired at the elusive figures. When the firing subsided, Captain Charlie pointed to three men. "You. Go and make sure they're dead."

The three men reluctantly reloaded their rifles and began advancing. The fog shifted, and they could see the figures still standing in the trail. Spooked, they fired again. Still, the figures didn't move. They fixed bayonets and took a few more steps forward, cautiously scanning the surrounding area.

"Are they dead?" Captain Charlie called.

In response the men ran at the silhouettes with their bayonets poised. To their surprise, the figures gave way easily and crumpled to the ground.

A large, colorful parrot in a nearby tree squawked loudly and rasped, *"Ahoy. Ahoy."*

Father chuckled.

In the path, the Robinsons had placed makeshift dummies made of branches and vines covered with their leather ponchos from the night before.

"It's a trick!" the men called.

"Get out of there!" Captain Charlie yelled.

The men turned to run when three flashes lit up the fog in an eerie glow and the three men dropped dead.

"Samuel? Lucas? Jeb?" Captain Charlie called. There was no answer. There never would be.

Seeing no way but forward, Captain Charlie pushed his men on with the guttural command, "Keep moving."

The diminished group quietly stood looking over the bodies of their friends.

"Shouldn't we bury them or something?" one asked.

"Lest grief overcome any of you," Captain Charlie answered, "Just think: With these men out of the way, there'll be more treasure for you!"

The men nodded; all thoughts of decency overcome by greed. The bodies were rolled off the trail into the brush, and the group marched on.

Captain Charlie walked next to Father.

"It's hard to believe you're the man my son told me about," Father said. "You don't resemble that man at all."

Captain Charlie said nothing as he stepped over the decoys lying in the path.

When the small group hiked above and out of the fog, the sky was blue and clear and they could see in the far distance the white-capped ocean and the *Independent* anchored in Safety Bay.

The trail led them along a rock wall on one side, and a steep four-hundred-foot cliff on the other. Unbeknownst to them, they were getting closer to the treasure.

Above them several loose stones fell from the rock wall. The men jerked their eyes, and their rifles, upward to see Fritz's leg pull back from the edge of the wall.

Knowing they were in a vulnerable position below, the men collapsed into a state of panic. As one man fired wildly into the brush at the top of the wall, Father swung his bound hands and knocked one of his captors over the cliff. The man's screams faded into a whisper as he plummeted to his death. The remaining men dove to the ground.

"Hold your fire!" Captain Charlie screamed, moving against

the wall.

Frustrated, but still full of bluster, Captain Charlie called to the Robinsons above. "Come down. You're outnumbered. You don't stand a chance."

When there was no response, Captain Charlie signaled for three men to sneak up the cliff and take out the Robinson brothers.

"Three are coming up!" Father yelled.

"Shut up!" Captain Charlie hissed, striking Father in the head with the muzzle of his gun. Dazed, Father fell to his knees. Enraged, Captain Charlie grabbed Father by the neck and pulled him to his feet. "Get moving!" Captain Charlie ordered the three men.

Father's face turned blue before Captain Charlie released his grasp. He had to keep him alive, at least for a little while longer.

The three men who were sent to deal with the brothers were quickly eliminated: two by arrows, and the other in hand-to-hand combat with Fritz. Fritz knocked his assailant off the rock wall where he fell at the feet of the men in the rear.

Captain Charlie ordered the rest of his men to move farther up the trail.

Johnny, frightened beyond reason, said, "This isn't for me. The only thing we've found on this island is death. I'm going back to the ship. No treasure is worth this nightmare."

"Get back in line!" Captain Charlie growled.

Johnny ignored the order and as he turned to leave, Captain Charlie pulled his pistol from his belt and shot him in the back.

"No one leaves," Captain Charlie snarled. "We came for the treasure, and that's what we'll leave with — all of us."

The seventeen remaining men stood silent. After this trip,

they would be fugitives. They could never return to England. With the riches promised them from the treasure, they could live out the rest of their lives anywhere in the world like emperors and kings. The treasure was what they had come for and, like it or not, they couldn't leave without it. Resolved, they turned and started back up the hill.

After another hour of hiking, Captain Charlie and his men approached the treasure cave.

"It's just around that hill," Father directed them. When they rounded the hill they could see a narrow pathway leading to the opening of a cave.

"The treasure's in that cave," said Father.

Captain Charlie's men gathered around. They saw that immediately off to the right of the path was another sheer drop.

"Tucker, Frank, and Mabel, you come with me," Captain Charlie ordered. Then turning to his men he said, "The rest of you stay here with Robinson, and keep your eyes open."

"Aye, aye, sir," the men responded, relieved to know they were finally within grasp of the treasure. For months, they had imagined what the treasure would look like and what it would be like to hold it in their hands. After months of anticipation, they were finally about to find out.

The three men walked carefully down the narrow path with Captain Charlie in the lead until they reached the opening of the cave. With the sun shining in, Captain Charlie could see the treasure gleaming at the far end of the cave. His eyebrows arched. His eyes opened wide.

"This is it!" he mumbled in awe to himself. He stepped into the cave, and one by one the other three men followed.

"Oh … my …"

"I can't believe it!"

"Dear Heavens!"

The men with Captain Charlie couldn't hold back any longer. They whooped and hollered, pumping their fists in the air. Captain Charlie stood back and watched, a smile on his face.

The men outside the cave could hear the celebration. They couldn't wait to get in and take a look for themselves.

"Okay, men," Captain Charlie said as he squared his shoulders, "Stop fooling around. We haven't got time to waste." They crossed over the planks spanning the drop to the river below and stood above the chests of treasure. With a quiet reverence they picked up pieces of gold and silver and touched the priceless jewels.

Captain Charlie tugged at the handles of the chests, which immediately broke off.

"Tucker, tell the men to bring the empty chests," he ordered.

"Yes, sir!"

"And make sure the rest of men keep watch," he added as Tucker ran from the cave.

Tucker stepped out of the dark cave and into the light. Raising his hands to his mouth he yelled, "We've found the treasure! Captain Charlie wants the empty chests brought in immediately."

The men burst into excited cheers and rushed forward, but Tucker yelled, "Those not bringing the chests stay behind and keep watch."

Those with rank and seniority volunteered themselves to take the chests. The rest of the men stood with guns ready, keeping watch on Father and staying alert to any other threat that might come upon them.

The men carried the empty chests along the narrow path and entered the cave. Now there were more men inside the cave than out, and they were immediately hypnotized by the treasure.

"We're rich!" one breathed.

"We're rich!" another yelled.

The men were ecstatic, their lust clouding their eyes. They were grabbing the treasure, letting coins and jewels run through their fingers. Like greed-driven children, they became giddy.

Captain Charlie alone kept a clear head. "Divide the treasure among the chests," he instructed. "Anyone caught stealing will be shot."

Outside the cave, the men were too focused on the cave to notice a distinct bird call, but Father recognized it and knew his sons were nearby.

As the men were loading the treasure, Tucker approached Captain Charlie. "Now that we have the treasure, what should we do with Robinson?"

"Kill him," someone shouted.

Captain Charlie, though, was thinking more clearly. "No," he said. "He's our ransom; our way out of here. We're down to seventeen men. As long as we have a hostage, we have control."

Outside the cave, Fritz, Ernest, and Francis were concealed in the trees and monitoring the scene. Without warning, two arrows were released and, with a quiet thud, two men dropped.

"Attack!" The yell came from the man closest to the fallen men. He looked at the direction the arrows had come, but all was quiet. The men quickly positioned themselves behind trees and boulders.

"We're under attack!" a man yelled to the cave.

Hearing the commotion, Captain Charlie turned to Mabel.

"Go now. We must not lose Robinson."

Mabel took his gun and carefully eased his head out of the cave opening. Father stood at the end of the path, alone and bound. A member of the crew slouched behind a rock aiming his gun at Father. Mabel quickly walked down the trail, his gun trained on Father. When he reached the crew he noticed the two men lying on the ground dead, and the other five men aiming their guns toward the trees.

"Where are they?" Mabel asked, keeping his gun pointed at Father.

"Don't know," said the man closest to Father.

A shot was fired and the ball hit Mabel in the hand.

"My hand!" he screamed, falling to his knees and dropping his gun. Clutching his bloody hand to his body, he stood and started running back to the cave, but, halfway down the trail, another ball hit him in the head. He crumpled lifeless to the ground, blocking the cave's entrance.

Two of Captain Charlie's men fired in the direction the shot had come from, when an arrow, seemingly from nowhere, hit one of the men in the chest. The remaining crew watched him fall to the ground. More shots came from the Robinsons, killing two more. The last man standing rushed toward Father but was struck with an arrow in the neck. He crashed to the ground just two feet from Father.

While Ernest and Francis watched from the safety of the trees, Fritz darted out to cut the ropes that bound Father. Father rubbed his wrists and then picked up the rifle and pistol from the man who lay dead at his feet.

With Mabel's body blocking the mouth of the cave, Captain Charlie and his remaining men were unable to exit the cave and pursue the Robinsons. They fired as best they could from the cave opening, but their aim was limited. Balls whizzed past Father and Fritz. Francis pulled an arrow from a man's chest, but there was no time to retrieve any more. Ernest shot at the cave, the bullet shattering the edge of the rock entrance, forcing the men to dive back inside to safety. The Robinsons took advantage of the break in action to escape and regroup in the jungle.

As they topped the hill above the cave, Ernest took a final opportunity to fire one more shot into the cave hitting a man in the leg. The man screamed in pain as he fell into the deep, dark crevasse in the cave floor.

Captain Charlie roughly pushed Mabel's lifeless body off the cliff and scrambled up the path, but once again, the Robinsons were out of sight.

Safe from Captain Charlie and his men, Ernest insisted on inspecting Father for injuries. He had bruises and a knot on his head where Captain Charlie had hit him with his gun, but other than that he was fine. Father, however, was more concerned about his sons.

"I overheard the men talking last night. Were one of you shot?"

"Yes. I was, Father, but I'm okay," Francis grinned, showing Father his bandaged side.

"Just a nick in the ribs," Ernest explained.

"Thank God," Father whispered.

Captain Charlie turned to his men in the cave. "Tucker, once the treasure is loaded, you and your men take the chests down the mountain."

"Sir, and you?"

"It's time to finish the Robinsons. We've lost too many men.

Caswall, Harrison, Curtis, and Lowrie — you'll come with me. We'll track down the Robinsons and put an end to this."

"Aye, sir," the men responded.

"We'll meet up with you soon," Captain Charlie continued. "Whatever you do, keep your eyes open and get that treasure to the beach."

"Aye, aye, sir."

"Let's go," he said, turning to his four-man team.

Chapter 38

Captain Charlie and the four men left the cave to set out in pursuit of the Robinsons. They began by inspecting the terrain outside the cave. Broken branches and footprints in the moist ground indicated that the Robinsons had retreated into the jungle.

"This way," Captain Charlie said, leading his men into the canopy of trees. Captain Charlie methodically followed every clue that would lead him to the Robinsons. *It's a nice change,* he thought, *being the hunter rather than the hunted.*

A few hundred yards away, Ernest held out his arm. "Shhh. Did you hear that?"

The Robinsons listened carefully. Then, *snap.* A twig broke. There was movement in the forest a short distance away.

"Charlie's on our trail. We need to get to higher ground," Ernest said as they grabbed their weapons and headed deeper into the woods.

A shot cracked through the leaves of the trees, and the ball whizzed past Fritz's ear; Captain Charlie's reputation as a top military fighter was well deserved.

"How did they catch up so fast?" Francis asked.

"It doesn't really matter how," Ernest said, picking up the pace. "We need to hurry."

They came upon one of the many large streams that flowed down through the jungle from the mountaintop and decided to use it to their advantage by traveling down through the river. Father, however, was weak and injured and was slowing their pace considerably.

"You go on ahead," Father said, leaning over his knees, breathing hard.

"No. We live together, we fight together, and we die together. We're family," said Ernest.

"I insist. I'll hunker down. They won't be able to find me."

"No, Father. We won't take that risk," said Fritz.

"Follow me," Ernest said, moving out.

They stepped off a shallow ledge into the river. They waded downriver, holding their rifles high over their heads. At one point, Father slipped, but Ernest and Fritz grabbed him under the arms and they trudged through the water as one. Finally, they came to a shallow portion of the river that made a sharp turn which created an overhang of rock and thick sod above them. The Robinsons hid beneath the ledge to let Father rest, hoping that their pursuers would walk right past them.

A few minutes later, Captain Charlie and his men came crashing through the brush stopping right above them on top of the ledge.

"Where're those bastards?" Captain Charlie fumed. "I'm

sure they came this way. They can't be far," he said, scanning the trees and river, completely unaware that he was standing mere feet from his quarry.

Sunlight was beaming down through the trees and onto the water creating a reflection. The Robinsons could see the images of the men standing above them. Ernest silently signaled with his fingers, *one, two, three*. Ernest and Fritz backed away from the overhang and shot two of the men who were turned away from the river. When the men fell backward into the water, Captain Charlie and the other two men pointed their guns toward the river looking for the telltale signs of gunfire, never thinking to look down.

Thinking quickly, Fritz and Francis lifted the body of one of the dead men above the ledge, drawing the fire of Captain Charlie and his remaining two men. When their weapons had been discharged Father tossed his rifle to Ernest who once again backed away from the ledge and fired, nicking a man in the arm. Fritz leveled the last loaded rifle on Captain Charlie, but when he pulled the trigger nothing happened — the gun had jammed. The two men lunged off the river's edge onto Ernest and Fritz. Still in pain, Francis jumped to aid Ernest and Fritz.

Captain Charlie pulled a pistol from his hip and aimed at Ernest. He fired, missed, and killed his own man. Ernest looked up at Captain Charlie, their eyes locking. Captain Charlie turned and plunged into the thickets of the jungle. Ernest jumped out of the river and chased after him.

Fritz and Francis were struggling to restrain the last man in the water, who was fighting for his life.

"I'm going to help Ernest," Father yelled, pulling himself from the river. He grabbed a rifle, bag of powder, and shot, and loped away.

Captain Charlie ran up a steep hill to a clearing high on the mountain overlooking Safety Bay. He threw himself on the ground and lay prone in the long grass that covered the clearing, gasping for air. He drew his knife and waited for Ernest.

When Ernest burst into the clearing, Captain Charlie jumped up and attacked, slashing into Ernest's arm. Ernest wheeled around and, drawing his knife, hissed, "This ends today."

"It will for one of us," Captain Charlie responded, "but it won't be me!"

In spite of Captain Charlie's age, the two men were extraordinarily well matched. They circled one another, thrusting and parrying, each seeking the advantage. Ernest grabbed Charlie's arm and drew him close enough to hit him in the face with the hilt of his knife, breaking his nose.

Captain Charlie backed away, wiping the blood from his face with his sleeve. "To think my best officer betrayed me."

"You betrayed yourself," Ernest countered, "and your country."

Captain Charlie lunged, cutting Ernest across the face. "Your family will hardly have time to mourn your death before they meet their own," Captain Charlie taunted.

Ernest suddenly dropped and grabbed Captain Charlie around the legs, both of them crashing to the ground.

"You've been blinded by your greed, Charlie," Ernest said. "You've lost your way."

"And you'll lose your life."

Rolling away from one another, Ernest gained his feet and kicked the knife out of Captain Charlie's hand. "Your luck has run out!" he said, breathing deeply.

Suddenly the roar of cannons in the cove reverberated across the island. A ship flying the Union Jack was sailing into Safety Bay. A cannon ball ripped through the *Independent's* main mast, sending the rigging crashing down. "Give up now, Charlie," Ernest said. "It's over."

"I'd rather die than go back to prison … and I'll take you with me!" Captain Charlie found his knife on the ground and with amazing speed, sprang to his feet with his knife once again in his hand.

The desperate men lunged at one another. Ernest was gaining the upper hand when his foot twisted on a rock and he fell onto his back.

Captain Charlie immediately dropped and pinned Ernest to the ground. Knife in hand, Captain Charlie went for Ernest's throat, pressing down with all his strength.

Ernest held Charlie's hands, but the knife inched ever closer as Ernest's strength began to give way. Captain Charlie smiled triumphantly as the blade touched Ernest's throat, when a shot echoed through the clearing, ripping into the silence.

Captain Charlie jerked back and quivered in surprise. Clutching his chest, he fell on Ernest. Ernest grabbed Captain Charlie's knife and threw it into the grass. Pushing his body off of him, he turned his head in the direction of the shot. Father stood at the edge of the clearing, a smoking rifle in his hands.

Ernest rose and stood over Captain Charlie. Blood from the gaping hole in Charlie's side was pouring onto the grass. Ernest quietly watched as he took his last breath. The man whom Ernest had once revered was a threat no longer.

Ernest dropped to the ground, his head in his hands, breathing hard. Father approached and put his hand on his son's shoulder, as Fritz and Francis burst through the trees.

"Thank you, Father," said Ernest.

Father squeezed his shoulder as if to say, "I love you."

"The other man?" Father asked.

"Gone," Fritz said simply.

Francis offered Ernest his hand and pulled him to his feet. The four stood on the cliff and watched Sir Montrose's ship send volley after volley into the *Independent.* Eventually, a fire started and reached the powder magazine. A terrific blast blew her out of the water. The Robinsons cheered.

"We're not done yet," Ernest cautioned. "There's still the men marching the treasure down the mountain."

"They must have heard the cannons. If they're smart, they'll put down their weapons," said Fritz.

"Whoever said they were smart?" Ernest said, picking up

his gear. He took one last look at his old captain before walking away.

Chapter 39

A sense of relief had come over the Robinsons knowing that help had arrived, but the feeling of grim determination stayed knowing that they had one last battle ahead of them. Dealing with Captain Charlie had delayed them longer than they would have liked, but Tucker and the remaining crew were moving slowly, and finding them wouldn't be too much of a problem.

The men transporting the treasure found it more difficult than they thought it would be to carry the chests. The chests were very heavy, and they required frequent breaks to rest their arms. "When do you think Captain will catch up with us?" a man asked as they slowly made their way down the mountain.

"Soon," said Tucker.

"What if he don't come … What if the Robinsons … "

"Don't say it," Tucker interrupted. "How dare you suggest such a thing?"

Taking a break, one man turned to his companion and whispered, "Just think, what if something did happen to him, this treasure will be all ours."

They looked at each other and smiled.

"Keep it moving, we haven't much day left," Tucker ordered the men.

"Keep your fingers crossed," the man whispered to his partner as they lifted the chest off the ground.

The *Conquest* dropped anchor alongside the *Independent*, which was badly damaged by the cannon assault and resulting explosion. Captain Briggs sent several men to board the *Independent* to salvage whatever they could and to take the crew into custody. It was only a few moments before Briggs's men stood at the rail of the listing ship with two of Captain Charlie's crew.

"Get them over here and throw them in the brig," Captain Briggs called from the *Conquest*.

"Aye, sir."

"You're going spend the next four months in hell, and when we get back to England, this hell will seem like paradise," one of Briggs's men said, shoving the bound men forward and into the boat. "You and anyone else still alive on the island are going to suffer greatly. Let's go!"

Many of Sir Montrose's merchantmen, including John Bennett and Captain Briggs, had been on the island before and were comfortable launching a rescue party.

Briggs divided the *Conquest*'s crew and the marines into two groups to march to Falconhurst on both trails. They marched with guns drawn, not knowing if or when they would encounter Captain Charlie's men. The group on the south trail noticed the headless man lying off to the side of the path.

"Well, that's a sight you don't see every day," a man said.

Later, the same group came to the Family Bridge that had been destroyed and discovered the bloated bodies of the dead men who had washed ashore along the bank of the river.

Admiration surged through the group. "This explains a lot about Captain Robinson," a man said, setting off a flurry of chatter.

"Yes," agreed another. "I've seen him fight like the devil."

"No wonder he rose so quickly in rank."

"I'm just glad he's on our side."

The men waded through the river to the other side.

The second group, consisting of Captain Briggs, Sir Montrose, and John Bennett, took the northern trail. The men passed by the pit where the man still lay impaled, his cloudy eyes open.

"Stay on the trail, men," Sir Montrose advised. "The Robinsons fortified the island well. Let's just pray they're still alive."

The two groups, guns in hand, were expecting a surprise attack. They didn't know how many men they would have to confront or where they would be, but they knew the criminals were out there somewhere.

The mood was somber as they moved forward. No one spoke a word as they encountered the bodies of dead men; it only reminded them of the seriousness of the task that lay before them. Led by the Royal Marines, the men were reminded to stay vigilant as they approached Falconhurst.

Suddenly, the sound of gunfire erupted. Balls whizzed past the heads of Captain Briggs and his men. The marines automatically got into formation and fired back. They quickly reloaded their rifles, anticipating return fire, but the jungle was silent.

When Captain Charlie's men saw the army of men advancing on Falconhurst, they ran back to First Mate Hicks and Cyril. "We haven't a chance," they informed them. "There're too many of them."

Charlie's men attempted to stand their ground as Briggs and his men moved forward, but after a short battle, the men surrendered and Falconhurst was reclaimed. Several of Captain Charlie's men were killed, but Cyril and First Mate Hicks, along with a few others, were captured alive. They'd found Cyril hiding under Ernest's bed in an upper room like a coward.

Captain Briggs designated a security detail to protect Falconhurst and assigned the remaining men to clean up and repair the damage done to the Robinson's home.

Captain Briggs had Cyril, Hicks, and the other survivors rounded up and shackled with chains to nearby trees.

"Take your hands off me!" Cyril demanded, resisting the restraints. "I am the son of Lord Wallace and a member of the royal family!"

"We know exactly who you are," Captain Briggs countered. "And soon you'll be joining your father in prison."

While sitting on the ground, Cyril was suddenly bombarded from above by a heavy spurt of wet, gooey bird excrement. The family parrot squawked on a branch above him before flying away, much to the humor of Sir Montrose's men.

"Where're the Robinsons?" Sir Montrose asked, standing over the shackled men.

Wiping his face, Cyril said nothing and neither did Hicks, but the other men spoke up quickly, hoping for good treatment.

"We haven't seen them since Charlie and the crew left yesterday."

"Where'd they go?" asked Sir Montrose.

"Inland. Captain Charlie had the father. He was going to guide them to the treasure."

"Have you seen the women and children?"

"No, sir," a man said.

"We never did see them," another affirmed.

This was good news to Sir Montrose. He knew that if Captain Charlie and his men hadn't seen the women and children, then they were most likely hiding.

"The Grotto," Sir Montrose said, turning to Captain Briggs. "If they're hiding, they'll be at the Grotto. You know where it is?"

"Yes," said Captain Briggs. He gathered several men to go with him, and they headed out with lanterns in hand.

The sun was falling fast, and Sir Montrose's men lit the candles surrounding Falconhurst. The establishment was glowing bright. Sir Montrose and his crew stood watch from surrounding positions, not knowing if Captain Charlie and his men would, at any moment, return to Falconhurst.

Inland, Tucker and his eleven men, descending from the mountain with the treasure, stopped to camp for the night. The men slumped to the ground, exhausted. The chests were extremely heavy and cumbersome on the narrow, rough trails. They assumed Captain Charlie would meet up with them soon, but unable to navigate the trail in the dark, they decided to camp for the night. The mood was heavy with uncertainty, swinging erratically between fear and hope.

"The Robinsons could still be out there. We need to be on alert," Tucker cautioned his men. "No fires, no noise. Understand? If you see or hear anything, shoot it!"

The moon, however, was nearly full, creating sufficient light for the Robinsons to quietly surround the camp.

The crew was jumpy, constantly calling out. "Did you hear that?" or "I think I saw something."

"No one sleeps!" Tucker growled, "or it'll be the last time you sleep."

Suddenly, Father was the first to fire. The man who was hit fell over, tumbling onto a fellow crewmate. "Lawrence is dead!" the man yelled, shoving the body off of him.

"Where'd the shot come from?" someone else called out, rifle drawn.

"It was over there," another pointed.

They all aimed their weapons into the trees and fired. Balls whizzed through the dark night, but Father was lying low behind a nearby tree.

Francis moved in close, aimed his crossbow, and hit a man in the arm. The man screamed with pain and fear. A fellow crewmate was attempting to pull the shaft out when an arrow hit him in the back and he fell over dead.

"Where are they?" several men screamed, jerking their heads in all directions.

Suddenly three flashes of light illuminated the shadowy jungle, each shot finding its mark. After each shot was fired, the Robinsons dropped, rolled out of sight, and reloaded their guns.

While Tucker's men were scrambling for more amunition, Francis scaled a tree and fired two more arrows, killing one man and hitting Tucker in the shoulder. Tucker groaned and moved to hide behind one of the chests. Unfortunately for him, he positioned himself directly in Fritz's line of fire. Fritz took the shot, hitting him in the neck. Tucker emitted one last gasp before he fell to the earth dead.

There were now four men left, and one had his sights on Father, but before he could shoot, he crumpled to the ground. Father took aim at another man, but he, too, fell to the ground before he could shoot.

Now there were only two men left. One ran behind a tree but, unbeknownst to him, he was standing within five feet of Ernest.

"I hope you've said your prayers," Ernest whispered. The man slowly turned to look in the direction of the voice, and Ernest fired.

The last man, terrified and confused, ran around in a circle, firing blindly into the jungle, and then he suddenly stopped and fell forward.

The Robinsons carefully moved into camp.

"How did you take those guys down without a shot?" Francis asked Father.

"I didn't. I thought it was you," Father replied.

Before Francis could respond, Fritz came up behind them. "Who killed that last man? I didn't hear a shot. Was it you, Francis?"

"No. I didn't do it."

They looked at each other skeptically, when Father bent down to examine the man. When he rose, he was holding a sharp dart by its feathered end.

"The Baraourou."

Father faced the trees and called out, *"Walica mutaggu de shati."* Which translated means, "We're glad to see you."

A strange animal call suddenly filled the air. Father smiled and returned the call. Lithe, dark figures quietly stepped into the clearing from out of the dark jungle. The leader stepped forward and put both of his hands on Father's shoulders.

"Zartuk," Father said. "Thank you for coming."

Zartuk, speaking in his native tongue, said, "My father had another dream and told us to leave immediately."

"How did you know we were here?" Fritz asked, extending his hand. The warrior shook it, and then reached out to Francis and Ernest to do the same.

"We saw a ship pass our island three nights ago. King Baraourou said it was an evil ship, and that Ernest was in its belly. We came as fast as we could, but our canoes are slow and the storm was fierce."

"But, how did you find us here? In this spot?"

"Father said you would be on the big mountain, and you

were easy to track. We could smell you," Zartuk laughed.

The Robinsons joined in the laughter.

"We smell that bad, huh?" Father asked.

"Not you. The bad men," Zartuk clarified.

The brothers laughed even harder.

"Are there others?" Zartuk asked.

"Not here, but there's sure to be a group at Falconhurst."

Then, they heard a moan. Checking the bodies on the ground, they found one man still alive. It was the man who had been shot through the arm with an arrow. One of the Baraourou warriors raised his blowgun to his lips, but Father held him off.

"We do not kill for killing's sake. The man is obviously unarmed and helpless," Father said. The warrior shrugged and lowered his blow dart.

While Father, Ernest, and Francis gathered up their gear, Fritz dressed the wound and wrapped the man's arm.

Leaving the treasure in place, they headed out. The warriors took control of the prisoner, prodding him along and keeping him terrified during the long night hike back toward Falconhurst.

Captain Briggs and his men were approaching the entrance of the Grotto when he suddenly stopped.

"Wait. I remember there being a trap nearby," he said, holding his lantern close to the ground.

"Everyone stay absolutely still," he said. There's a trip cord near here. Ah, here it is."

He carefully followed the cord to the trigger mechanism. "Stand back," he warned, releasing the trigger. The bent bamboo with sharp spikes suddenly gave way, violently swinging forward.

"Getting stabbed by those spikes would be very unfortunate," a marine mused.

"Indeed, it would," Captain Briggs replied.

The men followed him to the door of the Grotto. He knocked lightly.

There was no answer.

The men kept watch on the surrounding area while Captain Briggs spoke through the door.

"It's Briggs. Captain Briggs."

Still no answer.

"I'm here with a few of my men. I can name every member of your family. William, Elizabeth, Fritz and his wife Jenny and their children, Nicholas, Jacob, and Anne. Then of course there's Ernest, Francis, and Jack — who passed away, God rest his soul. I've come with Sir Montrose, Jenny's grandfather."

Jenny slowly opened the door, gun in hand. When she saw Captain Briggs she smiled and threw the door open wide. "What're you doing here?" she beamed.

"Come in. Come in," said Mother, lowering her rifle.

Captain Briggs and a few men entered the Grotto, leaving the marines outside to stand guard.

"When Sir Montrose learned of Ernest's abduction, he commissioned a ship as quickly as he could," Captain Briggs explained.

"Have you seen Fritz and the others?" Jenny asked, the worry plain on her face.

"No. We've taken back Falconhurst, and at first light we'll

send a party inland to search for them. For now, will you stay here or at Falconhurst for the night?" he asked.

"My grandfather's at Falconhurst?" Jenny asked cautiously.

"Yes he is," Captain Briggs answered, "and he's been very worried about you. He would have come himself, but he thought it would be too difficult hiking in the dark."

Jenny nodded. "We'll be safe now."

"Let's go home," Mother encouraged.

"Would you like to sleep in your beds tonight?" Jenny asked Nicholas and Jacob.

"Yes, Ma," they chorused.

The family gathered their belongings, wrapped Sunshine's body in a blanket, and hiked back to Falconhurst by the light of the lanterns. Friend flew on ahead, occasionally singing out, "Home. Fritz. Home. Home … " Just as they reached the clearing, the bird disappeared high up in the trees.

Sir Montrose was standing at the base of the huge tree with tears in his eyes. "Thank God you're all safe and well."

Jenny rushed forward to give her grandfather a hug. "Oh Grandfather! How wonderful to see you," she cried, tears running down her face as well.

"You too, my dear. It's been so long, and to know you're all alive and safe … " He reached out his arms to give Mother and Nicholas a hug. Jacob, who was quite young when he had last seen his great-grandfather, hung back holding Anne's hand.

"Come Jacob and Anne," Jenny encouraged. "It's time to be with family now," she said, pulling them into the group.

"We're so grateful you came," Mother said.

"It's not over yet," Sir Montrose cautioned, "not until we find your good husband and sons."

Just then, Mother looked up and noticed John Bennett.

"John? What's he doing here? Isn't he … ?"

Sir Montrose leaned close to Mother and Jenny. "Actually, he's the reason why we're here," he explained.

"But didn't he tell about the treasure?" Jenny asked.

"Yes, he did. He was drunk and foolish, but without him we wouldn't have known Ernest was taken, or realized the danger your family was in. He's very remorseful for what he has done," Sir Montrose finished.

"Of course," said Mother. She walked up to John, but before she could say anything, John spoke.

"I'm so sorry, Mrs. Robinson. What I did was terrible, but I hope in time you'll be able to forgive me. I had no intention of bringing harm on you and your family," he said humbly.

Mother's pure nature caused her to reach out her hand and take his "I forgive you, John. But I pray my husband and sons are found safe."

"I've been praying for the safety of your family and your home ever since leaving England," he whispered, head bowed.

"Thank you for working with Sir Montrose and doing all you could to help us," Mother said, stepping back.

"I'm sorry, John," Jenny said, coming forward. "I don't know if I can forgive you yet. I need to know that my family is safe first."

"I understand. That's all I could ask for," John replied.

The family gathered in the living room of the main tree house with Sir Montrose. It was getting late and the children were tired, so they joined hands for evening prayer. Mother prayed. First, she acknowledged the hand of the Lord in all things. She expressed her gratitude for Sir Montrose and Captain Briggs and for their help. She then fervently pleded with the Lord that her husband and sons would return home unharmed.

Chapter 40

As the sun peeked over the horizon, the jungle began to wake and the birds happily greeted the rising sun. The Robinson men and the Baraourou were already up and heading home. They passed the Wood of Monkeys where hundreds of primates were screeching and swinging from tree to tree. "Two more hours, and we'll be home," Father said.

"Let's hope Sir Montrose has Falconhurst under his control," Francis said.

"I'm sure he does," Ernest and Fritz both agreed.

"Most importantly, let's pray Mother and the children haven't suffered any harm," said Father.

A somber mood settled on the group as they hiked. Zartuk sent his men ahead to scout, searching for any remnants of Captain Charlie's men on the island.

After hiking for hours, they heard the distinct sound of men marching. Ernest and Francis ran to the top of a ridge to survey the scene, while Father, Fritz, Zartuk, and their prisoner remained around the bend. The Baraourou warriors spread out, blending into the jungle.

Forty British Marines were marching with guns drawn, Captain Briggs leading them.

Peeking over the crest of the ridge, Ernest said to Francis, "This is a welcomed sight," with a smile on his face.

"Indeed it is brother. Indeed it is," Francis said, slapping him on the back.

"Briggs!" Ernest yelled.

The marines stopped and pointed their guns in their direction.

The men were unable to see them, but Ernest yelled anyway, "Captain Briggs. It's good to see you!"

"Captain Robinson, is that you?" Captain Briggs yelled back, recognizing his voice.

"Yes, sir, it is. Tell your men to lower their guns. We'll meet up with you around the bend."

Ernest and Francis descended the ridge and returned to Father, Fritz, Zartuk, and their prisoner.

"It's Captain Briggs. They're around the bend ready to meet us," said Francis.

"Good news," said Father.

A few minutes later, Captain Briggs and the Robinsons greeted one another with a good deal of backslapping and hand shaking.

The marines, however, were standing in stunned silence. Flanking the Robinsons were a dozen or more fierce-looking Baraourou warriors, their faces covered in paint, spears and blowguns in hand, and bows and arrows slung across their backs.

The marines and the warriors eyed one another suspiciously.

Captain Briggs turned to his men to introduce them to the Robinsons. He noticed the tension on their faces and started to laugh.

"At ease, gentlemen. These native warriors are friends of the Robinsons."

The marines nodded but did not relax. The Baraourou grinned. One of them shoved the prisoner in their direction, officially handing him off. Relief flooded the prisoner's face. It was obvious that he preferred being a prisoner to the British rather than the natives.

"It's good to see you've survived in one piece," Captain Briggs said to Father.

"Yes," Father said. "Tell us, have you seen Mother, Jenny, and the children?"

"All is well," Captain Briggs reassured them. "They're with Sir Montrose now at Falconhurst. We collected them from the Grotto last night."

"Praise the Lord," Father sighed, the tension he had been carrying over the past few days leaving his body. "Thank you," he said, extending his hand again.

"We've secured the cove and Falconhurst," Briggs explained, shaking Father's hand. "Is Captain Charlie and his contingent still out there?"

"You needn't worry about them, Captain Briggs," Father answered solemnly. "Let's just say they've been 'secured' as well."

Briggs searched Father's face. There was no triumph there, only fatigue.

Ernest recognized a few fellow soldiers and greeted them heartily.

"Your appearance would not pass muster, Captain Robinson. We need to get you home and cleaned up," a fellow officer laughed. Francis and Fritz laughed as well.

"I think I've forgotten what a bath and shave feels like," said Ernest. "Unfortunately, my time on the *Independent* didn't include such accommodations."

The soldiers laughed.

"Let's move out," Captain Briggs ordered. "Let's get these men back to their family."

The last of Captain Charlie's men were shackled together and marched to the cove, where they would sail back to England on the *Conquest* to be tried for their crimes.

Sir Montrose had advised Elizabeth and Jane to stay aboard the ship until the island was secured. Now with the danger passed, they were finally coming to shore.

"Has anyone seen Captain Robinson?" Elizabeth asked as the longboat landed on the beach.

"No, Miss. No word yet," one of Sir Montrose's men answered as he lifted her out of the boat and carried her to the dry sand.

"Thank you," Elizabeth smiled.

"My pleasure, ma'am."

Just then the shackled men arrived at the beach. Elizabeth had been standing back, but when she saw Cyril, she marched up and slapped his face.

"I knew you were a scoundrel," she said hotly. "You are despicable! Enjoy the rest of your life in prison with your father!" Cyril smiled and mocked her with a deep bow. One of the marines watching the scene turned and punched Cyril in the stomach, ordering, "Get this scum out of here."

Cyril was dragged with the other prisoners up the beach and tied to trees until they could be transported to the ship.

Elizabeth and Jane were assigned escorts to walk them up the main trail to Falconhurst.

The marines, with the Robinson men and Captain Briggs following behind, entered the clearing at Falconhurst. A cry rose up, "The Robinsons are alive," followed by the cheering of Sir Montrose's men.

Mother and the children heard the commotion outside and rushed to meet the weary group.

"Excuse me, please," Jenny and Mother said, pushing their way to the front.

Nicholas and Jacob ran ahead, weaving their way around the legs of the men toward their pa. The last of Sir Montrose's men stepped aside and Nicholas and Jacob ran to Fritz, with Mother, Jenny, and Anne not far behind.

"Pa! Pa!" The boys yelled, their excitement barely contained as they jumped into Fritz's arms.

"I knew you could do it, Father," Nicholas said, smiling from ear to ear.

Jenny ran forward, straight into Fritz's arms.

Mother and Father moved toward one another and embraced, whispering, "I love you" to each other.

Mother then hugged all three of her sons.

The sailors and the officers stepped forward to shake hands with the Robinsons as they continued to walk to the center courtyard. One officer tugged on Ernest's long beard and laughed.

Sir Montrose was at the trunk entrance door to meet the family.

"Thank you for coming," Father said, stretching his hand forward.

"Thank the men," Sir Montrose said proudly. "They came on their own accord."

Father turned, looking the men in the eyes. "Thank you," he said simply, the emotion barely contained in his voice.

"Sir, did you happen to see Miss Cole before you set sail?" Ernest asked anxiously. "Did she ever learn what happened to me?"

Before Sir Montrose was able to respond, however, Ernest suddenly froze. "Excuse me," he said, looking over Sir Montrose's shoulder. John Bennett was sitting near the smokehouse. Outraged, Ernest rushed toward John.

John saw him coming and stood, bracing himself for the impact. Ernest plunged into him, the two crashing to the ground.

"You greedy piece of filth!" Ernest roared. "How could you betray me ... my family ... Elizabeth?" he yelled, holding John by the throat.

Captain Briggs rushed over and threw his arms around

Ernest, pulling him away.

"Captain Robinson. At ease! At ease!" Briggs yelled.

Exhausted and drained, Ernest went weak, slumping to the ground and weeping. John, too, was still on the ground.

"John, I loved you like a brother," Ernest whispered, tears rolling down his face. "How could you? How could you do this to my family? How could you separate me from Elizabeth?"

"I'm sorry, Ernest. I'm truly sorry," John said, also in tears.

Sir Montrose stepped forward. "It's not what you think, Ernest," he said quietly.

Fritz and Francis were looking on, angry, waiting for an explanation. Father turned to look at Mother, who gave him a nod.

"Ernest, we wouldn't be here if it weren't for John. He was left to die in the alley the night you were taken, but he managed to get to me to tell us about your abduction."

"I was drunk Ernest, a fool!" John cried. "I was jealous and hurt, and I lost myself in the moment. I never meant for any of this to happen. I'm so terribly sorry," he said to the entire Robinson family.

Ernest sat quietly. His family had been in such terrible danger because of John, but when Ernest looked into John's face, he saw a broken man. Gaining his composure, and taking a deep breath, Ernest slowly stood and moved toward John. He locked eyes with him and softly said, "I trusted you."

"Please let me make it up to you. I would do anything to earn your trust again. I just hope that one day you'll be able to forgive me."

Ernest studied John's face for several moments, seeing nothing but sincerity. Taking a deep breath, he bowed his head and sighed. "Of course, John. Of course. Thank you for sending help."

John said nothing, tears coursing down his face.

"You're tired. You need to eat and rest," said Sir Montrose.

Sir Montrose felt a tap on his shoulder. He turned to see several of his men pointing toward the main trail. Smiling, he turned back to Ernest. "We have a surprise for you. One you wouldn't have expected in a thousand years."

"There could only be one surprise that would qualify," Ernest said, brushing the dirt off his shirt and pants.

"Well, you know the Lord works in mysterious ways," Montrose said.

Ernest turned to the main trail, and gasped. A woman had just entered the clearing. Breathing fast, he looked to Sir Montrose, who smiled.

Ernest stood transfixed watching the woman, her graceful figure walking toward the crowd.

"Elizabeth?" he whispered, not trusting his voice.

Everyone stood quietly, enjoying the scene unfolding before them.

"Elizabeth!" Ernest cried, rushing forward.

"Ernest!" Elizabeth responded, running.

When they reached each other, Ernest and Elizabeth embraced for what seemed to be an eternity. As everyone looked on, everything around them was silent as they became lost in the moment. Tears streaming down their faces, they didn't want to let go. Although Ernest had hoped he'd be with her again, it felt like a dream after everything he and his family had endured.

Backing away, Ernest felt Elizabeth's arms as he took a moment to ensure that she was real. As he looked into her eyes, she placed her hands on his chest.

Then Ernest held Elizabeth's face in his hands, her eyes sparkling. "I can't believe you're really here. How is this possible?"

Before Elizabeth could respond, he leaned in and kissed her softly. He could smell her sweet perfume and feel the heat radiating from her body. It wasn't a dream. He reached out and twirled a tendril of hair that had escaped her bun. "You're really here," he whispered.

Ernest pulled her in for a second embrace, "I was so worried about you. I don't know what I would have done had something happened to you," Elizabeth whispered as she tucked her head into his chest.

"We'll never be separated again," Ernest responded as he tightened the hug and took a deep breath.

Sir Montrose walked up behind them. "Ah, here's our beautiful stowaway," he said laughing.

Ernest took Elizabeth's hands in his and asked, "Stowaway?"

"I wasn't about to stay in England, worrying month after month about what happened to you," Elizabeth smiled. "My only option was to sneak on board."

"Don't tell anyone," Ernest whispered, "but I'm glad you did."

"Let me introduce you to my fiancée," Ernest said proudly as his family came forward.

"Don't you think you ought to get cleaned up, Captain Robinson?" Briggs laughed.

Ernest suddenly became conscious of his appalling state. "Yes," he said backing away. "Please excuse me," he said, running to the tree house to clean up. As Ernest hurried off, Sir Montrose asked Doctor Spangler to follow Ernest and tend to his wounds.

"It wouldn't hurt for all of you to be looked at by the good doctor," Mother insisted.

"Splendid idea, Mrs. Robinson," Doctor Spangler said bowing. He pointed toward Father and Francis. "You two, come with me. We'll make it quick."

Obliging the good doctor, Father and Francis followed him to the tree house.

With the men gone, Mother took Elizabeth by the hand and led her up the stairwell, the rest of the family following.

Later that evening, Sir Montrose's cooks prepared a feast. As they prayed over the meal, and thanked the Lord for their bounteous blessings, a deep feeling of peace came over the family.

Dinner was coming to a close when Elizabeth gazed around the table. "This is remarkable," she began. "Ernest described your home, but I never imagined it would be this beautiful."

"Are you going to get married, Uncle Ernest?" Jacob blurted.

"Jacob!" Jenny scolded, embarrassed.

Ernest and Elizabeth looked at each other and smiled. "Yes, Jacob. That's the plan."

"Where'll it be?" Nicholas asked. "Will we be going to England?"

"Now, now, boys," Jenny said, once again reigning them in.

"Father was a pastor in Switzerland," Francis said. "I'm sure he could muster up a few Godly words. It seems to have worked just fine for Fritz and Jenny."

Elizabeth squeezed Ernest's hand, smiling.

"Actually," Ernest said, grinning. "We've decided to marry here, before returning to England."

"That calls for a toast," Father enthusiastically announced.

Mother remained quiet, deep in thought.

"My dear Elizabeth, I couldn't be more happy, but what about your family? Won't they be devastated?"

"That's very considerate of you, Mrs. Robinson," Elizabeth said quietly. "I've had a lot of time to think about this, and under the circumstances, I'm confident my family will understand, and wish me the very best. That is, if they haven't already disowned me for joining the rescue effort," she laughed.

Everyone smiled.

"Well, if that's your decision, we couldn't be more delighted to have the wedding here, and to have you as part of our family."

"Thank you, Mrs. Robinson," Elizabeth smiled. "It will be an honor to be a part of this family."

"Well said!" Sir Montrose cheered, to everyone's delight.

Changing the topic, Mother inquired, "How is your family, Miss Cole? Do they know where you are?"

"Yes," Elizabeth said, slightly uncomfortable. "I couldn't tell them of my plans before we left … they would never have agreed to let me go. But I did leave them a letter."

"And what did you write?" asked Ernest.

"I told them I would rather die then risk never seeing you again," she said simply.

Ernest cleared his throat. "You know," he began, "the long days and nights in the hold of that ship gave me plenty of time to think. To worry. To doubt. To fear. I worried about my family, of course, but I also worried about Elizabeth. Was she well? What if I never saw her again?"

Silence fell on the room.

"In my darkest moments, I would pray, and the one thing that always brought me peace was the thought of being reunited with Elizabeth. I could imagine raising children with her and the fine mother she would be. It was easy to see us growing old together."

"Elizabeth, do you remember when you gave me a sketch of yourself and I gave you one of me?"

"Yes, indeed," she said, gently touching the locket around her neck. "I've worn it every day since you gave it to me."

Ernest nodded. "Every night in the barracks, I gazed at it until I fell asleep. When I was taken hostage by Charlie, it was left behind. Night after night I would lay awake in my cell, unable to sleep, tormented by my situation. Then one night I carved an image of you into the wall of the ship. I'm a poor artist, but the image brought me comfort and helped me to sleep."

"And now here we are, together again," he said looking into Elizabeth's eyes. "I promise you now that nothing will ever part us again."

"I couldn't have said it better," Father intoned, raising his glass. "Here's to many years of happiness to the happy couple," he proposed.

"Hear, hear," was the resounding response.

Jenny and Mother nodded their understanding. Elizabeth would fit in their family perfectly.

When dinner was over the men gathered on the balcony to discuss the treasure.

"What have you decided to do? Has there been any discussion on the matter?" Captain Briggs asked.

"Were you able to learn any information regarding the treasure's origin?" asked Fritz turning to Sir Montrose.

"Well, I took the pieces you gave me to some trusted confidants," Sir Montrose began. "The treasure is just what you suspected. When Charles V abdicated the Spanish throne in 1556, it turns out much of the monarch's gold and silver went missing, and the pieces you gave me were determined to be from that time period. You said you found five chests?"

"Yes. It's sitting up on the side of the mountain as we speak," said Fritz.

"Hmmm," Sir Montrose mused.

"What?" Father asked, the tension in the room building.

"There's more."

"More?" Francis's eyes opened wide.

"Rumor has it that the entire cache was divided into five equal parts and placed secretly in five locations."

The mood deepened.

Sir Montrose continued. "Fortunately, no one has claim to the treasure, as the monarchy that it belonged to dissolved years ago."

"You mean … " Francis began.

"It's yours. Every last ounce of gold and silver is yours," interjected Sir Montrose.

Father remained silent, deep in thought.

"We should retrieve it and safeguard it from the elements until we decide the best course of action," Ernest suggested.

"Agreed," said Fritz.

"Briggs and I will employ some of our best men to help with the effort," said Sir Montrose.

"Can your men be trusted?" asked Fritz, thinking of John.

"Yes. I'd bet my life on it," Captain Briggs assured them.

"We should take up a few more empty chests," Ernest suggested.

"Empty chests?" asked Captain Briggs.

"Captain Charlie and his men knew the old chests were rotted and weak. They took new ones up to transport the treasure but they were extremely heavy," said Ernest. "A few more chests would lighten the load considerably."

"We'll need to bring back the old chests along with the treasure," Sir Montrose advised. "My sources told me that it's possible there may be a map with the treasure indicating where the other four repositories of treasure are hidden."

"And you think those maps may be hidden in the old chests?" Francis asked.

"It's hard to say, but I don't think we should chance it," Sir Montrose finished.

"I suppose we should inspect the cave more thoroughly to make sure we don't miss anything," Fritz added.

The conversation continued for a few moments longer before Father cleared his throat. "It's getting late. Why don't we join the ladies inside."

In the living room, Captain Briggs pulled out his banjo and Doctor Spangler pulled out his guitar, and they started playing. Elizabeth picked up Anne and placed her on her knee, bouncing her to the rhythm of the music. Fritz took Jenny's hand and pulled her to the center of the room to dance. Nicholas and Jacob followed their parents' lead and entertained the group with their creative dance steps. Mother and Father followed, and Francis surprised everyone by asking Jane to dance. Jane looked to Elizabeth for approval and Elizabeth simply smiled and nodded.

Ernest stood and extended his hand to Elizabeth and asked for a dance.

"I would be delighted, Captain Robinson," she said with a twinkle in her eye, setting Anne down on the chair.

"I won't be 'Captain' for long," Ernest said.

"What do you mean?" she asked, studying his face.

"Like I said, we shall never be parted again."

Elizabeth tucked her head close to Ernest's chest, smiling.

The family danced and sang late into the night. As they started to leave for their rooms they were startled when the Baraourou began to chant and dance around a large fire in the courtyard under the tree houses. Father was quick to inform the visitors that the warriors were blessing the island in their traditional way, and not to be alarmed.

From all around Falconhurst everyone paused to watch. They had never seen such an intense display of emotion. When it was over, a feeling of respect and reverence settled over the group. There was a lot of work to do over the next few weeks repairing and restoring Falconhurst and securing the treasure, but for now, peace had returned to Robinson Island.

The End

The story shall continue ...

Author's Notes

Growing up, my ultimate favorite movie was *Swiss Family Robinson*. Back then, I had a difficult time reading. Instead, I watched the beloved 1960 Disney movie version of the book repeatedly. (It was later in my life that I read the english edition of *The Adventures of Swiss Family Robinson* by Johann David Wyss.) In 2003, I pulled out my Disney version (on VHS). I hosted a movie night with my two sons, who were then three and five years old. We popped a little popcorn and cuddled together as we watched the movie. When the movie ended, I tucked my boys into bed and gave them my love.

After retiring for the evening, I suddenly awoke at one o'clock in the morning. In my mind's eye, a new idea for a sequel and continuation of the *Swiss Family Robinson* story was unveiled to me. My vision for the idea was clear. I had often wondered what had happened to the Robinson family after being shipwrecked on the remote island. Now the answers began to flood my mind. Because the images were so vivid and real to me, I got out of bed, sat on the sofa, and began to type. I typed as fast as I could, not wanting to forget any of the details. By six o'clock the next morning, I had typed more than fifty pages and *Return to Robinson Island* was born.

Much of what I've written comes from my own experiences in life. For example, I've created Fritz's family to resemble my own with two sons and two daughters.

The scavenger hunt was the exact way I won over my wife and we began *courting*. We were living in two different states at the time and I decided to surprise her by coming for a visit. However, I wasn't going to just show up on her doorstep, I had to be more creative for a first date. I wrote out five different clues and asked a neighbor boy to deliver the first one. Danielle followed each clue until she found me at a local park with a prepared picnic. The rest is history.

Flora and Turk were the Robinson's two dogs when they were first shipwrecked on the island. Although, they didn't live long enough to be in my book, they had an offspring. Her name was *Sunshine* — my favorite pet growing up.

Throughout the book I taught many survival skills. For example, on page 68, I described how the Robinsons made candles from the island's natural resources. You can see how this was done by going to YouTube and search: "How the Swiss Family Robinsons Made Candles.")

I also weaved throughout the story my own beliefs in terms of wholesome living, which the Robinsons also valued. You may or may not have noticed my book was free of any sexuality or crude language. I also share my views on the great law of health, which included living free from addictive substances. For the most part, the Robinsons took no part in drinking alcohol, chewing tobacco, or smoking.

I hoped to convey within my book the message that

goodness exists, but evil will reign if you stand idle. There will always be challenges and you must, with firmness, defend your God, your family, and your freedom.

You might be wondering ... Why are you just now getting to read *Return to Robinson Island* when the idea was born in 2003? Well, just like any good steak must be cured in order to fully appreciate the flavor, so did my story. Besides, life simply got in the way. Over the next decade (2003–2013), I tinkered with *Return to Robinson Island* when time allowed. The years went by and in May 2013, I felt a burning desire to finish the book. Between my speaking engagements, business responsibilities, and family priorities, I filled my time with writing the novel wherever and whenever possible. There is something sweet — and almost celestial — about burning the midnight oil while writing in the quiet space of my bungalow. Most writers and actors will understand what I mean when I say I had become personally acquainted with each of the characters. I could hear their voices and envision their mannerisms clearly and distinctly.

In May 2013, my original book idea for *Return to Robinson Island* had transformed from a side project I would occasionally tinker with into an important priority. As I continued to write, more ideas flowed. The manuscript eventually grew to forty chapters. I had a lot to learn. Thus, my historical journey began.

An author never creates a good book on his own. I am thankful for my entire writing team. Each reviewer and editor provided invaluable contributions to the project while keeping my vision intact.

If you have a burning desire and a dream to express your

passion, I say go for it. Believe in yourself. Be willing to put in the long hours and in time your dream will be realized. *If You Think You Can!*

For a more detailed description, go to
www.SwissFamilyReturns.com
and click on "**My Story**."

About the Author

 TJ Hoisington is a husband and father. He is also a *best-selling* author and professional speaker. His ability to tell stories and move audiences to take action with *'raving reviews'* has brought invitations to speak around the world. One way that he motivates and inspires his audiences, young and old alike, is through *telling stories that illuminate the mind and touch the heart.*

TJ is the author of the international best-selling book *If You Think, You Can!: Thirteen Laws that Govern the Performance of High Achievers* — sold in 34 countries. He is also the author of *If You Think You Can for Teens*, and co-author of *The Secret of the Slight Edge*. Additionally, he has authored numerous performance, leadership, and mindset development curriculums.

TJ's mission in life, whether speaking to one individual or 15,000 people, is to provide inspiration and insights that *help people unleash their greatness within*. **Return to Robinson Island** is a continuation of this mission as TJ weaves throughout the book many life lessons that lead to *success and happiness* — in an entertaining and adventurous way.

TJ resides in the state of Washington with his wife and four children.

Acknowledgements

Special thanks to all the reviewers and beta readers who read my book and gave great suggestions. Thank you for believing in me and my idea to create a continuation of the *Swiss Family Robinson* story. You are all a blessing to me.

To name a few, I am thankful to Stacy Jensen, Lynice May, Jeanette Withers, Emily Shelton, and my wife, Danielle Hoisington. Thank you to Renon Hulet who took the rough drafts of each chapter and cleaned them up, while suggesting many great ideas. Thanks to Krisette Spangler, who read an early edition and was instrumental in helping me make the book authentic to the early 1800s time period. Krisette was my go-to person when it came to the nuances and way of life during that time in history. I'm deeply thankful for Jenny Parkin, for her candor and desire to see this book become a success. As mutually agreed upon, she pushed back on ideas and wasn't shy to voice them. I quickly learned that Jenny has a talent for story development and flow. I am thankful for her efforts, ideas, and sacrifice as she read the entire manuscript twice to ensure a crisp and ideal read. Lastly, there were many other readers and reviewers who helped strengthen the book. I am thankful to you all!

CONNECT WITH THE AUTHOR

www.GreatnessWithin.com
www.facebook.com/tjhoisington
www.twitter.com/tjhoisington
www.instagram.com/tjhoisington

www.SwissFamilyReturns.com
www.facebook.com/SwissFamilyRobinsonReturns
www.facebook.com/SwissFamilySurvivalSkills

www.Goodreads.com
www.Goodreads.com/tjhoisington

eBook and Audiobook editions also available

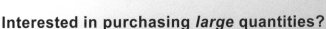

AYLESBURY
PUBLISHING